Child of Fire

Child of Fire

MAUREEN PETERS

ROBERT HALE · LONDON

© Maureen Peters 2002
First published in Great Britain 2002

ISBN 0 7090 7086 1

Robert Hale Limited
Clerkenwell House
Clerkenwell Green
London EC1R 0HT

2 4 6 8 10 9 7 5 3 1

Typeset in 11/13pt Baskerville
by Derek Doyle & Associates, Liverpool.
Printed in Great Britain by
St Edmundsbury Press Ltd, Bury St Edmunds, Suffolk.
Bound by Woolnough Bookbinding Limited.

ONE

Day by day she was shrinking. Day by day she was growing smaller, skin inching nearer to the bone, so near that when she held up her hand she could see the pale light from the window shining through it and making it transparent. Soon she would be so tiny that she could creep like a mouse through a little hole out of the grey stone walls in which she lay enclosed.

'Only think of the baby that's coming!' young Martha urged, spooning broth down her, bowl at the ready because it would soon be vomited back.

'I will think of it when it arrives,' she said, and felt under the bedcovers the hollow cavity that was her stomach. How could there be a child there? She had felt no fluttering, no leap of life, only the constant retching when her body jerked in spasms and blood ran out of the corners of her mouth. If a child was ever born it would be as small as one of the wooden soldiers that had been Papa's gift to Branny. It had been Branny's pleasure to share them with his sisters. They had breathed life into the figures, sent them on long journeys to the interior of Africa, given them voices. They had been lost long since, broken or thrown away.

'Miss Charlotte, try another spoonful,' Martha was coaxing. She shook her head, closed her mouth, fixed her eyes on the pale square of window. She ought to chide Martha because she was Mrs Nicholls now, a married lady. But Mrs Nicholls was only a disguise she had put on to satisfy convention. Underneath she was Miss Charlotte still.

'Hast tha seen the bonnet Miss Wooler sent for the bairn?' Martha was saying, holding up the little white cap on her hand.

Kind Miss Wooler! Happy Miss Wooler never to have known the invasion of a man! She had written to Ellen Nussey that

5

marriage was a solemn and perilous state. That had been before Arthur insisted on reading her letters, had ordered Ellen to burn them as she received them. Ellen, she hoped, would do no such thing!

'I'll let thee have a bit of a rest,' Martha said, and went from the room on tiptoe.

But she didn't want tiptoes and whispers and bright false smiles. She wanted the sound of laughter and argument, the noise of Aunt Branwell's wooden pattens clip-clopping about the stone floors. She longed to hear Emily playing a rousing march on the piano and Anne's sweet, weak voice raised in song and Branny's wild laughter as he set out his troops and conquered another tribe of Ashantees who all turned back into ninepins when the battle was done.

Mama had died in this bed at the same age as she herself now was. Why had they put her here? Papa was a tall man, over six feet, and Mama had been tiny like herself. Yet Mama had borne six children one after the other until the cancer claimed her. Why could she herself never do anything right?

In a corner of the room the old cradle waited, its wooden sides polished and the rockers mended.

'It was cradle for you all,' Papa had told her. 'The last to lie in it was dear little Anne. Soon my grandchild. . . .'

There wasn't any baby! If there had been she would have vomited it up by now, piece by piece! That would disappoint them. If she shrank even further she could lie in it herself and be her own baby with no need to suffer the labour of it. In her mind she slipped from the bed and drew close to the wooden rocker and saw already there a dolly thing wrapped in wool, with a shining being standing near the pillow, face a blank for her to draw her own features upon.

'Papa! Papa, there's an angel by our Annie's cradle!' she said excitedly, bursting into the room where her parents sat drinking tea.

Outside it had been raining, big, fat drops of water and Nancy had run out into the back yard to unpeg the clothes from the line and bring them into the kitchen to drape them on the clothes-maiden that was let down from the ceiling on ropes and then pulled up again. Papa said it was very dangerous to dry clothes near a fire, and it was forbidden to go too close. Papa was very tall with red hair and he knew everything in the world that was fit to be known. His name was Patrick but only Mama ever called him that. Other people called him Mr Brontë or 'sir' and the children called him Papa. That is those who could talk properly called him Papa. Branny and Emily and little Annie were the tail of the family, Papa said. She was in the middle – right in the middle before Annie had been born.

'Middle children are important,' Papa had said once, 'since they hold the two halves of a family together.'

Maria and Elizabeth were the head children. Maria was about seven and Elizabeth was just on five and they could both talk very well, though Maria was the one who said the clever things and Elizabeth said things like, 'More bread and butter, please.'

'An angel! My dear Charlotte!' Papa looked over his spectacles at her.

'Floating in the air!' Charlotte said excitedly. 'All shiny. Come and see, Papa!'

'Very well.' He cast an amused look towards his wife and rose, allowing himself to be pulled along by the hand into the room with a cast-iron fire-dragon on each side of the hearth. 'Now where is this angel?'

'It's gone,' Charlotte said in a disappointed voice.

'Perhaps you dreamed it?'

'It was here!' she insisted. 'It was, Papa!'

'Could it be a sign of divine favour, Papa?'

Maria had followed them and stood within the door, her face pale and eager, a stray beam of pale sunlight turning her long hair to gold.

'That is always possible,' he said gravely, 'but such signs are rare on earth. You will recall that in the *Pilgrim's Progress*, Christian sees few signs of divine radiance until he enters the celestial city.'

Papa read the *Pilgrim's Progress* to them while they ate their supper, altering his voice so that he became all the characters.

'Perhaps it is a sign that Anne is special?' Maria said.

'That may be so.' He went over to Maria and smoothed back her hair. 'We must hope that Anne is blessed by this mark of grace.'

But she was the only one who'd seen the angel, Charlotte thought indignantly. The baby had had her eyes tight shut all the time! She knelt down by the cradle and pushed it gently with her hand. Maybe the angel was going to come back and take Anne away to the celestial city.

They would all be very sad if that happened but it would make her the middle child again, binding up both ends of the family. Though she loved her newest sister very much it would be exciting if an angel carried her off to the celestial city.

It had stopped raining and the windows were bright with little golden stains where the water was drying. Charlotte gave the wooden cradle another little push and stood up, walked through into the other room and stood by the door looking at the rest of the family. Papa was seated at the table with Maria standing within the circle of his arm, and Mama was combing Granny's mop of red curls, and Elizabeth was sitting with Emily, arm about her shoulders. There was nobody for Charlotte.

She wandered back towards the kitchen and peeped in, but Nancy and Sarah were supping a mug of ale between them and didn't notice her. Charlotte sucked her thumb pensively. If she got to the celestial city first that would be a mark of divine favour and make her special again.

She slipped noiselessly through the side door which had been opened to let out the steam and went down the steps into the cobbled yard. The cobbles were all wet and shining with busy little puddles in between them but she didn't waste time playing. Instead she went through the open gate on to the main road.

This place was called Thornton, where she had been born. She was the first child to be born in the house behind her because Maria and Elizabeth had been born at Hartshead before Papa had come here to be the minister. She squinted up into the sky and traced the pale rim of the emerging sun. The celestial city would lie there, full of pearl and ruby gates and singing angels. Charlotte smoothed down her pinafore and set off sunwise, marching forward on her thin little legs.

The buildings ended and there were fields on both sides with stone walls running alongside them. The road was muddy with lumps of horse muck steaming in the waking warmth. It looked a bit like the Slough of Despond in the book Papa read to them, Charlotte thought, marching on with her lower lip stuck out.

A cart was being pulled along the road by an ambling horse, its driver at his ease with the reins slack between his knees and a pipe clenched between his teeth. Charlotte vaguely recognized his shape as the equipage drew nearer. She waved her hand.

'Miss Charlotty! What ever art thou doing out on't road?' he exclaimed, waking up suddenly.

'I'm going to the celestial city,' Charlotte said politely.

'Carry on this road and tha'll reach Bradford!' he told her. 'Thy mither and feyther will have a fit, child! Tha cannot get to the – where tha said in this life! Come, I'll take thee home!'

She didn't want to go home. She wanted to go to the celestial city and be special again. She wanted to kick and cry and bite his hand but she was very small and he was as square as his cart. She let herself be lifted and plonked on a pile of damp sacks as the horse ambled on again.

'You might've been run over or taken away by cruel people,' Mama said.

'At least the child displays a sense of adventure,' Papa said tolerantly. 'When I was a child I often went off for long walks in the hills near my home in Ireland. My parents never fretted.'

'Your parents,' said Mama edgily, 'had nine other children and in any case, my dear Patrick, you were a boy. There is all the difference in the world!'

'Surely the Good Lord will protect a child who sets off in search of the celestial city,' Maria said.

'This child,' said Papa, 'gives the lesson to us all. Come, Maria, we must walk into town. I have the proofs of my latest volume of poetry to correct – and you may assist me in the task.'

Maria was the cleverest and the prettiest of them all, Charlotte thought. She was good too which was more important, Papa said.

She went into the kitchen where Nancy and Sarah Garrs were packing china into a big box half-filled with straw.

'May I help?' She stood on tiptoe to look above the top of the table.

'Now tha keep thy hands to thysen, Miss Charlotty!' Nancy scolded. 'We'm packing up ready for t'move.'

'To Haworth up on't moors,' Sarah supplied more kindly. There had been a lot of talk about Haworth since before Anne had been born. Papa had been appointed perpetual curate there by the bishop but the people of Haworth hadn't wanted him so the bishop had given them someone they liked even less.

'Poor Redman got up into the pulpit and the entire congregation started yelling and catcalling while a drunken oaf with his face blacked with soot sat backwards on a donkey as it trotted up the aisle,' Papa said. 'He had to be escorted out of the village by local constables!'

'My dear Patrick, such conduct is insulting to the Church itself and hence to God!' Mama said, shocked.

'You are perfectly correct, my dear, but it must've been a fine scrap all the same!' Papa said.

He sounded wistful, as if he would have enjoyed joining in.

At Haworth they would live in a larger parsonage with a proper garden and the church just across the road, and there would be the moors to play on and a higher pulpit from which Papa could tell them all about hell-fire and the dangers of sin.

'But will there be any congenial society there?' Mama wanted to know. 'Our teaparties with Miss Firth . . .'

'There are some genteel people in the environs of the village,' Papa said consolingly. 'The Heatons are a most prosperous and important family and we must not forget that the great preacher William Grimshaw was spiritual leader there! To follow in his footsteps will be a great honour and a great responsibility.'

'And of course as perpetual curate we shall never have to move again,' Mama said, giving a sigh as someone dropped something in the next room.

Charlotte went to where Maria was reading the newspaper, and tugged at her pinafore.

'What's perpetual?' she wanted to know.

'Perpetual means for ever,' Maria told her.

'Ever, ever, ever, ever!' Branwell chanted from the corner where he was trying to stand on his head.

So Haworth must be like the celestial city, Charlotte reasoned. They would all live there for ever and ever and ever.

They were moving there on 20 April which was the day before her own fourth birthday. When she woke up on the Friday morning she would look out over moors full of flowers and she would be a whole year older! Perhaps she would be taller and prettier and her nose would have shrunk to match her face! Or perhaps she would be clever like Maria and able to read the newspapers and help Papa to correct the books of poetry he sometimes published.

'There is nothing I love more than sitting alone and writing poems,' Papa said. 'It surpasses all other pleasures!'

'All pleasures?' Mama queried mildly, glancing at the group of children.

'I confess that I do enjoy the company and conversation of Miss Firth,' Papa admitted. 'When you are unable to walk far in public she is always ready to accompany me on a ramble.'

'Miss Firth is very pretty,' Mama said.

'She is indeed!' Papa rose, stepping over Emily who was lying full length chewing the fringe on the rug. 'You remind me that I have not yet paid my respects at Kipping House this week. I shall take Miss Firth your love, my dear.'

'Naturally, my dear,' Mama said. 'Emily, stop that! You are ruining the carpet!'

Unusually for Mama she sounded quite sharp.

Some days never came. Judgment Day hadn't arrived yet though one morning it surely would and then there would be two lines of sheep and goats. Charlotte wasn't sure if pepple were going to be riding on them or turn into them. She didn't want to do either. Strange animals looked dangerous though Emily toddled up fearlessly to the huge carthorses that pulled the delivery wagons and laughed up at them. Emily was pretty too, with dark hair curling over her head and dark blue eyes. Perhaps a horse would bite off her head one day when she went too close to them. That would be a terribly sad thing to happen!

Moving day did come. Two men with bulging muscles carried the furniture and all the trunks and boxes out to the covered carts and then the little group of people who had come to see them off kissed the children and Mama and shook hands with Papa. Papa kissed Miss Firth's hand in a very gallant manner and everybody said that five miles as the crow flies was no distance at all and there would still be visiting to and fro!

They were all crammed into the lead wagon except for Papa who had elected to walk with Branwell on his shoulders. Mama was holding Anne and Nancy was squashed up next to Sarah with Maria and Elizabeth on their laps, and Emily and Charlotte were lifted up and slotted into the remaining space. Charlotte could see the outside through a rent in the canvas and she held on tightly to a rope at the side as the wagons jolted over the cobbles. They could hear but not properly see the people waving and the chorus of farewells.

'Miss Firth is quite tearful to see us leave,' Papa announced, coming alongside the wagon.

'I've no doubt she is, dear,' Mama said.

Sarah giggled and yelped as Nancy dug her in the ribs.

Five miles was a very long way, longer than the years that Charlotte had lived. Papa liked taking long walks, as long as fifteen or twenty miles at a stretch. He had long legs, did Papa, and a handsome face and a head of red hair that was only just beginning to turn grey. She was like Mama, small and thin with a big nose and brown hair that frizzed up when it was curled.

After hours and hours – well, three anyway – they stopped to water the horses and Nancy lugged out the big picnic basket where sausage pies and cupcakes and bottles of lemonade had been packed.

They had left the paved road behind and the track was a narrow, pebbly one winding between great swathes of grass and turf with patches of blackish brown which, said Papa, were peat bogs such as they had in Ireland. He had left Ireland when he was a young man and gone somewhere to get a Degree which meant he could put letters after his name and stand up in a pulpit and tell people what hell was like.

Elizabeth was whining softly in the way she sometimes did. She wasn't pretty like Maria but narrow-faced with her eyes set wide apart and stringy gingerish hair that always looked grubby even when it had been washed. Now she was whining more loudly, screwing up her face.

'What ails the child?' Papa asked, setting Branwell down.

'She'm wet hersen!' Nancy exclaimed. 'Shame on thee! A great girl of five to wet hersen!'

She administered a slap and Elizabeth wailed louder, seconded by Branwell who let out a great roar.

'Why are you howling?' Papa enquired.

'Emily sat on the sandwiches!' Branwell roared.

Elizabeth stopped wailing and lifted Emily out of the way. Maria said anxiously,

'Ought we not to say grace, Papa?'

'Of course, my love!' Papa swallowed the rest of a meat pie. 'We must thank God for bringing us this far safely on our way and for the food that He has provided.'

Nancy and Sarah had bought the food and made the pies and

the sandwiches, Charlotte thought, screwing her eyes shut and putting her hands together. Wasn't it a bit mean of God to take the thanks? She said a loud 'Amen!' very fast in case He had been listening to her thoughts. When they'd eaten, squashed sandwiches and all, and Sarah had wiped Elizabeth's legs with a dry cloth, they climbed back up into the wagon. This time Maria chose to walk, holding tightly to Papa's hand, and Branwell sat in the little seat next to the driver after loudly threatening to be sick. Charlotte would have liked to sit there and pick out the places on the way to the celestial city but she wasn't a boy and anyway she felt sleepy after eating and dozed off with her head in Sarah's lap and her thumb in her mouth.

She was woken with a jolt as the horses stopped and the wagon swayed to aa standstill.

'Out tha comes!' A big man was lifting them down into the road, exclaiming as he did so, 'Why, these bairns are so titchy tha could fit 'em all in a laundry basket with room t'spare!'

The hill ahead of them was so steep that it looked like a great wall. That was as it should be because the celestial city where they were all going to be perpetual was at the top of a hill. There were houses down both sides of this hill and the hill itself had small cobbles set at right angles. There were people standing out in front of the houses or leaning on the sills of the open windows, all staring.

Papa set Branwell on his shoulders again, and took Maria by the hand and strode ahead of them. Mama took Elizabeth's hand and Emily held on to Nancy's skirt and Sarah carried the baby. Charlotte trotted at the rear of the small procession and laboured up the slippery setts that went up and up and suddenly flattened out into a piece of ground with a big church with a high tower to the left, just above an inn with its name in big letters over the front.

THE BLACK BULL, Charlotte read and hoped there wasn't a real bull there. They turned into another lane at the side of the church gates and went on past leaning headstones and through a side gate with a square house of grey stone on the right and a piece of garden with a wall and lots of yellow dandelions.

'Our new house!' Papa said, and kissed Mama on the cheek.

'It looks – most suitable, my dear Patrick,' Mama said.

'Go along inside, children! The men will bring in the furniture and the boxes under my direction,' Papa said. 'The sofa first, my good fellows! My wife will wish to rest for a while.'

They went up the front steps into a hall with a round archway beyond which was a staircase that went up to a narrow landing and then turned to the left. The floors were stone like the walls and there were wooden shutters on the windows which Papa was folding back against the pale-grey walls. There was a room on the left and one on the right.

'I shall take this as my parlour,' Papa said. 'Here I can compose my sermons, receive visitors. The opposite room will do well as the dining-room, don't you think?'

'Yes, dear. It will do very well,' Mama said, sinking on to the black-upholstered sofa that the carters had just carried in.

'Where's 't kitchen?' Nancy was asking.

'Reckon this is it,' Sarah said, bouncing into a small room at the foot of the stairs. 'Tha cannot swing a cat in here!'

'The door leads into the back kitchen,' Nancy discovered, pulling it open. 'Eh, there's a flagged passage and another room – with a pump!'

'You may pump water from the well directly into the sink,' Papa said, bustling past her. 'The stairs there lead up to a storage space. The privy is in the yard – it has two seats.'

'Reckon we won't know oursen,' Nancy said with a grin.

Charlotte was staring at a part of the wall behind the dining-room.

'What's there?' she asked.

'There is a small lumber room at the side behind that wall,' Papa told her. 'The door is on the outside. We can stack peat in it or store potatoes.'

'And get sopping wet going round in't rain to get the 'tatoes,' Sarah muttered.

Sarah was a big girl of fourteen, Charlotte thought, but she still grumbled about the housework.

She left Sarah grumbling and climbed up the stairs and on past the landing to the top of the stairs.

There was a bigger landing here with doors leading into three empty rooms and a tiny chamber sandwiched between two of them. This last had a big window and Charlotte went in and stood on tiptoe to look out at the church tower with the big clock on it.

'This room is to be our study,' Maria said, joining her. 'Papa says this is to be our own room. I shall tell you about everything that happens in Parliament down in London.'

'Is there a room behind that wall too?' Charlotte asked.

'Aye, there is!' Sarah trailed up the stairs with a pile of bedding. 'Tha can only get up to it by a staircase on th' outside wall! Aye, we'll get soaked bringing in stores and catch our deaths going round in snow to get to our beds,' Sarah said. 'Aye, it's a grand life!'

'Only come and see, my dear!' Papa was escorting Mama up the stairs. 'We can use the bedroom over my parlour and the room behind will do very comfortably for Branwell. Since it is over the kitchen it will be pleasantly warm for him. We shall keep the room over the dining-room for when your sister visits us from Cornwall! You will wish to see her very soon. . . .'

'But my dear Patrick, where will the girls sleep?' Mama asked.

'The girls?'

'We have five daughters,' Mama said.

'Anne's cradle must be in our room while she is so small,' he said promptly. 'The others – why, they can sleep in the children's study! We can easily furnish two folding beds of canvas which can be taken down in the morning. You are not dissatisfied with my arrangements, I hope? It would be a cruel disappointment for me to learn that my plans were not approved by the one person on whose good opinion I depend!'

'I am sure you have arranged everything for our comfort,' Mama said.

Charlotte, listening, thought she sounded very tired.

'Guess,' she piped up, 'what happens tomorrow?'

'Tomorrow is Friday,' Mama said.

'Tomorrow will be our first full day in our new home!' Papa said. 'Is that what you mean?'

'Yes,' said Charlotte, 'but—'

'Branwell is out in the yard!' Mama had glanced through a window. 'Maria, go and fetch your brother before he does himself an injury! Is Emily with Elizabeth? Sarah?'

She hurried down the stairs.

'Your mama frets too much,' Papa said. 'I must go down. . . .' He turned and ran down the stairs.

Charlotte sat down on the bare boards. This wasn't the celestial city after all even if it was perpetual! And tomorrow wasn't important enough to remember.

TWO

Mama was screaming again. Although the bedroom door was shut the shrill, piercing sounds splintered the quietness and drowned the ticking of the clock on the half-landing.

Charlotte sat on the bottom step and tried to stop listening but it wasn't possible to stop. Scream after scream descended into long sobbing moans. Feet clad in wooden pattens clattered down the stairs.

'My dear Charlotte, what are you doing here?' Aunt Branwell said.

Aunt Branwell, who was Mama's sister, had come up from Cornwall after Mama first became ill to take charge of the household and help with the nursing. She looked like Mama with her bunchy dresses and long nose so that it was queer to see her trotting about the house as if Mama had split herself into two, one version of herself lying in bed and the other walking into the kitchen and tasting the soup.

'Is there going to be a baby?' Charlotte asked.

'A – no, my dear, your mama is suffering from a serious illness called cancer,' Aunt Branwell said. 'Go and put your cloak on and play out with the others.'

There had been something a couple of nights before, Charlotte thought, reluctantly obeying instructions. She had woken to the sound of voices and feet on the upper landing, and leaned up in the canvas bed she shared with Maria to look through the partly open door.

There were two gentlemen there in frock-coats with black bags – they were doctors she knew – and behind them Aunt Branwell with her mob-cap shading her face. Then one of the doctors had turned and she had seen that he had an apron tied about his waist all covered with stains that looked brown in the light from the lamp Aunt Branwell held. And he had a bundle wrapped in a cloth. Charlotte heard him say,

'This must be buried at once. The prognosis is not hopeful.'

Then they had passed from view and she had heard a long-drawn-out sobbing cry from the direction of the room where Mama and Papa slept.

They hardly ever saw Mama these days. Charlotte had made a little shirt for Branwell, Aunt helping her to cut it out and thread the needle, and making sure the stitches were all even and tiny, and she had taken it in to show Mama who was propped up in bed, watching the daily woman lay the wood in the fireplace.

Mama was smaller than she had ever been, her bones sticking out in her face, her eyes rimmed with black. When she smiled she looked like the skull mask that Papa sometimes wore when he played ghosts with them in the arched and echoing cellars that ran right under the house. Charlotte had the oddest feeling that she was the one lying in the bed, her bones sticking out, her eyes the only thing that had grown big about her.

'Did you make this by yourself? How clever you are!' Mama had said.

'Aunt helped me,' Charlotte said honestly.

'Aunt is very good to you,' Mama said.

'Come along, Charlotte.' Aunt was guiding her out of the room.

There had been another day when Mama had been well enough to come downstairs and Charlotte had paused at the dining-room door to see her on the sofa propped up with cushions. She was leaning forward, her small hand stroking Branwell's red curls as he prattled away and the firelight had bathed them both in a rosy glow.

That was how she would remember Mama she thought, going quietly away. Playing with Branny in the firelight.

Now she went into the kitchen where Nancy was washing pots.

'I'm to go out,' she said.

'Tha'll catch them up at bottom of th'lane,' Nancy said. 'Where's th'old tyke?'

'Aunt Branwell is – somewhere,' Charlotte said.

'Very likely guarding th'cellar door in case I go down for a nip of ale,' Nancy said darkly.

Charlotte went out and turned up the lane. It ran past the

parsonage towards the stile and the low fields that led towards the moors. Charlotte ran to catch the others up, seeing them strung out in a line, four grey-cloaked little figures and Sarah carrying the twenty-one-month-old Anne, who slowed everybody else up as she toddled along.

It was cold and threatening to rain. Charlotte pulled her hood over her head and hurried to join them. On the moors one could be free, able to run and jump and skip and shout instead of creeping around the house and keeping one's voice low for fear of disturbing Mama.

Emily had broken away from the others and was running ahead. She was going to be tall like Papa, Charlotte thought, and Sarah often said she was the prettiest of them all.

'She is a Brontë!' Papa would say. 'Long legs, blue eyes. If her hair was golden she'd be the image of my own dear mother and Eilys McClory was the most beautiful girl in Ireland!'

They had never met any of their Irish relatives though Papa often told stories about them, of how his brothers Hugh and Welsh used to dress up as ghosts and ghouls and go about to scare the neighbours, and how his five sisters danced all in time with their arms straight at their sides and their legs criss-crossing faster than the eye could follow.

'And their name was Prunty before it became Brontë,' Papa would say. 'O' Pruntaigh some say. And wasn't my father cheated out of his whole inheritance by a wicked uncle his grandfather took pity on and brought into the family? A black gypsy-cub he was, and married my father's own great aunt, Mary, and treated her with cruelty. Now that's a grave sin in a man! One cannot say that I ever treated you with cruelty, eh, Maria?'

He looked across to where Mama sat on one of her rare visits downstairs.

'At least I can be grateful that you have never given me an unkind word, Patrick,' she said.

But now it was October and all the heather was gone from the moors and Mama didn't come downstairs any longer.

That night she was woken by Aunt opening the door of the little room and saying in a harsh whisper,

'Maria, Elizabeth, Charlotte, Emily! Get up and dress yourselves as quickly as you can! You must come and say goodbye to your Mama.'

They filed into the bedroom which was lit by candles. Papa sat by the bed and in the bed something small and bony gasped and moaned.

'She is not reconciled to her death,' Papa said.

Death? The word bounced around the room. She had heard the word before many times and not heard it properly until now. Charlotte stared at Mama and heard her say hoarsely and gaspingly,

'Oh God, what will become of my poor little children?'

Mama wanted to scream and rage but she couldn't. She could only lie gasping until with a dreadful rattling sound the gasping ceased. Everybody was crying, even Papa, but Charlotte's eyes were dry. They were shepherded down to the kitchen and given hot drinks and then sent back to bed where they lay silent and wakeful listening to footsteps coming and going and low voices and an occasional burst of sobbing from Nancy and Sarah.

I will not remember any of this, Charlotte thought. I will only remember Mama playing with Branny in the firelight.

She ought to have felt important as they walked to church behind the coffin in which Mama had been put, because quite a lot of people had come – the men in their black suits and the women with black shawls. She could hear whispers of: 'Eh, the poor bairns!' Papa walked with Maria and Elizabeth with Emily and Aunt with Branwell and Nancy and Sarah took turns to hold Anne who wanted to get down and play. Charlotte walked by herself, scowling from under the brim of her black bonnet. Mama hadn't really known anyone in the village so why were they so upset?

Inside the church was dim despite the flaring lights in their sconces along the walls. A friend of Papa's was to preach the sermon and there were people from Thornton already in the pews. She saw Miss Firth in a flounced black dress and a bonnet with a little veil concealing her face.

They were putting the coffin down into a hole under the church floor. They were putting Mama down in the crypt where nobody could hear her if she woke up! Charlotte heard the sliding of stone, the sound of sobbing, someone intoning in a loud voice. But Mama couldn't scream any more.

'There is wine and coffin cake in the dining-room,' Aunt said. People were crowding into the parsonage, shaking hands with Papa, embracing Aunt, ruffling Branwell's hair.

Charlotte opened her mouth and screamed loudly, on and on and on. She couldn't stop screaming. Someone shook her and still she screamed until her throat was raw and only whimpering sounds came from it.

'Let me take Charlotte home with me for a few days! She is very upset.'

That was Mrs Atkinson who was a friend from Thornton. She was a nice lady who often had sweets in her pocket.

'She is sensitive,' said Miss Firth. 'Poor little mite!'

They were giving her sips of brandy, rubbing her hands, putting a big shawl round her. Nobody was taking any notice of the other children at all. Charlotte stopped screaming and whimpered more pitifully. She couldn't stop but part of her seemed to stand aside and watch her, to whisper silently, *She was the one most affected, poor child!*

When she came home again it was as if Mama had never been. Maria came and hugged her, whispering she was glad she was come home, and Aunt gave her an extra piece of curdcake for tea. Then life settled down again and went on as before except that Papa went off to visit Miss Firth, wearing his best suit and with his boots polished until they shone.

'Reckon tha's getting a new mither,' Sarah said. 'Well, she's got a bit of brass and she's bonnie enough!'

Charlotte didn't want a new mama. She wanted the old one back but she couldn't find the words to explain how she felt. Only Maria appeared to understand, cuddling her as they lay in bed that night and whispering,

'I shall be like your mama, now. I promised.'

Maria was too young to be Mama, but she was growing up all the time, not in height but inside her mind. It was Maria who helped Aunt to teach them their letters and how to count and Maria who hummed songs when the candles were extinguished and only the ticking of the clock could be heard in the stone house.

In the spring Charlotte was six years old. Sarah made a cake but it wasn't a very jolly day because Papa called them into his parlour to tell them that his own mother, Eilys of the golden hair, had died far away in Drumballeyroney.

21

Miss Firth hadn't become their new mother. She'd gone and got herself a husband called Mr Franks and Papa, after sulking round for a week or two, had ordered Sarah to polish his boots and gone off to see a Miss Isabella Dury who was twenty-one and had a little money.

Nothing came of that either, for as Sarah said,

'A lass would be clean daft to tek a widowman in his forties with no brass!'

Then just after her seventh birthday Charlotte saw Maria and Elizabeth going off in the hired gig to school.

'Quite an expensive school,' said Aunt, 'where Mrs Franks went when she was a girl. I believe that the girls will do well there.'

It was strange without Maria and Elizabeth though it made more room in the tiny study where they put up the canvas beds every night. Aunt slept in the guest-room and Anne had a little bed in the same chamber. Only Branwell had a decent-sized room all to himself over the warm kitchen. Papa, whispered Sarah, was writing letters to a lady who lived down in the south. She had taken the letters to the postman and asked him to spell out the name for her. Charlotte wondered who Mary Burder was. Whoever she was Papa was very moody when he finally received a letter from down south. He preached a very long sermon about the evils of the flesh and how hell-fire waited for those who lusted.

Charlotte was eight when Maria and Elizabeth came home from their school at Wakefield. That meant nobody remembered her birthday again but she didn't mind because she had Maria back again and Emily had her Ellis as she called Elizabeth. The latter was still slow and clumsy and apt to look blank in the middle of a sentence but Papa said she would make an excellent housekeeper when she grew up.

'Another ten years, Miss Branwell, and you will be at liberty to return to Penzance,' he said.

'Where there is sunshine and sea and the flowers bloom far into the winter,' Aunt said.

She didn't like Haworth at all because it was so often damp and cold and there were no palm trees. She seldom left the house except to go to church and as she grew older she looked less like Mama and more like somebody who has been disappointed too many times.

Maria and Elizabeth had liked the school. They had found the other girls friendly and the teachers kind.

'But it is far too expensive for Papa's means even with Aunt and Mrs Franks contributing,' Maria said with a little sigh. 'Papa tells me that a new school has opened at a place called Cowan Bridge on the border with Lancashire. It is for the orphaned daughters of clergymen.'

'Are we orphans?' Emily demanded.

'We are half-orphans,' Maria said sadly, 'but at Cowan Bridge everybody has lost one or both parents.'

So they wouldn't be particularly special, Charlotte thought. It seemed that she would never be very special at anything. Maria was the eldest and Elizabeth was going to housekeep for Papa and that made them both special. Branwell was the only son and Emily the prettiest and Anne the youngest and that made them special, but there was nothing special about her at all. She thought there might be when she got a dreadful headache and broke out in spots but when Aunt investigated it turned out they all had the measles and some of them had the scarlet fever and whooping cough as well! The doctor came and said it was a mercy they'd only caught the diseases very lightly else they'd've died for sure! All that Charlotte could picture were six little coffins being carried into the church with herself being not very important among them all.

They none of them died. Aunt had the two eldest girls up in her room sewing tapes on school uniforms for hours on end.

'Instead of letting 'em play out on't moor and get some fresh air!' Sarah grumbled under her breath.

But there was one day when Papa was out parish-visiting and Aunt had actually bestirred herself to go out too and Sarah came to tell them that they might as well play out while they had the chance.

'What shall we play?' asked Elizabeth who never had any ideas.

'Today is Oak Apple Day!' Maria cried. 'During the Civil War Prince Charles Stuart who became King Charles the Second hid from the Roundheads in an oak tree. Shall we play that?'

'There's a tree outside Papa's bedroom window,' Emily said. 'I can be Prince Charles! I like climbing!'

'Not in a skirt tha cannot!' Sarah said.

'I can wear Branny's trousers,' Emily said.

'Your legs are too long!' Branwell said.

'Doesn't matter!' Emily gave him a shove.

23

'I'm not sure,' Sarah began doubtfully, looking slightly alarmed at what was developing.

'Some of you go outside and start looking for the prince!' Emily bossed, running upstairs.

A few minutes later the opening of Papa's window and the shaking of the upper branches of the tree announced the arrival of the royal fugitive.

'Oh, where can the prince be?' Maria cried.

'Up in the tree!' Elizabeth said.

'You're not supposed to tell!' Branwell said crossly. 'You have to pretend you can't see – ooh!'

Emily, leaning out too far, lost her footing, slithered down several feet of trunk and landed in a heap.

'Emily is killed dead!' Branwell shouted.

'No I'm not!' Emily picked herself up calmly. 'I'm alive.'

'But the lower branch is broken off!' Maria sounded agitated and upset. 'This is Papa's favourite tree.'

'It's the only tree,' Elizabeth said sensibly.

'We can cover the scar with soot and hide the branch in the woodshed!' Sarah said. 'Hurry up now, Miss Emily, and get back in thy frock. Happen t'maister won't notice.'

By the time Papa arrived home Aunt Branwell had returned and taken a tray of tea and scones up to her room and they were all seated round the dining-room table.

'Someone,' said Papa, coming in, 'has damaged my tree.' Papa was like God. There was no hiding anything from him.

'Maria, was it you?'

'Not I, Papa,' Maria said.

'Elizabeth?'

'Not I, Papa,' Elizabeth said.

'Charlotte?'

'Not I, Papa.'

She was telling the truth but she felt as if she was telling lies so fierce and piercing were Papa's pale blue eyes.

'Branwell?'

'Em—?'

'Not I, Papa,' Branwell said smugly.

'It were me, maister!' Sarah burst out from where she was standing. 'I were playing a game wi'th'childer and I climbed the tree and—'

'At eighteen, Sarah Garrs, you are rather too old to be climbing trees!' Papa said. 'At least you have told the truth but I am very disappointed in you. You ought to have more sense of responsibility. I shall take my tea in my parlour.'

He stalked out followed by Sarah.

'Emily, you should have told Papa,' Maria said. 'Not telling means that Sarah has had to tell a lie.'

'She cannot confess now,' Charlotte said, 'because then Papa will know that Sarah told a lie and she will be dismissed!'

'It's a terrible sin to let someone else take the blame,' Maria said sadly.

'I don't care!' Emily pushed back her chair and stood up. 'I like being a sinner!'

She stalked out of the dining-room, leaving the others silent and stunned.

Nobody ate much tea except Branwell who sneaked Emily's sandwiches, and when the clock struck seven they trooped off to bed without any argument.

There was no sign of Emily. Charlotte lay awake, eyes open in the darkhess. She was never going to speak to Emily again of course but perhaps the hardened sinner had run away or hanged herself! Charlotte lay still, listening to Maria and Elizabeth's peaceful breathing.

The door opened and Emily came in, pulling off her frock and her shoes and pulling on her nightdress.

'Emily, where've you been?' Charlotte whispered.

'In the cellar,' Emily whispered back.

'Who put you there? Did Papa?'

'Nobody,' Emily whispered. 'I put myself there. I thought that Mama might come and talk to me. She's the other side of the far wall in the crypt you know. I thought she might tap on the wall and say it was going to be all right.'

'Dead people don't do that,' Charlotte said.

'Sometimes they do,' Emily said. 'Branny and I hear her.'

'Did she. . . .?'

'No, but I saw a light flash across the wall and I heard an angel,' Emily said.

'What?' Charlotte sat bolt upright.

'A voice singing. I wanted to die and see it properly, but then there was only Sarah there, scolding me and telling me to come up to bed. I'm sleepy now. 'Night, Charlotte.'

' 'Night,' Charlotte said, lying down again.

Had there been an angel? She'd seen one once herself by Anne's cradle but had never seen it since. Had one come to Emily or had it been Sarah swinging her lantern as she crossed the yard and letting its light enter the narrow window that was at ground level outside? She hoped it had been that because if people started seeing angels all over the place then her own memory wasn't so important after all.

She put her arm round Emily's shoulders and tried to sleep. Not long afterwards Papa took Maria and Elizabeth off to Cowan Bridge School in a hired coach. They looked very small as they climbed in after Papa.

'You will join them in a month or so,' Aunt said. 'They say that the Reverend Carus Wilson is a most worthy man. I hope it may be so for the girls are still very apt to catch colds. And the school is very cheap. However – come inside, Charlotte. You have not finished your line of hemming for today.'

THREE

The winter had been a harsh one. Walking to church had been an agony to be endured every Sunday. Charlotte, trudging across the bleak fields, had felt the wind cutting through her skin and the chilblains on her hands and feet had cracked and bled.

Four of them were at Cowan Bridge now, Emily having joined them in December. Emily was still the prettiest even with her hair clipped close to her head.

'Vanity of vanities, thy name is vanity!' Mr Carus Wilson had intoned when he visited the school.

He was a tall, heavily-built man and he looked, Charlotte thought, like a black tombstone with a carved white face on top. He stood before the girls and lectured them on the evils of fine dress and curled hair and of raising one's eyes from the ground and of speaking before spoken to, and all the while his own wife and daughters sat in their fur wraps with long ringlets peeping from their feathered bonnets and looked scornfully at the silent rows before them.

If this was school then school was like hell without the fire. It was bounded by a high wall so that nobody could get in or out, with a gate that was always locked, and the space within before the buildings was criss-crossed with small plots where they were supposed to grow vegetables. There was a walkway where they took exercise, walking in pairs with their heads down and their cloaks clutched about them. At night they slept two to a bed in a long dormitory with patched and darned sheets and bedcovers, and washed in icy water when the rising-bell went.

'Mr Wilson runs this school for the good of our souls,' Maria told her. 'Christ taught us to submit, Charlotte. In this place Mr Wilson does the Lord's work.'

27

She spoke sincerely, her eyes shining in her thin face. For the first time in her life Charlotte felt like arguing with her beloved sister. If Mr Wilson was like the Lord, she thought, then she didn't think much of the Lord.

'Papa would never have sent us here if he had known how cold and hungry we'd be,' she said mutinously.

'Papa must not be told,' Maria said. 'He is paying for us to be educated, Charlotte. Imagine how bad he would feel if he thought his sacrifice was not appreciated!'

There was no telling Papa or anybody else anything anyway since any letters home were carefully read by the teachers and no visitors came. She didn't count Miss Firth who was now Mrs Franks and had called in with her husband while they were on a trip somewhere or other. The weather had been warmer then and the Franks had met them in the comfortable staffroom where there were carpets and sofas and even a small fire burning. They had given the three girls, Emily not yet having arrived, half-a-crown each and had not asked to see the sleeping-quarters or the kitchen where the meagre meals of food already stale or left-over from an earlier meal were boiled up together in a big pot in which traces of meat that had gone green and maggoty could still be seen.

'Papa would be very angry to know we were hungry and cold,' she said now.

'But we are receiving an education,' Maria said. 'One day you and Emily and I are to be governesses and Elizabeth will keep house for Papa so that Aunt can return to Cornwall. We must take every chance we have to study hard and to perfect our characters. Promise me you will try.'

Of course she had to promise. Maria was fretted to bits about them already. She dreaded an outburst from Charlotte and she feared for Elizabeth who walked round with a dazed look on her face. Most of all, Charlotte knew, Maria feared for their souls. She really believed that Mr Wilson was a good man and doing God's work.

'I promise,' Charlotte said.

'You will get your reward in heaven,' Maria said.

She hadn't even been allowed to keep the half-crown, Charlotte thought. Mr Wilson had taken the money from them after Mr and Mrs Franks had left 'to put the money in the poor-box'. Nobody, she had vowed, watching the coins disappear into the slit, would ever take her money from her again. Nobody!

At least the winter had gone. There were no holidays at Christmas time and after the extra long prayers – 'Let us in celebrating the birth of Christ never forget His life ended in agony upon the Cross!' – the Wilsons had gone home to their roast goose and plum-pudding and Miss Andrews had sneaked the pupils some slivers of fruit-cake she kept in her own room.

Now it was spring and with the spring had come the sickness. Girls were complaining of headaches and pains in their joints and laying their heads on the desks even when one of the assistant teachers went round with a birch switch to make them sit up again.

'It is the low fever,' one of the girls whispered to her. The girl was one of the big girls – at least fourteen, Charlotte had heard. Most of the big girls spent their time shoving the smaller ones away from the one fire that burned in the schoolroom or grabbing their pieces of bread and cups of lukewarm coffee which comprised their suppers, but Mellany Hale had shared the bread she had with Charlotte and stood up for her when one of the big girls had pushed her over.

Mellany had darker skin than other people and bright black eyes. That was because she came from the West Indies, from a place called Jamaica, which was an island where the sun always shone and every flower grew at every season.

Maria would have looked after her but Maria was ill. It wasn't the low fever. Maria had a terrible racking cough that kept everybody awake at night and sometimes when she coughed blood spotted her handkerchief and she cried because any pupil who required more than three clean hankies a week must be a slattern and should be punished. Maria had been punished already for not being able to get out of bed one morning. One of the teachers had come into the dormitory and dragged her off the bed into the middle of the dormitory floor and shouted at her that she was a dirty little slut who disgraced the school.

'Charlotte Brontë, come with me!'

One of the teachers had come into the schoolroom. Elizabeth and Emily were with her.

'Yes, ma'am.'

Charlotte stood to attention, her eyes on the floor. Mellany Hale sidled away.

'Your papa has come to take Maria home for she is not well,' the teacher said.

Papa was come! When he saw them surely he would take them all home again! Charlotte's heart leapt with hope.

'You and your sisters may wave to them from the upstairs window,' the teacher said. 'Your papa does not wish to disturb your lessons.'

What lessons she thought blankly? There were hardly any lessons now because too many girls were ill. Papa would go away without seeing the classroom where pupils sat limply with their heads on the desks or the kitchen where the pans were thick with grime and the food tasted so awful that nobody could eat it.

From the landing window they could see the coach outside the main gate and then Papa came down the path. He was carrying Maria who was bundled in a shawl and the three girls waved and waved but he never looked round and Maria never waved back.

After that the fever got worse. More coaches came and more pupils were removed. Mr Wilson gave orders that the remaining girls were to be allowed to play outside the walls along the banks of the river. Lessons would be suspended.

Spring really did make a difference, Charlotte thought, her eyes raised to the green leaves through which the sun was shining. On the surface of the river the sunshine was dancing in little golden motes that dazzled her eyes. Charlotte took off her shoes and stockings and waded out to where a large flat stone rose up above the water. The stone was warm from the sun and slightly gritty. She wrapped her arms about herself and stared at the water, imagining herself as a bright fish or a bird swooping and diving below the sky. The voices of the other girls as they ran about among the trees faded into silence. The world fell away. She stood so still that Mellany, splashing towards her, cried,

'You look like a statue! Are you dead?'

Charlotte came out of her reverie and allowed herself to be led back to the bank.

'Where's Elizabeth?' she asked as Emily came running up.

'Don't know.' Emily shrugged her thin shoulders.

Elizabeth wasn't in the schoolroom where they nibbled their thick slices of bread and drank the weak coffee. She wasn't in the long dormitory that stretched along the upper floor. The bed where Maria and she had slept was empty. Perhaps she had run away? Charlotte, sliding out of the bed where Emily was sleeping, tiptoed to the door and opened it. When she glanced back she could see the beds and the row of washstands glimmering in the moonlight that came through the unshuttered windows. 'Child, what are you doing here?' The shadow of Miss Andrews fell across her.

'I'm looking for Elizabeth,' Charlotte faltered.

'She is sleeping in my room for a few days,' Miss Andrews told her.

'Is she very ill – like Maria?' Charlotte ventured.

'There has been an – accident,' Miss Andrews said. 'Your sister fell and hurt her head. She has been very brave and I am watching over her until the wound is better. Go back to bed, child.'

Charlotte went back to bed. She wished Maria would hurry up and get better and tell Papa what had happened so that he would come and take them all home. She wondered what had happened to Elizabeth. Ellie was always slow and a bit clumsy and the assistant mistress often pushed her or slashed the backs of her legs with the cane.

A few days later Elizabeth appeared among them again. She had a plaster behind her ear held in place by a bandage and her eyes looked funny as if she couldn't make them look in the same direction together.

'Mr Wilson wishes to speak to the Brontë sisters,' one of the teachers announced.

Charlotte's heart sank into her boots. Surely Miss Andrews hadn't told him that she had strayed out of the dormitory! She went into the staff room with her fists clenched in the folds of her skirt and her mouth set so firmly that her jaw ached.

'Girls, I regret to have to tell you that your sister Maria has died,' Mr Wilson said. 'Of course you will feel this loss but she has risen to a higher sphere. She died of consumption of the lungs – her blood entered her lungs and she drowned in her own blood. That is called Consumption. Your papa writes that when she died her mind was beneath divine influence. Let us pray for her soul and for the time when we shall all be translated into a higher sphere. The Lord has taken Maria. Let us rejoice!'

You made her sick, Charlotte thought. You made her die. The Lord didn't want her dead. He doesn't want twelve-year-old girls dead! You're a liar and a murderer and one day I shall tell the whole world about you and your awful school.

31

'Amen!' said Mr Wilson in a loud voice.

'Amen,' Charlotte said meekly.

They would never see Maria again. She had been put down in the crypt with Mama. Mama had company now.

'When is Maria coming back?' Elizabeth asked.

'She's not coming back.' Charlotte stared at her when they were out in the passage again. 'Maria is dead, Ellie.'

'Yes I know,' Elizabeth said, 'but when is she coming back?' Her eyes looked funny and she wasn't walking straight.

Emily said, 'She's with Mama, Ellie.'

'Yes,' said Elizabeth and began to cough. There was blood at the corners of her mouth.

The next evening when she went into the dormitory Miss Andrews was there.

'Your sister, Elizabeth, isn't very well,' she said. 'The housekeeper is taking her back to Haworth. Come with me and you may see her leave.'

They stood at the window again and saw in the gentle dusk the bulky figure of the housekeeper lifting a second shawled bundle into a coach. They neither of them waved.

'Mr Wilson has arranged for you and your sister to be taken to his own house,' Miss Andrews said. 'You will be happier there. He is doing his best for all his pupils but his motives are sometimes difficult to fathom. Come! I will help you to pack your things.'

Everything was happening too quickly. There was no time to say goodbye to Mellany Hale, no time to go out and stand where the stone rose out of the sparkling river. They were being bundled into a private carriage and driven away from the high walls and the classroom where the pupils drooped and sickened.

It was a handsome square house with lights in the windows and a driveway. When the carriage stopped Charlotte could hear a murmuring sound. She thought it sounded like the wind soughing through trees and then she remembered that Miss Andrews had told them once that Mr Carus Wilson lived by the sea.

They went into a wide hallway with a handsomely moulded ceiling and Mrs Wilson, whom she recognized, greeted them kindly and took them into a small room where they had coffee and toast on clean plates and then they were led up the stairs to a bedroom with a big bed in it and velvet curtains draping the long windows. It was so different from Cowan Bridge that it didn't look quite real.

'My dear, I shall take the younger one.'

Mr Wilson had appeared in the open doorway, his outline filling up the space.

'She is very tired,' Mrs Wilson said.

'You are not contradicting me, my love?'

His voice was perfectly genial but Charlotte sensed rather than saw a shiver run through her.

'Not for the world, my dear,' she answered and Mr Wilson took Emily's hand and led her away.

'Get into bed, child,' Mrs Wilson said to Charlotte. 'Your sister will not be long. Say your prayers first.'

Charlotte knelt down and folded her hands together.

Mrs Wilson had left the room, leaving a lamp glowing softly over the green velvet and buff of carpet and curtains. The sound of the sea had faded. She wondered if they might see it in the morning. It would be wider than the river and there would be boats upon it which took people away to strange and wonderful lands.

Her head drooped against the side of the bed and she slept. When she woke up she felt cramped and chilly and the lamp had burned low. She couldn't remember whether she had said her prayers or not so she gave herself the benefit of the doubt and got into bed.

She didn't know how long afterwards it was when Emily came in. She had her nightdress on and she padded across the carpet and climbed up beside Charlotte.

'What did Mr Wilson want?' Charlotte asked, lifting her head from the pillow.

'I went in the red room,' Emily said. Her voice sounded flat and cold.

'What's that?' Charlotte leaned on her elbow.

'Nothing,' said Emily, turning her back. 'Go to sleep.'

In the morning they still didn't get to see the sea. Mrs Wilson came in with their clean garments and told them to get dressed and then she brushed their short hair and took them down to the little room where she sat them down at the table in front of the shiny clean dishes piled with eggs and bacon and sausages and told them to eat heartily.

Charlotte wanted to eat heartily but it was so long since she had had a decent meal that she could only pick at the edges around the plate and Emily ate nothing at all.

'Girls, your papa is come.' Mrs Wilson arrived in the doorway.

'Papa?' Both were on their feet. 'Papa is here?'

'To take you home to see your sister Elizabeth,' Mrs Wilson said.

And there was Papa, top hat in hand, shaking hands with Mrs Wilson and thanking her for her kindness, and then they were in yet another coach speeding through the morning.

'I set out at once for Cowan Bridge the instant I saw Elizabeth,' Papa was telling them. 'The mistress there informed me that Mr Wilson had very kindly taken you both to his house and I came on here at once. I have not closed my eyes all night.'

'How is Elizabeth?' Charlotte asked eagerly.

'She is very ill,' he said gravely. 'Very ill indeed. We can only pray – you know about Maria, of course? She died peacefully. Her soul was with God.'

Charlotte could have told when they were coming to Haworth even with her eyes closed. She knew the cobbles over which the horses strained and the coach wheels rattled and the smell that rose up from the midden heaps behind the cottages. Aunt Branwell stood at the front door and for the first time she didn't look like a pale copy of Mama but like herself alone, not particularly loved but safe and familiar.

Emily slipped past them and ran through towards the kitchen.

'You look fagged out, child!' Aunt said, untying her bonnet. 'Mr Brontë, you must be exhausted! I shall have food and tea brought to you at once.'

'Is Elizabeth . . .?' He paused, exchanging glances with his sister-in-law over Charlotte's head.

'The same,' Aunt said.

'Where are Nancy and Sarah?' Charlotte enquired.

'Nancy got married and Sarah went with her to Bradford,' Aunt said.

'Married?' Charlotte stared at her in astonishment.

'To a very respectable young man,' Papa said.

'An Irishman.' Aunt sniffed. 'And a Papist!'

'One must regret that of course,' Papa said, 'but it is better to be a good Roman Catholic than a wicked Protestant, Miss Branwell.'

'But who is going to do all the work?' Charlotte said.

'Mrs Tabitha Aykroyd from the village is come to act as house-keeper for us,' Papa said.

'Surely general servant, Mr Brontë?' Aunt had drawn herself to her full height. 'I was given to understand that I would act as your housekeeper until such time as—'

'General servant – of course, Miss Branwell,' Papa said. 'I am so tired that I scarcely know what I'm saying.'

Charlotte went slowly into the kitchen. The house hadn't changed at all but everything else had. In only ten months she had lost her dearest Maria, and Nancy had married and Sarah had left too and the small, elderly woman stirring something on the stove looked like a rather good-natured witch stirring a caul-dron.

'Tha'll be Miss Charlotty,' said the witch. 'I'm Mrs Aykroyd but tha may call me Tabby. I've seen thee and t'rest afore when I were in't fields gathering harvest up. '

'I have never seen you at church,' Charlotte said.

'Nay, tha has not and that's because I'm a Joined Methodist! But if t'maister desires me to come to his church then I'll not be the one t'say no! Tha's not asked after thy sister.'

'Elizabeth is going to die, isn't she?' Charlotte said.

'We mun hope and pray, Miss Charlotty,' Tabby said. 'Thy brother and Miss Annie are up in t'study.'

Charlotte went up the stairs, past the ticking clock on the half-landing.

Branwell was drawing pictures with a stick of carbon on the bare white walls and Anne was sitting in a little rocking chair by the window. She looked up as Charlotte appeared and frowned for a moment as if she wasn't quite sure who she was.

If she had stayed away for ten years instead of ten months none of them would remember her at all. They would all look at her as if she were a stranger.

'Tallii!' Using the name he'd used ever since he'd begun to speak proper words, Branwell flung himself at her.

'Is it Ch–Charlotte?' Anne said.

She was still babyish even though she was five now, her fair hair curling limply over her head, her eyes bright blue.

'Yes! Annie, it's me!' Charlotte cried.

'M–Maria went to heaven,' Anne lisped. 'W–we saw!'

'Don't talk about that! Stop talking about that!' Branwell threw the piece of carbon at her and banged his fists on the wall.

'Children, hush! Your poor sister is trying to sleep,' Aunt said, bustling in. 'Dinner is on the table. I held it back for your coming. Come downstairs and wash your hands. You too, Branny!'

Emily was already at the table, looking prim and neat.

'Your papa is having something in his parlour,' Aunt said. 'I must go up and sit with Elizabeth. Do as Mrs Aykroyd tells you now.'

The bread was fresh and well buttered and there were sardines and some sliced ham on the table and a curdcake. Charlotte took some ham and a piece of bread and butter and her throat closed up. She couldn't eat, not with the memory of Cowan Bridge food so close. She would never eat meat again she resolved.

Being at home again seemed ordinary after the first few days. They were used to walking very quietly and to whispering so as not to disturb an invalid. Now it was Tabby who went out with them on to the moors which were green and lush with wild flowers dancing in the wind and lambs still bouncing about in the fields.

Once or twice they were allowed to peep in at Elizabeth but she simply stared back at them with nothing behind her eyes. Then after a couple of weeks Aunt told them to go in very quietly to say goodbye to Elizabeth. But what lay on the bed in Aunt's room wasn't like Elizabeth: it wasn't like any little girl at all.

'She would have grown into a useful woman,' Papa said, 'for she had plenty of good sound sense. We can only be glad that we had her for ten years.'

I will not remember this, Charlotte thought. I refuse to remember this!

Closing her eyes she saw Mama playing with Branny in the firelight.

FOUR

When she looked back over the past year Charlotte found great blanks in it as if her mind had rubbed out some months, thus making other times stand out in sharp relief.

Immediately after Elizabeth's funeral she and Emily had been sent back to school. She had gleaned part of the argument.

'My dear Miss Branwell, since I did not give the customary three months' notice the fees which I paid in advance are forfeit! I am not a rich man and the actual instruction given at the school was, I feel, entirely satisfactory!'

'And the inedible meals, the lack of sanitary arrangements, the excessive discipline? Maria told me—'

'I am assured that the situation has been greatly improved. The cook has been dismissed and the building sweetened, and Mr Wilson has been criticized for his over-zealous methods.'

'But Mr Brontë—'

'I must be permitted to act as I see fit where my children are concerned!'

So they went back to a school where there were fewer pupils and where meals, though far from hearty, were at least properly cooked, more time allowed for recreation, but the carved white face atop the black coat and the hectoring voice were exactly the same, and the vacant bed where Maria and Elizabeth had cuddled together for warmth still stood.

The six weeks they had spent there stayed in her memory like a reopened wound. Emily had lapsed into silence, eyes darting from side to side like a small animal seeking escape, voice inaudible. Mellany Hale had left but the stone that rose in the river was still there and since the pupils were now permitted to spend some time by the river Charlotte regularly waded out to stand on it, ears lulled by the rushing of the water, eyes fixed on the sky where small clouds flitted above the trees.

Then, without warning, Papa had come and taken them home, not a word being said as to why he had arrived, though Charlotte, recalling what she had overheard, suspected Aunt Branwell's hand in it.

Whatever the reason it made no difference. They were at home again with Aunt to fuss over them and Tabby becoming familiar in the kitchen.

'There must be order and method in this family or we shall never get on!' Aunt Branwell said.

They were the watchwords of her Methodist upbringing and though Charlotte was irritated by her pernickity ways she had to admit that order and method did make life run more smoothly. So they rose early and went to prayers in the parlour before breakfast and then Branwell went to do his lessons with Papa while she and Emily and Anne went up to Aunt's room to do their lessons there, though there were frequent interruptions because a delivery boy had called or Tabby needed a hand in the kitchen. Papa usually went out after dinner and sometimes took Branwell with him while the girls sat sewing in Aunt's room, the task made more bearable because she read them stories out of the magazines she had sent up from Cornwall. They were allowed to read all the newspapers and *Blackwood's Magazine* once Papa had finished with them, and they could read any book they came across.

'The mind will impose its own censorship,' Papa said when Aunt suggested that murder, incest and adultery might unsettle young minds.

The Bible, of course, was full of all three and Charlotte read it with her heart pounding and her eyes growing wider.

Then there were the moors. Tabby went out with them every day, trudging along behind as they ran and jumped and screamed.

At least she was the eldest child now. That was something special though Branwell, being the only boy, was the really important one.

When Charlotte looked at her brother her heart ached with loving. He was close on nine, but he was small for his age and thin though Tabby affirmed he ate twice as much as anyone else!

He had the white skin and the long upper lip which Papa said was typical of a real Irish lad, and pale-blue eyes and red hair just like Papa. He was clever too, his mind brimming with ideas that bubbled off his tongue faster than most people could follow them. When Branwell was a man grown he was going to be rich and famous and take care of his sisters.

'For this house is ours during my lifetime only,' Papa told them solemnly. 'When I am dead another curate will come and live here.'

So perpetual didn't mean for ever and ever, Charlotte thought, and found herself from time to time eyeing her father anxiously for signs of approaching demise. Death, she had learned, could creep up and take someone away almost without warning.

She was woken up on this morning by Branwell shouting 'Tallii! Ems! Get dressed quick and come and see what Papa brought me from Leeds!'

He was in the tiny bedroom before the words were out of his mouth, a wooden box in his hands.

'Soldiers!' he was continuing. 'Twelve wooden soldiers! Look at them! For my birthday!'

'Is it your birthday today?' Emily wanted to know.

'In a week or so but Papa doesn't often go to Leeds and this was the only set of soldiers there. You may each choose one for yourselves though it's only a borrow, mind!'

'Anne too!' Emily said, jumping out of bed.

'Is s–somebody hurt?' Anne enquired, emerging from Aunt's room.

'Papa has given me soldiers for my birthday and I shall give you one each as a borrow,' Branwell told her.

'As a loan,' Charlotte corrected.

'Do you want one or not?' Branwell demanded.

'I shall have this one! He shall be the Duke of Wellington!' Charlotte cried, seizing a painted wooden figure.

'Then my chief one shall be Bonaparte!' Branwell shrilled.

'Yours is Gravey, Ems!' Charlotte said.

'What's mine called?' Anne enquired.

'Yours is called Waiting Boy,' Branwell said, tossing her a soldier.

'Why?' Anne wanted to know.

39

'Because she never gets to go anywhere!' Branwell chortled.

'That's not fair!' Emily slapped her brother.

'Children, there is no need to squabble,' Papa said, pausing in the doorway on his way downstairs. 'I bought toys for the girls too. A set of ninepins for you, Charlotte, a miniature village for Emily and a little doll for Anne. Now hurry and get dressed.'

'Does that mean we have to give the soldiers back?' Charlotte asked Branwell.

'We c–could sh–share everything,' Anne suggested.

'Not my whipping-top!' Emily scowled.

She had a striped top that spun round and round when she whipped it. She sometimes went off by herself and whipped the top over and over and Charlotte, coming upon her, had wondered why her sister's face was so full of hate.

'Not your whipping-top,' she said now. 'Branny, we must give the others names too, and send them off on adventures. . . .'

'By themselves?' Anne said in surprise.

'Don't be silly, Annie! We can move them about and make them do what we want,' Branwell told her.

There had been other sets of soldiers before for Branwell to play with but they had been made of tin and easily got twisted and bent.

This was the first time they had all been together sharing the toys. It really didn't matter that Papa had completely forgotten that Charlotte had been ten two months before and probably wouldn't remember that Emily was going to be eight in a month's time.

After that they played with the soldiers at every spare moment they could find. Branwell was the best at inventing games and the wooden figures fought constant battles up and down the floor of the children's study until Aunt called the girls to their sewing and Branwell was sent down to con his Latin or his Greek.

Even when they went out on the moors the games could continue with themselves taking over the roles of the Twelve as Branwell called the soldiers.

Branwell and herself were the leaders, turn and turn around, and sometimes as they sat, planning the next adventure for their heroes, it felt as if they were two heads speaking in alternate voices on the same body. Emily and Anne were there too, of course, joining in, making their own suggestions but generally lagging behind or going off to play their own games.

'You must play more quietly,' Aunt scolded.

'Is somebody sick?' Charlotte looked up, an old fear clutching her heart.

'No, child, of course not! But your papa has his work to do and needs some peace in order to do it,' Aunt said. 'And the noise does rather bring on my megrims.'

'We could write down their adventures,' Branwell said when Aunt had pattered back to her own room. 'We could make books like Papa did and get them published.'

'Emily and Anne can't spell properly,' Charlotte said.

'Oh yes we can!' Emily gave her elder sister a shove.

'Not that I've noticed,' Charlotte said in a grown-up way.

'When we feel like it,' Emily said sniffily.

'We can make little books,' Charlotte said, not troubling to complete the argument. 'With covers on them. Tabby would let us have some empty sugar-bags and we could cut them up and stitch them up the middle.'

But before that happened there was a party to attend.

'Mrs Heaton has very kindly invited the four of you to a party at Ponden House,' Papa announced after prayers.

Mr Robert Heaton was an important man with a handsome estate and shares in a couple of mills. He and his wife came to church with their sons, he remaining to chat with the villagers in the broadest of dialects and to Papa in faultless English. He was a trustee of the church and came to all the meetings, riding his big bay horse.

'What's p–party?' Anne asked.

'A gathering of people all playing games and enjoying themselves,' Aunt said. 'When I was a young girl we attended frequent parties.'

'Did Mama go?' Branwell asked.

Charlotte lowered her head and stared at her plate. She didn't want to hear about Mama going to parties. She couldn't remember her and it wasn't fair that Aunt who was often cross and fussy should.

'It will be an opportunity for you children to begin to make social contacts,' Aunt was continuing happily. 'It is not good to be too introverted.'

'My brothers and sisters and I never lacked social contacts,' Papa said. 'We had one another. Too much social activity cannot be good, my dear Miss Branwell, though I would exempt the Heatons from that stricture. It will make a pleasant treat for you all. In fact I shall hire the gig and drive you there myself.'

'That will be expensive, Papa,' Charlotte said.

'A little expense is sometimes justified,' Papa said grandly.

On the day itself they could easily have walked the four miles for the afternoon was fine and dry but Papa piled them into the swaying gig and climbed up into the driver's seat with a fine flourish.

Ponden House was a long, low building, with an orchard at the side. There were tales about the orchard. Mr Heaton's sister, Elizabeth, had run away to live with a gypsy from Keighley and borne a son and the gypsy had to be bribed to wed her. After that he beat her and she fled back to her home and fell sick and died, her mother catching the fever and dying too. Papa had told them that old Mrs Heaton and her daughter walked in the orchard after dark, weeping and wailing. The bastard boy lived with the Heaton family still and worked on the farm.

'But is the s–story real?' Anne had asked.

'It is possibly exaggerated, my love,' Papa had admitted, 'but it's certainly true that when someone is to die the Gytrash leaves its lair in the Heaton house and rolls, flaming and with the devil's eyes, across the moors seeking victims.'

'Mr Brontë! These are not tales to send the children to bed on!' Aunt had protested.

'Nonsense! Children thrive on a little second-hand horror,' Papa had said.

'I like these stories,' Emily said.

'Of course you do! Aren't you half-Irish and don't the Irish have the finest imaginations in the world!' Papa cried.

'The Cornish are descended from a Celtic tribe too,' Branwell supplied. 'We are pure Celt!'

'The Branwells,' said Aunt with dignity, 'are not connected with any tribe, Mr Brontë. We are respectable Methodists!'

Emily uttered a snort of laughter as Papa winked at them.

Now Papa got down and shook hands with Mr Heaton and kissed Mrs Heaton's hand in a manner that always irritated Charlotte and then they were ushered into the huge high-raftered hall with its panelled walls.

Papa must have gone because all she could discern was a

crowd of children. They were laughing and chattering and crowding and they wore frilly and embroidered frocks and had their hair twisted into ringlets or velvet breeches and shirts with frilled jabots. Their voices were blurred as were their faces, as if they existed at a distance in another world.

'We are going to play musical-chairs!' Mrs Heaton announced, clapping her hands together briskly. 'Get in line now, children.'

A couple of servants were putting chairs in a long line. The children were pushing and shoving one another.

'There's one chair less than the children,' Branwell whispered, tugging at her sleeve.

There was a pianoforte at one end of the hall. Mrs Heaton had seated herself at it and struck a chord. The other children were marching round and round the chairs, still pushing one another.

'W–what are we supposed to do?' Anne asked, bewildered.

'I don't know.'

Charlotte pressed herself against the wall, conscious of her bunchy green frock over which Aunt had so diligently laboured. She felt all wrong because she looked all wrong! She knew that.

The music stopped abruptly and all the children rushed to sit on the chairs. The child left over promptly set up a wailing and was hastily removed with the bribe of a large slice of cake which she munched while spilling crumbs all over the floor.

'Are you not playing then?' a voice boomed. Mr Heaton, dark and broad, was looming over her.

'We prefer to watch, thank you,' she said primly. 'We are not accustomed to these kinds of games.'

'We shall play hunt the slipper next,' he said genially. 'Dost tha not like that game then?'

He had lapsed into dialect, addressing her as if she were one of the children who worked in the mills or laboured on the farms instead of the daughter of the perpetual curate of Haworth. Charlotte said stiffly:

'We are happy to observe, thank you, sir.'

'Please thysen!' He gave her an amused grin and went off. There was no sign of Emily. She wasn't joining in the games so she had probably wandered off somewhere. She stood protectively next to Branwell and Anne ready to defend them if one of the children pushed or jostled them. In her head she was rewriting the scene, imposing a picture over the blurred reality before her.

A great palace made of glass with foundations of marble surrounded her, Turkish carpets laid over the mosaic floors. A tall dark man, cloak flung carelessly over one broad shoulder, strode through the guests, his lip curling sardonically. This was not her chief Wellington but someone else, someone who came of a royal line in a far land.

His name was Zamorna. Duke of Zamorna. She watched him cross to where a lady waited to greet him, her head raised as proudly as his, a long veil floating from the diamond tiara she wore, one hand idly fingering the magnificent rope of pearls looped about her white throat.

In the corner a younger girl, fair and frail, her gown a soft leaf-green unadorned with jewels, her hair simply styled, stood in the shade. She it was whom the Duke loved best. Mina Laury would dress as his page, shear her long hair, follow him into danger knowing that at the end he would return to his abandoned duchess.

She wondered vaguely where the people had come from. They had appeared out of the shadows, more brilliant than life, blotting out the children and the chairs being scraped along the floor. The children, seated on the floor now and passing round a parcel to the insistent drumming of the piano, were no more than outlines drawn in fading chalk on a white wall. Brilliantly gowned and jewelled ladies and men with daggers at their hips were dancing together, Zamorna leading the steps with his proud duchess while, unnoticed save by him, Mina Laury stood in the shadow.

'Teatime everybody!' Mrs Heaton, rising from the piano and clapping the palms of her hands together, banished the scene.

It made no difference, Charlotte reflected, allowing herself to be chivvied to the long table. She could conjure them up again when they were needed. They would come and mingle with Branwell's people. He had spoken recently of a new character for their play – a powerful nobleman whom he thought was called Northangerland.

Emily drifted back into the room with Mr Heaton at her side. She looked quite animated and pleased with herself. Usually she shied away from grown-up people but she was chatting away to

Mr Heaton, letting him help her to some jelly. Charlotte found a custard tart on the plate before her with a sprig of redcurrants on top of it.

Tiny red jewels like the earrings that Mina Laury wore under the long tresses of hair that covered her ears. A gift from Zamorna.

'Did you have a good time?' Papa enquired when they had piled into the gig for the homeward journey.

'It was wonderful!' Charlotte said. 'We had a lovely time.'

'And thanked Mr and Mrs Heaton for having you, I hope?'

'Yes, of course, Papa.'

'We had trifle and jellies and cakes,' Branwell said dreamily.

'Mr Heaton has a considerable library,' Papa said. 'He has invited me to borrow whatever I choose and in a year or two he plans to extend the same courtesy to you all. That is quite a privilege, children, for he is a well-read gentleman who does not lend his books to those incapable of appreciating them. While I cannot pretend that I have met with any mind commensurate with my own since leaving Thornton I shall not stand in your way of friendship with the Heatons.'

'Mr Heaton is calling upon you tomorrow,' Emily said.

'He didn't mention – you did behave yourself?'

'He asked me if you would like a dog,' Emily said. 'He says he has one and will bring it over tomorrow – and a pear-tree for me.'

'Emily, are you making up some silly story?' Papa demanded.

'We had a talk in the orchard. I saw the bastard boy,' Emily told him.

'Unfortunate boy!' Papa frowned at her. 'It is unkind to blame children for their parents' follies.'

'Why did you talk to Mr Heaton? You never talk to people,' Branwell asked.

'Mr Heaton was out shooting on the moor when the eruption of Crow Bog occurred – that was just after I had taken you to join your sisters at school,' Papa said to Charlotte. 'Sarah had taken the others out to play and they were almost caught in the landslide. Emily will remember that day, don't you?'

'All the hill fell down and the rocks and stones flew up into the air,' Emily said with unwonted enthusiasm. 'It was like an earthquake!'

'Exactly so!' He shot her an approving glance. 'I preached a sermon upon it which was printed and distributed as a warning to our neighbours and parishioners. Of course *The Times* newspaper insisted on publication in its own columns though I regret to say several scientists disagreed with my thesis, but then science cannot in the end stand against faith.'

They had reached the lane. He stopped, lifted the children down.

'Go in quietly and don't disturb your aunt too much,' he said.

'May I come with you to take the gig back, and hold the reins?' Branwell was scrambling back up over the wheels.

'Very well, very well! Now carefully, lad! Go indoors, girls. Better not mention the dog to your aunt. She is nervous of strange animals and must be brought round to the notion of our having a dog by degrees.'

Anne went in ahead of them to find Aunt. Charlotte pulled at Emily's sleeve as they reached the door.

'Why did you talk to Mr Heaton?' she asked curiously. 'He's as fierce-looking at times as Mr Carus Wilson used to be.'

'No he isn't!' Emily scowled at her sister. 'Mr Heaton isn't . . .'

'Isn't what? '

'It's a secret,' Emily said.

There was something sly in her face as she turned and marched inside.

FIVE

The snow had clogged the lanes and the ditches and lain so thickly on the moors that taking Grasper for only a short walk had been more like an Arctic expedition than anything else. In the Great Glasstown Confederacy ice had scrawled patterns on the palace walls and the ladies of the court had worn their finest furs and been pulled on sledges across the glistening surface of the roads.

'The sheep are all penned up because the shepherds cannot get to the newborn lambs,' Emily said, clumping into the kitchen.

'Aye, it's a hard winter,' Tabby observed. 'Scatter more snow over t'floor, why don't tha? I've nowt else t'occupy me but clean up after thee!'

'I shall see to it,' Emily returned, cheerfully unrepentant.

'Aye, come Thursday!' Tabby seized a broom and shooed girl and dog out of the way.

'I can smell rain coming,' Emily said.

'Aye, first snow and then floods! Nowt but problems. Miss Annie, the cakes are for tea, not for thee t'dibble-dabble thy fingers in! A great girl of near eleven should have cleaner ways!'

'I was m–making patterns,' Anne said, getting down from the chair on which she was kneeling.

Charlotte left them to argue and started in search of Branwell until she remembered he'd gone sledging with John Brown. John was the sexton's son and a big strong young man whom Branwell followed round like an eager puppy.

'The boy needs a friend,' Papa had said tolerantly when she had complained about it. 'John's a lively young man and will look out for Branwell. '

'I can look out for Branny,' Charlotte muttered.

If anything happened to Papa she would have to look out for them all, Charlotte thought. Aunt wouldn't be able to though she did her best but the cold weather drove her to her room where she spent much of her time writing long letters to her numerous relatives in Cornwall.

Papa was in his study. She could hear his cough as she paused outside the door. It sounded, she thought, straining her ears, less tight and painful than before. He had been ill throughout the autumn, flushed and feverish and confined to his bed while Aunt and Tabby made steaming bowls of broth and the local doctor came and went, muttering about the dangers of lung fever.

If Papa died, and he was midway through his fifties, then they would have to leave the parsonage. Where would they go? Papa had only his stipend and Aunt couldn't keep them all on her fifty pounds a year. Mr Heaton had five sons of his own and certainly wouldn't take them in, and as for the relations in Ireland and Cornwall! For the first time she began to wonder why only Aunt from the Cornish side had rushed up to help when Mama had died and the Irish Brontës evidently never crossed the sea.

By the time the doctor had pronounced Papa out of danger she had made her decision, one which she announced to him on the first day he came downstairs for weeks to sit by the fire.

'Go to school! My dear Charlotte, you hated Cowan Bridge.' He looked at her in astonishment.

'Not to Cowan Bridge, Papa! There are better schools in Yorkshire than Cowan Bridge. Should anything happen to you—'

'My dear, I am swiftly recovering and for the future we must depend on the Lord.'

The Lord had let Mama, and Maria and Elizabeth die. She would rather not depend on Him!

'The Lord also expects us to help ourselves, Papa. Aunt does her best but her time has been taken up with nursing and in any case her own education was limited. If I am to teach then my standards must be high.'

'Schools cost money,' he said uneasily.

'I don't mean that we should all go to school again. If I had a couple of years at a good school then I could return and instruct Emily and Anne. They are woefully ignorant! Perhaps Mrs Franks might know of such a school?'

'Branwell cannot be sent away. He is too sensitive for a rough boarding-school. Later on I hope he may consider University.'

'And then he will take care of us all. I know that, Papa, but I would like to feel useful myself. As the eldest—'

'I shall think about it,' Papa said.

He had thought about it to good effect. Mrs Franks had replied to his query with a letter recommending a school at Mirfield some fifteen miles off.

'The Misses Wooler run the establishment,' Papa said. 'They are women of probity and education and the regime is humane there. It is however beyond my means to send anyone there. I have written already to acquaint her with my disappointment over this. There may yet be a way. In the meantime, my dear Charlotte, if you spent rather less time scribbling in those childish little notebooks you all seem to favour in a hand that no normally sighted person could possibly decipher and more time in doing the grammatical exercises that your excellent aunt sets for you then I will be the more inclined to find a way round the difficulty.'

At least neither he nor Aunt had ever tried to read the pages filled with minute printing and backed with sugar-bag covers coaxed out of Tabby. He had no idea that his four children were Genii, fierce and wonderful creatures from whom the Twelve derived life as did the citizens of the secret kingdom. He knew nothing of the terrible battles fought out between the royal rivals, nor the adulteries in which she was more interested than the battles. If she went to school again she would have to lay the secret world aside for a time. Branwell would have to carry on alone and keep her informed as to how events were unfolding in Verdopolis.

The snow had turned to lashing rain before matters were finally settled. Mrs Franks had agreed to defray half the costs on Charlotte's behalf and she was registered to spend a year and a half at the school.

Only when the arrangements had been settled did she tell the others. She went up to the tiny study where she found Emily, lying on her stomach on the floor and playing with one of her soldiers.

'I have news for you,' Charlotte said.

'The siege is over?' Emily sat up.

49

'Not Glasstown events. I am going to school.'

'Don't be silly! Papa says that there is no school in Haworth worth attending,' Emily said.

'I am going to a school in Mirfield. It's called Roe Head and has a very fine reputation.'

'You cannot!' Emily, springing to her feet, was at twelve taller than her sister. Her face had whitened.

'Unless I get a more comprehensive education I shall never be able to get a post as a teacher or governess.'

'They kill you in schools,' Emily said.

'They didn't kill you or me,' Charlotte said sensibly.

'They killed Maria and Ellie! And you can't leave the Twelve because they depend on us!'

'They're wooden figures. They have no life!'

'Yes they have! We give it to them! We built the Glasstown Confederacy and gave the people there life too. You can't desert them! Schools are terrible places, Tallii! Don't go. Don't leave Haworth!'

'At least you'll have a bedroom to yourself,' Charlotte consoled.

'I'll go and share with Tabby! I won't sleep alone! We have secret games when Maria and Ellie come alive again—'

'We can have them when I come back for the holidays.'

'No! You can't stop something and then start it again! I won't let you go! I will not!'

'Its all arranged. I can't stop it.'

'You never stopped anything, did you? You never stopped the red room!'

'Emily, that was a long time ago – at Mr Wilson's!'

'There are red rooms everyplace,' Emily said, her face contorted though her voice remained flat and dead.

'Then tell me what happened there, you never would.'

'It's a secret,' Emily said. 'I promised.'

'Promised whom? Mr Wilson? I can stop—'

'No you can't! You never could! You never will! And the Twelve are all dead too – there he goes! Dead wood!'

She flung the soldier across the room and turned, her eyes grey as melted ice, lashing out with her fists.

'Children! What on earth is going on here?' Aunt pattered across the landing.

'Emily is angry because I'm going to school,' Charlotte sobbed, shielding her face with her hands.

'Emily, go downstairs and brush the carpet,' Aunt ordered. 'You may take out your temper on the dust. To strike your sister who is only thinking of your future welfare! You should pray to God to make you better and give you a gentler heart!'

Emily dashed out of the room and down the stairs. Charlotte sat tremblingly on the edge of one of the canvas beds, tears running down her face.

'That Irish temper! It must be curbed or she will never fit into society.' Aunt patted her shoulder. 'She takes things to heart too readily. She will come round to the idea and meanwhile you may take comfort in the fact that you are doing your duty. You will meet some girls of good family there so we must look over your wardrobe and curl your hair.'

'You approve of my going, Aunt? It isn't for my own pleasure,' Charlotte said earnestly.

'I think you have taken a wise decision, my dear,' Aunt said. 'Now we must make a list of what you will require at Roe Head.'

They went across the landing to Aunt's room which, though stuffy and overcrowded with the good lady's bits and bobs, was always warm.

The sudden clamour that erupted from below made them both jump. 'Emily is venting her temper on the furniture it seems,' Aunt said. 'We shall ignore it.'

Meaning she couldn't deal with it, Charlotte thought cynically.

When she finally went downstairs it was to find Tabby clattering the pots in the back kitchen and Anne tipping her chair back and forth in a rapid, frantic rhythm. Branwell, seated cross-legged like an apprentice pisky on the hearthrug, looked up and said brightly,

'Emily just tried to cut her throat.'

'What?' Charlotte stared at him.

'She went down in the cellar and helped herself to the ale, and then she came in here and grabbed the kitchen knife and said she was going to cut her throat and then Papa came in and pulled her into the back yard.'

'Are they . . .?'

'They went down in the cellar together,' Branwell said.

'Tabby, what happened?' Charlotte flew into the back kitchen.

'Miss Emily made a great fool of hersen,' Tabby said, clattering more pots in the sink. 'Threw a fit of temper and wouldn't brush t'carpet and rushed down in't cellar and—'

'She was b–bleeding,' Anne said, appearing in the doorway.

'Bleeding! Then she did—'

'Nay, lass, she never touched hersen.' Tabby laughed suddenly. 'She's started t'curse, that's all! It upsets some folks.'

'She's too young! She's only twelve!'

'Comes to some sooner than others,' Tabby said. 'Means she's a woman now.'

'What's it like being a woman?' Branwell pushed Anne aside.

'Mind thy own business, Master Branwell!' Tabby ordered.

It wasn't fair, Charlotte thought. She was nearly fifteen and there was no sign of the curse. It wasn't fair that Emily should become a woman before her elder sister.

She went back into the kitchen and thence into the hall. The door to the cellars was closed. She put out her hand to open it and then, changing her mind, went back upstairs again.

Within days all had been settled. Her trunk was packed, her hair frizzed into corkscrew curls and a local carter deputed to take her the fifteen miles to Mirfield.

'For you cannot expect me to be always hiring the gig,' Papa said. 'The fees alone—'

'No, of course not, Papa. I shall manage very well,' Charlotte assured him.

Everybody came to the end of the lane to wave her off. Even Aunt Branwell, arrayed in a fearsome number of quilted wraps, ventured on to the half-frozen ground. Papa had on his thickest muffler and the gloves she'd knitted him for Christmas, and Branwell was jumping up and down as he declared she was lucky to be going on such a great adventure.

'You will keep me up to date with what happens in Angria?' she whispered to him.

The secret world was Angria now and Emily and Anne took little part in it.

'I promise,' Branwell whispered back, and stepped away from the covered cart to stand by his sisters who stood together with arms linked. Charlotte looked towards them for as long as she could. Then the cart turned the corner and they were all gone, leaving her with the odd impression that she might never again see them as she had just seen them, that if she survived school they would be changed as the people in the secret world changed when she took her attention from them.

They had started out early before it was properly light and it was afternoon before the horse began the long slow pull into Mirfield. Charlotte had eaten the muffins that Tabby had made and the driver had stopped at a tavern and brought out a cup of hot punch for her to sip while he watered his horse and refreshed himself, but she was frozen to the marrow as the cart rattled up the drive towards a large handsome house surrounded by lawns thick with frost and trees dripping icicles that were slowly melting. There was a figure standing in one of the bay windows on the ground floor looking out. Charlotte caught a glimpse of a red dress and then a short, stout lady in a light-grey dress and a long shawl was coming down the steps to greet her, face smiling under a high crown of plaits.

'Miss Charlotte Brontë? I am Miss Wooler, your headmistress, my dear. The man will bring in your trunk. You must be frozen!'

It wasn't like Cowan Bridge at all but first impressions could be deceptive. Charlotte climbed down stiffly and followed the other up the steps into a wide panelled hall with a staircase curving gracefully upwards and double doors on all sides.

'The other pupils are at their lessons,' Miss Wooler said. 'I will show you the dormitory where you will sleep. You will be sharing a bed with Miss Ellen Nussey who is another new pupil though she has not yet arrived. Let me take your shawl. It's very damp indeed! Have you indoor slippers?'

'Yes, ma'am. In my trunk,' Charlotte faltered.

'And here comes your trunk! Find your slippers quickly, dear, and then you must have something to eat and drink. The dining-room is being washed so you shall have a tray in the library. There is a fire there which will help to thaw you out. Mary Taylor, what are you doing out of class?' She spoke to a girl in a red frock with her hair curling golden over her shoulders who had just peeped in.

'Nothing, Miss Wooler,' Mary said.

'Nothing except satisfying your curiosity about our new pupil,' Miss Wooler chided, so mildly that Charlotte was astonished. 'You will meet Miss Brontë later when she comes into class. Now go back to your lesson.'

'Yes, ma'am,' Mary said, dipping a curtsy and vanishing again.

'Come along downstairs, Miss Brontë,' Miss Wooler said. Charlotte, slippers on her feet, followed the short but statuesque figure down the stairs again.

The library was a long room lined with bookshelves with a large table and a number of chairs. A tray on the table held a bowl of soup, a dish of rolls and a pot of coffee which smelled delicious.

'Help yourself and then you may occupy yourself with a book until I return for you,' Miss Wooler said. 'We shall require you to be tested on the standard you have reached in your schooling so far.'

She went out noiselessly. Charlotte went to the table and broke a bit off one of the rolls. It was fresh and white and spread with butter. She chewed it and swallowed, took a spoonful of the soup and forced that down. Her throat felt as if it was closing up and choking her. This was no Cowan Bridge. This was a splendid school with a kindly headmistress, and she would never fit in! She had seen the slightly scornful glance that the girl called Mary Taylor had given her. Mary was exceedingly pretty and her red dress was of velvet. Her own frock was old fashioned with too many pleats in the bust and a skirt that showed her thick boots and her hair looked dreadful, all frizz with two silly bows holding it behind her ears. They would all laugh at her and despise her. Tears rushed into her eyes and she sat down on the carpet and wept.

The library door opened and she tried to stifle her sobs as someone came in. From where she crouched by the table she could see a pair of kid slippers and the flounce of a pink skirt and then the feet advanced along the side of the table and stopped. The person to whom pink skirt and kid slippers belonged knelt down and regarded her gravely.

'Why are you crying?' she asked.

'I want to go home!' Charlotte whimpered and felt shamed.

'Oh, so do I,' the newcomer said earnestly. 'I have only just arrived and if you go on crying then you will set me off too. We will be a sad spectacle, both of us bawling!'

She had a round pale face with large brown eyes and smooth dark hair tied in two long bunches with white braid. As Charlotte sniffed and dug out her handkerchief the girl made a woeful face, turning down the corners of her mouth in a manner that made Charlotte giggle.

'My name is Ellen Nussey,' the other was continuing. 'I think you must be Miss Charlotte Brontë. Miss Wooler told me that you were come and we were to share a bed. Have you met Mary and Martha Taylor yet?'

'I believe a pupil called Mary Taylor came up to the dormitory.' Charlotte stood up and scrubbed her eyes with the handkerchief.

'That is Mary Taylor!' Ellen uttered a crow of laughter. 'She and Martha live quite near to us and we know them very well. Our fathers were acquainted but my papa died quite recently.'

'I am terribly sorry!' Charlotte stared at her.

'I was very sad,' Ellen said. 'Fortunately I have older brothers who can take care of Mama and my sisters and me. I am the youngest of twelve. That is probably why I am so small. How old are you?'

'I shall be fifteen on the twenty-first of April,' Charlotte said, adding, 'Nobody ever remembers it.'

'I shall remember it,' Ellen said, 'because I am going to be fourteen on the twentieth of April! That makes us twins save for a year and a day! Mary Taylor is fourteen next month and Martha is eleven.'

She broke off as Miss Wooler came in.

'I see that you have introduced yourselves,' she said. 'Were you not hungry, Miss Brontë?'

'I'm sorry . . .' Charlotte began.

'Never mind! You may have worked up an appetite by suppertime. Come into the schoolroom now. You must be tested so we shall know whether to put you in the higher or lower class.'

She led them across the hall and down a passage to a large room where seven or eight girls were seated at a row of desks. Charlotte saw Mary Taylor amongst them.

'Recreation, girls!' Miss Wooler clapped her hands. 'Now can you sit here and write down these words with their correct spelling and their correct attributes – whether verb, noun, adverb or adjective?'

The test had begun. Charlotte's heart sank as she heard Miss Wooler begin to read out words where she was never certain if one put the i before the e or doubled the s. Aunt had done her best but lessons had been piecemeal and so often interrupted.

The calculations were worse. How did one multiply fractions

and show the method by which one reached a solution?'

'My dear!' Miss Wooler, collecting the sets of papers and running her eye down them, looked embarrassed. 'Have you never learnt grammar or arithmetic? Or spelling?'

'Not properly, ma'am.'

'But you can read? I was assured—'

'Yes, ma'am. And I know about politics,' Charlotte said desperately. 'I can list the members of the king's privy council and I can recite most of the *Tales of the Arabian Nights* for Aunt gave it to us as a New Year gift.'

'Nevertheless I cannot place you in the first grade until you have learned the principles of grammar and arithmetic – my dear child, what on earth is the matter?'

Charlotte had burst into tears and stood sobbing while Ellen Nussey gave her ineffectual little pats.

'I cannot bear it!' Charlotte wailed. 'I must be in the first grade or Papa will be mortified! Please, please, couldn't I learn the rules of grammar and suchlike in my spare time in the first class?'

'It will be a great deal of extra work for you,' Miss Wooler said doubtfully, adding hastily, 'However if you feel equal to the task then I shall be pleased to place you in the first grade with Miss Nussey and Miss Mary Taylor. Now dry your eyes and come along in to supper!'

'I shall work until I drop, ma'am. I swear it on my life,' Charlotte vowed.

'Just do your best, dear. We cannot expect more than that. Now come along to supper or the beef will be cold – what is it now?'

'I cannot swallow meat, ma'am. I can only eat the vegetables.' Charlotte gulped.

'Can you eat fish?'

Charlotte nodded.

'Then we shall find some fish for you. Miss Nussey, do you . . .?'

'I can eat anything,' Ellen said cheerfully.

'Then let us go to supper.'

Miss Wooler, ushering them towards the dining-room, hoped that Miss Brontë would recover from her fits of crying before the school was washed away!

SIX

Charlotte was dreaming, her arms and legs twitching, her breath coming fast between her parted lips. Maria and Elizabeth had come to visit her. She stood in the library and watched the door open and the two of them sweep in, both quite grown up and clad in red velvet frocks and bonnets tied with white ribbon. She wanted to run to them but she stayed rooted to the spot though her heart was bursting with joy. Cowan Bridge had been a nightmare but she was awake now, reunited with her sisters. She tried to call out their names but no sound came out and they took no notice of her. Instead they were walking round the room, picking up a book here, a cushion there, feeling the nap on the long curtains and all the time they made scornful comments in high, affected voices.

'Miss Brontë! Charlotte! Wake up!'

Mary and Ellen were both shaking her and their voices drowned the titters of Maria and Elizabeth.

'They've gone,' she said blankly, sitting up and opening her eyes.

'Who have gone?' Mary demanded.

'My elder sisters, Maria and Elizabeth.'

'The ones who got killed at Cowan Bridge?'

Martha Taylor, who shared a bed with her sister bounced up, her piquant face lively with curiosity.

'Maria was so good,' Charlotte said. 'She was the best and the brightest of us all, Papa says, and Elizabeth was so patient. We didn't see Maria again after Papa took her home, and Elizabeth – that was seven years ago. They were grown up, visiting me here in the library. I was so pleased to see them again that my

57

heart stood still. They had on the most fashionable dresses and bonnets.'

'What happened then?' Ellen enquired.

'Nothing.'

'Make it up!' Mary urged. 'You know you can!'

'No, I can't.' Charlotte shook her head, her eyes filling up. 'They were different – terribly grand and snobbish. They went round and criticized the furniture and they took no notice of me. No notice at all!'

'Don't cry, Charlotte!' Ellen put her arm round her. 'It was only a dream.'

'Dreams are portents,' Charlotte said, scrabbling for her handkerchief. 'Aunt says – I hope all goes well at home!'

'No news is good news,' said the practical Mary. 'The rising-bell's due to go. We'd better get up.'

'Yes,' Charlotte said, still choking back tears.

She had been at Roe Head for almost a year and was happier there than she had ever imagined possible. It was as different from Mr Wilson's school as heaven from hell.

There were only twelve pupils in the whole school, each one with her own private chamberpot, and an unlimited supply of handkerchiefs. The foods were beautifully cooked and she had even begun to eat a little meat sometimes without gagging on it. She wished her frocks weren't so ugly but Mary and Martha, despite their velvet dresses, were even more poorly clothed than she was with coats that were inches too short and darned gloves.

'Papa was cheated by his business partners and had to go bankrupt,' Mary had cheerfully explained. 'He will make his fortune again and meanwhile it's no shame to be poor.'

'Nobody respects you if you're poor,' Charlotte argued.

'If people only respect me because of the brass in my pocket they needn't bother to come calling!' Mary said blithely. 'You are a goose, Charlotte!'

'Perhaps we shall make good marriages,' Ellen suggested.

'I will never marry,' Charlotte confided. 'I'm too ugly.'

'You're very ugly,' Mary said with devastating candour.

'I know,' Charlotte said.

She had long since ceased to wake up in the morning and look at her face in the glass in the prayerful expectation that the miracle might have occurred. The same face always stared back at her, the high overhanging brow, the large nose, the reddish complexion, the wide mouth with its twist at the corner of her lips and the discoloured, crowded teeth.

'Sorry!' Mary grimaced uncomfortably. 'I didn't mean to be unkind.'

'If you can't be beautiful be clever,' Charlotte said, misquoting Aunt Branwell.

'You're certainly that!' Eager to say something both truthful and pleasant, Mary linked arms with her as they went down the stairs. 'You know about things that the rest of us never heard about – all the poems you can say by heart and the pieces from the Bible and that Milton thing—'

'*Paradise Lost.*'

'That's what it is! And you know about artists and the men in Parliament – I think that you could write a book yourself.'

'I already do,' Charlotte whispered.

'What?'

'We all of us do.' Charlotte drew her aside. 'Branwell and I and sometimes Emily and Anne too – we write stories in little books that we make ourselves with covers and sometimes drawings in too. We use tiny printing so that we are the only ones who can read it. It's a great secret. Papa and Aunt don't know – and you must never tell anybody either, not even Ellen! One day I might show you some of our magazines. We are like four authors labouring in secret.'

'You sound more like potatoes growing in a cellar,' Mary said.

'I suppose we do,' Charlotte admitted.

It had been a mistake to mention it to Mary. She wouldn't tell but she would never understand either.

At break they went out into the garden at the back of the school. There was a long lawn here where they played ball and exercised with hoops and dumbbells. Charlotte, who had long since stopped trying to catch a ball which was no more than a blur to her, wandered into the shrubbery at the side and stood gazing up into the sky. She loved to watch the clouds as they changed shape and formed faces and angels and animals high above her.

'Charlotte, come and play! We need someone else on our side,' Mary invited.

'You know I will merely miss the ball or drop it. I prefer to stand here,' Charlotte told her.

'Skygazing!'

'At Cowan Bridge when we were allowed to go out into the woods down along the river there was a big stone in the middle of the river,' Charlotte told her. 'I used to wade out and stand on the stone for hours.'

'Doing what?'

'Looking at the sky and the water.'

'You'd've been more useful catching a fish!' Mary bubbled with the silvery laugh that didn't mean to be unkind.

There was a wonderful surprise a few days later to make up for her friend's thoughtless remarks. Branwell arrived, hot, dusty and with the sole of his boot flapping.

'Your brother has walked here,' Miss Wooler said, hardly able to contain the shock in her face. 'Walked the whole way from Haworth!'

'Is Papa dead?' Charlotte gasped out.

'No,' Branwell said.

'Aunt? Tabby? Oh God, not Emily?'

'Nobody's dead,' Branwell said. 'Don't be so dramatic, Tallii!'

'Not ill?'

'Not ill either! I told Papa I wanted to come and see you and he said that he couldn't afford to hire the gig but he wondered how you were so I said I'd walk,' Branwell said airily. 'I set off at first light and I must start back in a couple of hours. You haven't grown!'

'Neither have you very much,' Charlotte said, laughing. 'Are they all well at home?'

'Never better. Papa sends his love as does Aunt – as does the whole family! This looks like a fine school.'

'It is,' Charlotte said fervently. 'Oh, it is!'

'Your brother must have something to eat,' Miss Wooler said. 'You are excused lessons while your brother is here, my dear. When he has eaten why not take him into the garden? If you will give me your boot, Mr Branwell, the handyman here will fix the sole on for you. Take your brother into the library, Miss Charlotte. I shall send in a tray for him.'

'She seems very cordial,' Branwell said.

'She is indeed. She has four younger sisters who also help out

60

by teaching here.' Charlotte waited impatiently until a hastily prepared tray of sandwiches and coffee had been brought and then went on, her tone eager. 'What news from Angria? Is the rebellion over? Is Zamorna reconciled with his duchess?'

'I'm thinking of killing the duchess off,' Branwell said.

'Branny, could you be so cruel? Poor lady, she has had so many trials and tribulations,' Charlotte protested.

'Not the least an unfaithful husband!' He grinned at her.

'And Emily and Anne – do they—?'

'They went off and founded a new country,' he told her. 'Gondal they call it and as far as I can tell it's full of women. Tallii, I wish you were at home again. I cannot write well until you are there to strike sparks from!'

'Another few months and I will be at home again, teaching Emily and Anne.'

'Emily grows like a beanpole and has a face about as big as a penny,' Branwell said.

'And Anne?'

'Anne is absolutely nothing at all,' he declared. 'Tallii, I have persuaded Papa to buy a piano and to invest in a course of art lessons for me. I have the genius but I need to master the technique.'

'The university—?'

'I am fitted for neither the pulpit nor the lecture hall! I am torn, Charlotte, between literature and art. Then there is music! I play the flute as well as any man, I believe, and my own compositions may well place me among the illuminati of that discipline.'

'The world is wide open for you,' Charlotte said.

'And I will conquer it as the Twelve conquered the Ashantees and Zamorna and Northangerland conquer the beauties who throng about them!'

He had surrendered his boots and now rose in his stockinged feet, striding up and down the library carpet, half a sandwich in his gesticulating hand.

'Your boots, Mr Branwell.' One of the servants tapped on the door.

'Shall we walk in the garden, Branny?' Charlotte suggested, watching her brother tie on his boots. 'If you can stay a little longer you shall see my great friends, Miss Nussey and Miss Taylor. They are the most—'

'I want you to myself, Tallii! I have it in mind to write a novel – a serial for *Blackwood's Magazine*. We can sit in the garden if you wish.'

Taking his arm as they strolled in the shaded avenue beyond the lawn she said tentatively,

'What does Papa say to your ambitions?'

'He is most encouraging. Papa understands how it feels for people to want to strike out a path for themselves! Men feel these things. They are not content to be seamstresses and milliners.'

'Neither are many women,' Charlotte said with spirit. 'I want to strike out a path for myself too, Branny.'

'And once I am established I shall be able to help you, introduce you to the right people. I am half-inclined towards portrait painting you know. It provides a welcome relief from writing.'

'But you love writing!'

'As a man loves a demanding mistress. You know there are times when I feel as if the secret world is crushing me, suffocating my mind, making it impossible for me to breathe real air! I am fifteen years old and have already created a universe!'

'Will it cost a great deal to train you as an artist?'

'Papa will do what he can and Aunt has promised to give part of her savings for my training. London, Tallii! Think of it!'

'While you are finding your feet in the great city I must help to support myself and the girls.'

'Well, it'll not be for a year or two yet. You must teach the girls first,' Branwell said, laughing. 'Emily prints most of her letters backwards and spends half her day out on the moors, bringing back any sick or wounded creature she can find. And Anne follows her like a shadow. You will have a task of it to make them mind you!'

'I miss them,' she said wistfully. 'Branny, I dreamed once that Maria and Elizabeth—'

'She calls,' he said.

'What?' Charlotte stopped abruptly and stared at him.

'From the crypt.' His voice had dropped and he hunched his narrow shoulders uneasily. 'Mama and Maria and Elizabeth – though she doesn't call so often or so loudly. I hear them, Charlotte. They want to get out.'

'Have you told Papa?'

'I have written about it. I do hear them. Such things are possible if the dead are restless and unhappy.'

'But they were all so good,' Charlotte said.

'Better than the rest of us can ever hope to be! We can never achieve their particular heaven and so they refuse to enter it. They wait in a half-way stage for us to join them so they can sneak us into heaven behind God's back. It is a kind of Purgatory.'

'That's a Papist belief!'

'Shall I tell you a secret?' He looked at her with mischief in his expressive face. 'Our Irish grandmother, Eilyis McClory was a Roman Catholic. All the McClorys were. That's why our grandfather, Hugh, had to run away with her to be married. Her family forgave her but the old faith is still there, in the blood and the bone!'

'Papa supported Catholic emancipation,' Charlotte said uneasily. 'You don't think—?'

'Papa is staunch Protestant and pities Catholics for their ignorance as he despises Methodists for their ranting, but he believes in equality for all. He's a man of principle. I wish I were more like him.'

'You lack the height,' Charlotte said, laughing.

'But I have the colouring, the energy – who's that?'

'The girls are come out for the afternoon break. Let me—'

'Then I must start back!' Branwell said. 'Papa only agreed to my coming on condition I returned before full dark. He fears the Gytrash may get me! Goodbye, Tallii! I shall write and tell you how our fellow Angrians get on!'

He kissed her cheek, waved his hand and vanished into the foliage.

'Who was that? Charlotte, you haven't got a sweetheart?' Ellen came up with Mary at her heels.

'My brother, Branwell, walked all the way here just to see me,' Charlotte said.

'He didn't ride here?' Ellen said in surprise.

'Not everybody goes galloping about on horses!' Mary said, giving her a sharp nudge. 'Some of us use our legs!'

'Why didn't he wait to meet us properly?' Ellen asked.

'He had to rush back which disappointed him very much, but he asked me to make his apologies,' Charlotte said.

Perhaps Branwell had inspired her because that night, after lights out, when she was urged as usual to tell them a story she found herself relating one that seemed to be unfolding in the darknesss even as she spoke.

'The girl left her bed and went out into the long moonlit corridor which divided the bedchamber from the tower. She knew this place well because she had spent her whole life within these walls. Her father came once or twice a year to check on her height and her looks and then rode away again into the darkness of the surrounding forest.'

'Did her mother come?' Martha enquired.

'Her mother was dead,' Charlotte said.

'Her grandmother?'

'Dead too. All her family except her father were dead.'

'But what—?'

'Shut up, Martha!' Amelia said. 'Go on, Charlotte.'

'Into one room of the castle she had never been, for it was forbidden to her,' Charlotte said. 'But on this night nature overcame her training. The girl dreamed that she awoke and in that state left her bed and made her way down the long passage to the tower and so, her mind still dreaming and her body asleep though it moved, she climbed up the spiral staircase and opened the forbidden door and saw. . . .'

'Saw what?' Mary urged. 'Do get on with it!'

'The room was red,' Charlotte whispered. 'The forbidden room was red. The door closed behind her and she tried to wake up, tried to find the handle of the door but the red was all about her, forcing its way into her mouth, her nostrils, her – oh God!'

She screamed out suddenly so loudly that half the occupants of the dormitory screamed too and Amelia fell into sobbing hysterics.

The door opened and Miss Wooler, in nightcap and shawl, holding a lamp aloft, hurried into the room.

'Is someone sick or hurt? What is it?' she demanded.

'Charlotte was telling us a story,' one of the other girls sobbed out. 'She's frightened us all to death! My heart's stopped.'

'Nonsense, Leah Brooks, your heart is beating quite normally,' Miss Wooler said impatiently. 'Charlotte, stop that silly moaning at once! It is past ten at night and you all should be peaceably asleep. In future you will restrict your story-telling to the daylight hours. One more word and I shall issue you all with a bad conduct mark. Now good night!'

She withdrew herself and her lamp and closed the door firmly.

'Charlotte?' Ellen raised her head from the pillow. 'What was in the red room that made you scream ?'

'I don't know. I was never there,' Charlotte said dully. 'Go to sleep, Ellen.

She turned over, pulling the bedclothes over her ears, and for no reason she could fathom wondered suddenly if Emily was still sleeping in Tabby's room.

It seemed to her that the months were flying by. She would soon be sixteen and ready to begin the task of educating her sisters to a higher standard than Aunt Branwell had been able to achieve. More enticing than that was the prospect of being with Branwell again, sharing in their dream universe of Angria, writing their poems and stories in the home-made volumes, some hardly bigger than postage stamps, in the minute print that nobody else could decipher.

'Charlotte, my dear, you hold your book far too close to your eyes,' Miss Wooler remarked one day, pausing by the window seat where Charlotte was studying. 'I have told you before that it looks most odd.'

'I find the print blurs, ma'am, when I hold the book further away,' Charlotte said. 'My brother suffers from the same problem as does Papa.'

'Your brother wore spectacles when he visited you.'

'Yes, ma'am. He is to be an artist so it is important for him to see clearly.'

'And spectacles are expensive. Yes, I do understand.' Miss Wooler nodded understandingly.

'Miss Wooler!' Charlotte stumbled over her words. 'Please don't think me impertinent but I believe you have it in mind to tell Mrs Franks of my predicament. I would be grateful if you would not. She has been more than generous since I came here as a pupil, having me to stay with her for parts of the holidays. She and Miss Outhwaite, who were our neighbours when we lived in Thornton – Mrs Franks was Miss Firth then, of course – they have presented me with a dress and shawl for formal occasions and – I would really prefer her not to know that my sight is – inadequate.'

'You don't wish to be placed under any further obligation. I applaud your independent spirit, my dear. I shall say nothing to Mrs Franks.'

'Thank you, ma'am.'

Charlotte resumed her seat, her cheeks rather flushed. Of course Papa would buy her spectacles if he realized how poor her sight really was, but in a year or two every penny would be needed to support Branwell while he was in London and pay for his tuition at the Royal Academy.

Leaving day was almost upon them. Charlotte and her friends stood in the dormitory sorting their clothes. Papa was sending the gig for her the next morning. She hoped the expense hadn't been too great but was relieved not to be going home in the covered cart.

'What are you thinking about?' Ellen enquired.

'I was thinking that my schooldays are over and I don't feel – I've spent so much time studying,' Charlotte said.

'Apart from telling scary stories after dark,' Ellen teased.

'I will miss you dreadfully, Ellen,' Charlotte said. 'You and Mary and Martha and Amelia and the Brooks sisters.'

'We shall go on being friends,' Ellen said. 'We shall write to each other and one day exchange visits.'

'We shall write in French,' Charlotte said. 'We both need to perfect our skills in that language. Even so . . .'

'Even so what?'

'I would like to behave like an out-and-out schoolgirl just for once and run round the garden as fast as I can, yelling and waving my arms!'

'I'll come with you if you like,' Ellen offered.

'It's too late.' Charlotte shook her head. 'I am in the habit of being staid and prim.'

And the next morning as she received the silver medal for excellence from Miss Wooler she was glad she hadn't given way to the impulse.

'A leaving present from my sisters and myself,' Miss Wooler said.

In her hands was a black-leather spectacles case with C.B. inscribed on it in gold, and within a pair of gold-rimmed spectacles through which for the first time she would be able to see the beauties of the world.

SEVEN

'Tabby, have you seen Emily and Anne?' Charlotte enquired, putting her head round the kitchen door.

'Miss Annie's sewing in Miss Branwell's room,' Tabby said, looking up from her knitting. 'Miss Emily's out on't moor. '

'She hasn't finished the exercise I gave her,' Charlotte said crossly, taking her cloak from its peg in the hall and hurrying out into the warm afternoon.

Going down the lane and over the stile she paused to put her spectacles on her nose, tracked the tall figure at a little distance and put the spectacles back into their case. Though their usefulness was immeasurable she still felt self-conscious about wearing them in public.

'Emily, wait!' She trotted over the grass to where her sister was throwing a stick for Grasper.

'What?' Emily turned with a faint frown on her face.

'I didn't know that you'd come out.'

'I don't have to report to you every time I leave the house,' Emily said.

'But you are supposed to make some effort at doing the work I set for you! Papa questions me about it and I don't know what to say to him.'

'Tell him it was too difficult for me,' Emily said.

'That wouldn't be true! You could do the exercises perfectly well if you would only make an effort.'

'I don't choose to make an effort,' Emily said calmly. 'You don't really enjoy teaching us and I, for one, certainly don't enjoy trying to learn. You would much prefer to be writing stories about Angria and I would much prefer to be out here.'

'With no bonnet on and your skirt all over grass!'

'Tallii, you're turning into Aunt!' Emily gave a sudden peal of infectious laughter. 'You want to turn me into a fine lady, don't you? It's been coming on ever since you visited Miss Nussey last year. You want me to wear corsets and half a dozen petticoats to plump out my skirt and a little bonnet under which my hair can be decently coiled.'

'If you had seen Rydings,' Charlotte said, 'you would understand. It is one of the most elegant houses one could hope to visit – there is a rookery and a battlemented—'

'Branny told us all about it after he had driven you there. He said he'd left you in paradise. Is Miss Nussey as elegant as her home?'

'She has a simple elegance,' Charlotte said, forgetting about the unfinished exercise. 'She is not exactly pretty – her features are serene and regular, her eyes brown, her hair dark – she suits pink and white – and she has beautiful manners.'

'Then be content with her and leave me to my own devices!'

'Emily, you're fifteen,' Charlotte argued. 'You're almost an adult now. You cannot spend your days on the moor or scribbling up in the little study.'

'One day when there's no help for it I will behave like a lady,' Emily said.

'You could start by taking your hands out of your pockets and stop listening to the birds when you should be practising your scales. You don't set a good example to Anne.'

'Leave Anne alone. She does well as she is. If you want prunes and prisms then write to Miss Nussey.'

'I did write,' Charlotte said, forgetting her irritation. 'She is coming here for two weeks' holiday – here to stay with us! Papa and Aunt both approve and—'

'You want me to move out and sleep with Tabby again while she's here. Why didn't you say so in the first place?'

'There is room for three but it would be rather crowded. Do you mind?'

'No, of course I don't mind,' Emily said. 'I'm pleased your friend is coming, truly! We shall have two weeks without lessons, I trust?'

She laughed again and ran on, the breeze flattening her narrow skirt to her long legs, her curly dark hair tumbling over her shoulders.

There was something about Emily that made people look at her twice when she wanted them to look, Charlotte thought as she walked back along the lane. When Emily didn't want to be noticed she could come and go as invisibly as air. Dear Anne was quite different – slender and small with a long neck and light ringlets framing her face. While Emily would stamp about or disappear with Grasper and the pet hawk she'd found up on the heights and nursed back to health, Anne was always demure and gentle. One knew where one was with Anne.

By the day Ellen arrived Charlotte had chivvied the family into a state of readiness, with the floors scoured, carpets beaten, hearths cleaned out and laid ready for an evening blaze, dishes polished and even the spines of the books in the bookshelves carefully waxed.

'Is the privy freshened?' she demanded of Emily as the latter came in from the yard.

'It smells of lavender,' Emily assured her. 'Do stop fussing over everything, Charlotte!'

'She wishes everything to be nice for her friend,' Anne said.

'I hardly think that Miss Nussey is going to go on her hands and knees to inspect behind the privy,' Emily said. 'Hark! I hear the rumble of wheels!'

It was Ellen, stepping out of a smart little carriage, wearing a pink dress embroidered with white, her hair in glossy bands under a straw bonnet. Charlotte rushed to embrace her friend, scarcely able to believe that after almost a year's absence she was here.

'Aunt, Papa, may I present my friend, Miss Ellen Nussey of Rydings in Birtstall,' she said proudly.

'Miss Nussey, this occasion is one that we have long anticipated.' Papa was at his most stately. 'We shall endeavour to render your visit as agreeable as possible though our humble home must strike you—'

'As warm and welcoming, sir,' Ellen said, dropping a curtsy. 'Miss Branwell, my mother sends her compliments and a box of crystallized violets. She understands they grow in the woods round Cornwall.'

'Indeed they do and have remained one of my favourite flowers,' Aunt said, looking gratified.

'My sisters, Emily and Anne. Miss Nussey.'

Both girls, hovering in the background, dipped into curtsies.

'I'll take your bags upstairs,' Emily said unexpectedly. 'They look heavy.'

She picked them up from where the driver had placed them and went up the stairs.

'Come upstairs and you can freshen yourself up before we come down to tea,' Charlotte said, taking Ellen's arm and bustling her up the stairs.

As they reached the landing Branwell came across the hall, paused and looked up.

'Branwell, Miss Ellen Nussey is come,' Charlotte called.

'Miss Nussey!' He sketched a salute and headed for the front door.

'My brother is always in such a hurry that we swear he will trip over himself coming back one day,' Charlotte said. 'Emily, go and tell Tabby to brew the tea, will you?'

'Right!' said Emily, for once not arguing.

It was going to be a perfect visit. She could feel it in her bones. Happily she led Ellen into the tiny study and threw her arms about her in a loving embrace.

It was unfortunate that after a convivial evening Charlotte should wake in the morning with a thick head and watery eyes.

'You look,' said Papa over breakfast, 'as if you have a cold coming on.'

'It is a touch of migraine, Papa, nothing more. I had planned to take Ellen for a walk—'

'After lying awake half the night giggling and whispering!' Aunt said coming in.

'You must lay the fault at my door, Miss Branwell,' Ellen said promptly, 'for I had a great deal to say. I am very sorry if you were disturbed though.'

'I was not much disturbed, my dear.' Aunt Branwell relented. 'It is, after all, several months since you and Charlotte met. I am sure that if I were to meet some of my old friends from Cornwall I would be chatting the whole of the night!'

'I will take a walk with Miss Nussey if she likes,' Emily said unexpectedly.

'Thank you. I shall be happy to walk with you, Miss Emily,' Ellen said.

They set off shortly after breakfast, Charlotte stationed at the window as they went along the path, Emily's tall figure contrasted with Ellen's small, trim one.

'Emily has never volunteered to go for a walk with anybody outside the family before,' she said blankly.

'We've never had a visitor before,' Anne said placidly.

'I do hope that Emily realizes that Ellen is not accustomed to tramping over rough ground or fording streams.'

'Oh, Charlotte! You fuss too much,' Anne said, laughing.

It was an hour before they returned, an hour during which Charlotte hardly budged from her vantage point. Emily could be so unpredictable! Sometimes she would tease her by leading her close to the cows and sheep that wandered over the moor and then tell her she ought to wear her spectacles, and once she had draped a grass snake over Charlotte's arm and told her it was an adder.

They came through the front door, both talking amiably, Ellen with scarcely a hair out of place.

'I must go and help Tabby!' Emily made for the kitchen.

'Did Emily behave herself?' Charlotte asked Ellen.

'I like your sister,' Ellen said placidly. 'She is a pleasant girl.'

But Ellen was her own friend! Emily and Anne had each other. Ellen was her own special friend. Charlotte said with an effort, 'Well, my headache is almost conquered so I shall not neglect you during the rest of your visit!'

The conquered headache stayed away for two whole weeks. Ellen quickly established herself as a favourite with everybody. Papa joined them as usual for breakfast and even sat with them once or twice after supper when he regaled them with a few of his more horrific ghost stories.

'The poor woman had, of course, eaten her own children. Only their heads remained and they pursued her everywhere, leaping and tumbling through the air.'

'Papa!' Charlotte protested, catching sight of Ellen's face.

'The story was told to me as a true one,' Papa said. He glanced sideways at Ellen as he spoke, a little smile on his lips.

At least he didn't walk out with them on the moors. The four of them spent happy, sunlit afternoons on the heights, sometimes with Branwell though he usually grew bored with the conversation and wandered off. They went almost as far as Ponden House and found a shallow valley through which water gushed over rocks to fall into a pool below.

71

'We ought to form a Society,' Charlotte said.

'The Philosophical Society,' Anne suggested.

'Anne is the only philosopher among us,' Emily said, lying on her stomach at the edge of the pool and chasing tadpoles with her fingers.

'Anne!' Charlotte laughed.

'She believes that all is for the best in the best of all possible worlds,' Emily said.

'Indeed I do not!' Anne spoke with unwonted vivacity. 'The world is a sad and sorry place in many respects but I do believe that we by our own efforts can make it better. I believe that's why we're here.'

'I don't believe we can influence other people at all,' Emily declared. 'We are born either good or bad and we either accept our own natures or fight against them and so do great damage to ourselves and upset the balance of Nature herself. Look at these tadpoles! Some of them swim up to investigate my fingers while others swim away very fast.'

'We are not tadpoles,' Ellen said, giggling.

'We may appear as such to higher beings,' Emily said.

'Oh, I cannot believe that!' Anne sat bolt upright. 'I think that we each of us have a guardian angel who looks after us during our life times.'

'I . . .' Charlotte stopped. Never would she talk about the angel she had seen hovering over Anne's cradle.

'Then some guardian angels,' said Emily, taking her hand out of the pool and shaking drops of water from it, 'are falling down on their duty! The crime rate proves that!'

She jumped up and whistled to Grasper who was chasing an imaginary rabbit and strode off.

'Your sisters are very clever,' Ellen said to Charlotte as they made their way back to the parsonage.

'Clever?' Charlotte looked at her. 'You are very kind to say so, dear Ellen, but in truth they remain woefully backward in their schooling despite my best efforts. Emily can barely spell and neither of them can sew a straight seam without spotting the material with blood.'

'They both play the piano very well,' Ellen defended. 'And Anne sang so sweetly yesterday!'

'Her voice is pleasing but still somewhat weak,' Charlotte

allowed, 'and her playing is correct but lacks spirit. Emily has all the spirit but not the technique. It is a pity that my own short sight made it impossible for me to study music.'

'I expect you would have been very good,' Ellen said.

'That just proves that you have no inkling of what makes a fine musician,' Charlotte said, laughing. 'I would not have excelled, believe me! Branwell now is a different case. He plays the flute wonderfully when he can be persuaded to stay still for long enough and has composed some splendid tunes! Music has always inspired my brother. Sometimes he becomes so excited by it that he has to plunge his head into cold water to cool the disturbance to the brain.'

'Your standards are very high,' Ellen said. 'My own are not so well informed as yours. I enjoy pretty music but of books and pictures I still cannot separate the great from the mediocre.'

'You may rely on me to guide you in that,' Charlotte said, fired up at the notion of instructing her friend. 'I would advise you to eschew novelty and stick to the tried and true. For novels I would suggest Scott. Nobody writes so beautiful as he does these days. In art try to find prints of the great Italian artists. Their mastery of line and colour is superb. In matters of fashion you must guide me. You have exquisite taste, my love!'

Ellen, she thought fondly, was almost perfect.

The end of the visit loomed. Papa, looking gratified as he always was when he could perform a kindness without trouble to himself, told them that he had hired the gig so that they could accompany Ellen back as far as Bolton Abbey.

'Your brothers will meet you there, Miss Nussey, so you may enjoy a few hours still with my little family before you are parted for a spell. Branwell will drive the gig so we must contrive to pack you all in, together with your bags.'

'This is very good of you, Papa,' Charlotte said gratefully.

'I have already written to Rydings to tell them of the arrangements.' Papa smiled at them.

'At least we shall be together for a little longer,' Ellen said to Charlotte as they packed away Ellen's things.

'Have you truly enjoyed yourself here? The parsonage is not as grand as your home. We have always lived very simply,' Charlotte said anxiously.

'I like this house.' Ellen spoke with some of Mary Taylor's

forthright manner. 'It doesn't pretend to be what it is not. And I like your sisters very much indeed. Emily has a way of smiling with her eyes that is most attractive!'

'Not a blessing she bestows on many people,' Charlotte said drily. 'Emily will have to be civilized soon or she will be fit for nothing and Anne still stutters on occasion.'

'I didn't mean,' said Ellen, smiling slightly, 'that I liked them as well as I like you.'

'We have a very special bond,' Charlotte agreed. 'If neither of us marries perhaps one day we could take a cottage together and relish our independence?'

'That would be rather shocking, surely,' Ellen said.

'I fail to see why! Two close friends making a home together could exist very happily without giving offence. Or, if the neighbours made a fuss, I could put on breeches and call myself – Charles Thunder!'

'Charlotte, you come up with the most astounding ideas!' Ellen cried, shaking her head. 'It would be amusing though! However it is our lot to be married sooner or later. I would hate to be a despised old maid, wouldn't you?'

'Oh, nobody will ever want to marry me or my sisters,' Charlotte said. 'We are too eccentric and not in the least beautiful, not to mention that we have no dowries. You will be snapped up very soon I don't doubt, and I shall dislike him exceedingly so I warn you!'

'Girls! Hurry down! Branwell has brought the gig round,' Aunt called from below.

'I have a little gift for Mrs Aykroyd,' Ellen remembered, and hurried down to the kitchen where a moment later Tabby was heard.

'Eh, Miss Ellen! I never thought as how tha'd give me owt! It's been a right pleasure to look after thee, Miss Ellen. A lace handkerchief! Now tha mun call me Tabby! I'm Tabby to all the family.'

'Tabby then,' Ellen was saying as Charlotte came downstairs. Behind Charlotte Emily was lugging down the bags.

And finally they were off, Branwell with his red hair curling over his collar had taken the reins and Papa was helping them up into the swaying vehicle.

'I am trusting you to drive carefully,' Papa said.

74

'I shall protect the girls with my life, Papa!' Branwell cried. 'Might I not borrow one of your pistols for extra protection?'

'You are quite right, my son,' Papa said drily. 'You might *not* sally forth armed! Goodbye, Miss Nussey!'

It was a lovely morning with quite a lot of traffic on the roads. Branwell frequently waved his whip towards other drivers or called out a greeting, prompting Ellen to comment,

'Your brother knows a great many people.'

'Branwell is the most sociable of us all,' Charlotte said. 'He makes friends wherever he goes.'

'It's my fatal charm,' Branwell said, turning to smile at them.

'Keep your eye on the road, Branny,' Emily advised, 'or you will have to call upon that fatal charm to explain to Papa how you managed to throw us all into the ditch!'

They reached the ruins of the abbey without any untoward accident and piled out into the yard at the side of the inn where Ellen's brothers were to meet them.

There was already a handsome carriage drawn up there and a small group of stylishly-clad young people towards whom Ellen hastened.

'George! Henry! You are come already! Oh this is splendid! You already know my dear friend Charlotte,' she cried.

'Miss Brontë.' Henry Nussey bowed gravely.

'And this is Miss Brontë's brother Branwell and her sisters. . . .' Her voice chatted on, entirely confident as she made the introductions. Charlotte's heart had sunk into her boots. For two weeks she had relished her friend's company without really stopping to thick too much how they would appear *en masse* to Ellen's relatives.

Branwell, hair unkempt and shirt-collar open á la Lord Byron looked – untidy, and Emily and Anne seemed to have been struck dumb for they stood together, arms closely entwined, their eyes fixed firmly on the ground.

'I have taken the liberty of ordering luncheon,' George Nussey was saying. 'However we shall first have a glass of wine and then after our meal we shall stroll about the ruins for an hour. Mr Brontë, you will not refuse a glass of wine after your driving so far?'

'Very kind of you, sir, very kind indeed,' Branwell said a shade too loudly.

They looked all wrong, Charlotte thought in agony. Their hair was all wrong, their boots too thick, their garments badly made.

'Miss Brontë, would you do me the honour of taking my arm?' Henry Nussey had crooked his arm with a little bow.

'Thank you, Mr Nussey.'

Taking his arm with a slight inclination of her own head she decided grimly that one Brontë at least would show how to behave well in polite company!

EIGHT

Charlotte put down her pen and gazed unseeingly across the classroom. Her head ached and the scratching of nibs from every desk grated as if they were drawing acid along her nerves. Everything was going wrong, she thought miserably. Yet the previous year they had been so full of plans and projects.

'Branwell must complete his course of anatomy lessons before he presents his letters of introduction to the Royal Academy,' Papa had told them.

Charlotte's smile had been forced. It had been, after all, two drawings of hers and not of Branny's which had been accepted for an exhibition in Leeds the previous summer, but it was Branwell who was going to London where he would see all the magnificent monuments and statues, the Tower with its romantic and tragic associations, the art galleries crammed with masterpieces! It was only right since Branwell was the son but it galled her bitterly all the same.

'At least you will not be going to a strange place,' Aunt had consoled her. 'It is most kind of Miss Wooler to offer you a post at Roe Head, is it not? You are thoroughly familiar with the house and the grounds and the staff too.'

And fourteen pounds a year would buy clothes for her and one of her sisters. Miss Wooler had also offered a free place to one of her sisters. She had decided upon Emily though Papa had raised his eyebrows.

'My dear Charlotte, Emily is seventeen, hardly a schoolgirl. She will not take kindly to discipline.'

'Which is precisely why she will benefit from a year or two at Roe Head. Papa, she must realize she cannot waste her life away.'

'She seems to me to be constantly busy,' Papa said.

'Looking after her pets, cleaning the kitchen, wandering off with Anne in tow! Papa, it won't do.'

'So only Anne will be at home. Well, at least she will be able to move into the study bedroom and give your aunt a room to herself!'

'Anne,' said Aunt, who was listening, 'will continue to sleep in my room, Mr Brontë. I could not dispense with her company.'

It had taken longer to persuade Emily that she required further education.

'Miss Wooler and her sisters are the kindliest of women and the conditions there are extremely comfortable,' Charlotte had pleaded.

'I shall hate it,' Emily said stubbornly. 'I shall hate every single moment of it. I will die there.'

'That's ridiculous!' Charlotte lost patience. 'How can you hope to work as a teacher if you have had no formal training?'

Emily had returned no answer but gone out slamming the door so violently that the cups rattled.

They had travelled together the day before Emily's seventeenth birthday, her sister sullen-faced and taciturn.

And that was when it had all begun to go wrong, Charlotte mused. They had been greeted kindly but from the start Emily had set her face not only against learning anything but against eating or talking. Meal after meal she took a forkful and pushed her plate away. Charlotte, trying to accustom herself to the role of teacher rather than pupil, had seen her sister's slender figure grow painfully thin as the weight dropped off, had desperately tried to cheer her up with talk of the pleasant walks round the neighbourhood the pupils took.

'Two by two,' Emily said dully. 'Animals going into the Ark.'

'Try to make friends,' Charlotte urged. 'Some of the pupils are agreeable girls—'

'I don't need friends,' Emily said.

And the other pupils thought she was strange anyway, Charlotte thought. She was the oldest pupil there and the tallest and she walked round in a kind of daze, her eyes fixed on the ground, her mouth set in a sneer.

Within three months she had given in and, at Miss Wooler's suggestion, written to Papa telling him that Emily was ill and that her place could be supplied by Anne.

'Your youngest sister is—'

'Anne will be sixteen in January, ma'am. She is quiet and very conscientious. More malleable than Emily.'

'Then I feel she will fit in with us more happily,' Miss Wooler said. 'I must confess, dear Charlotte, that I cannot feel any kinship with Emily.'

'She is homesick,' Charlotte defended. 'In Haworth she is used to following her own routine, and in arranging her own time.'

'Yes, well – we shall see how your other sister gets on,' Miss Wooler had said, tactfully refraining from further comment.

Inside she felt bruised. She had looked forward to drawing closer to Emily but Emily had been unresponsive, merely shrugging when they heard that Branwell had returned from London within a few days, his money apparently stolen and his letters of introduction never even presented.

'How could he be so careless?' Charlotte had raged. 'To lose – for I cannot believe it was stolen – his money in such a careless way and then to come drudging home again without making the least effort! I had such high hopes of him.'

'He likely gambled or drank it away,' Emily had said.

'Branwell would never—'

'Wake up, Tallii,' Emily said and walked off without another word. At least Anne had settled in nicely, Charlotte reflected. She had simply become another pupil, obedient and demure.

And I, thought Charlotte, am simply another teacher, driving grammatical rules into the heads of oafs and dolts.

It wasn't Miss Wooler's fault. The routine of the school was as gentle and unvarying as ever, but it was one thing to be a pupil, to study the lessons and do the exercises, and join in the walks round the neighbourhood while Miss Wooler told them exciting tales of the Luddites who had lain in wait on the moors to smash the new looms coming into the mills and attacked the owners of the mills in their own homes.

It was quite a different matter to have to prepare and mark the exercises, to have to listen to someone read out a poem or a piece of magnificent prose with as much feeling as if it were a shopping list.

And during the evenings when the girls sat out of doors or, as darkness fell, linked arms and walked up and down the long drawing-room, she, as a junior mistress was expected to deal with a pile of mending.

She closed her eyes, seized a pencil and began to write – words spilling out of her into the darkness, her hand moving rapidly.

'I am going to write because I cannot help it . . . what is there in all this to remind me of the divine, silent land of thought, dim now and indefinite as the dream of a dream, the shadow of a shade? Why cannot the blood rouse the heart, the heart wake the head, the head prompt the hand? to do things like these?'

'Miss Brontë, are you all right? Are you asleep?' Voices breaking into the scene unfolding in her head.

'She can't be asleep! She's writing.'

Charlotte opened her eyes, instinctively placing her arm across the wildly slanted writing, her eyes seeing the bewildered faces of several girls clustered round her desk. Vomit rose up in her throat.

'Miss Brontë, shall I fetch Miss Wooler?'

'No indeed!' She heard her own voice. 'I was merely conducting an experiment. Is this your exercise, Miss Lister? Leave it there for me to mark. Ah! the supper bell. Leave your compositions on my desk and file out quietly.'

She walked to the window and opened it, letting the wind cool her face and ruffle her hair. Branwell and Emily would likely feel the same wind as it swept across Yorkshire. Branwell had resumed his drawing lessons and was writing poetry – she had received a letter from him though he had neglected to include any of his poems, and he had told her nothing of how events unfolded in Angria. He had been made secretary of the Temperance Society – she could imagine Emily's lifted eyebrow at that news! And he had been initiated into the Masons though he could tell her nothing about that!

Branwell was moving away from her. She could feel the bond weakening. It would have been bearable had he been in London establishing himself in a powerful position. She could have been proud of that, but learning of his various social activities, the hours he spent in the local boxing club, his bursts of enthusiasm that invariably descended into apathy, she felt a burning frustration rise up in her. She was here earning her living and clothing Anne as well as herself so that Branwell's ambitions could be paid for and he was doing nothing constructive!

As for Emily! Emily had recovered her appetite and her cheerfulness within hours of arriving home and in the months since had elected herself as assistant servant, helping in the kitchen, struggling with the weekly wash, tramping across the moors with the new dog, Keeper, her hawk on her shoulder, living in her world of Gondal which she shared with Anne, though Charlotte guessed that Anne's absence at school would make little difference to what the characters in Gondal were doing.

'Charlotte, my dear, are you well? The girls said. . .' Kind little Miss Wooler had entered the room.

'A slight headache, ma'am.'

'I shall brew you a tisane. Come to supper now.'

It wasn't a tisane she needed. It was time and leisure and space in which to involve herself once more in the colourful world she had shared for so many years with her brother.

'You work too hard, Charlotte,' Miss Wooler was saying. 'You were exactly the same when you were a pupil here, conning your books long after it became too dark to see.'

'Mary Taylor always vowed that I could see in the dark,' Charlotte said, smiling faintly.

'You must take more advantage of your free Sundays,' the other advised. 'Ellen Nussey and Mary Taylor both invite you to spend that day with them as indeed does Mrs Franks. You must accept more frequently, my dear.'

'Thank you, ma'am. I will,' Charlotte promised.

Neither Ellen nor Mary lived in the secret world nor knew of it, though Mary had sometimes tried to remind her that she had once said she would let her read one of the little books they composed. On the other hand she did relish her visits to them though for different reasons.

'The point is,' said Mary, turning up unexpectedly on the next free afternoon, 'that while you teach here month in and month out you're not doing anything positive with your life!'

'I'm clothing Anne and myself,' Charlotte said defensively.

'But not saving anything? You will be middle-aged before you turn round. Don't you want to get on in the world?'

'Yes, of course. When Branwell—'

'On your own account!' Mary said, her grey eyes flashing. 'Why must your brother be responsible for taking care of his sisters until some unwary male falls into their clutches and carries them off? I intend to seek further education for myself

81

and then obtain employment abroad. Mother thinks I am mad and undisciplined but Father supports my aims.'

Charlotte found herself smiling. Her brief visits to the Red House at Gomersal where the Taylors lived had stimulated and amused her. Mrs Taylor was a cantankerous woman who found it difficult to be amiable even with a guest but Mr Taylor was a shrewd, outspoken man who spoke French as readily as English, encouraged his two daughters to be as independent as possible and treated Charlotte when he saw her as an intelligent being who deserved to harbour ambitions on her own account.

Ellen was a different matter. When Charlotte thought of Ellen her heart melted into tenderness. Ellen's company was soothing. When Charlotte closed her eyes she could summon up Ellen's image, the small, trim figure, the bands of dark hair and large brown eyes.

She wrote often to Ellen, pouring out her feelings, telling her how much she loved and missed her. The thought that Ellen might visit the school brought tears of anticipation to her eyes and at night, as she lay wakeful in her bed with images of the secret world rampaging through her head, she could only find a measure of sleep by hugging her pillow and imagining it was her friend.

At least there was Christmas to enjoy! There was time to write, time to hear from Branwell what was happening in Angria, time to satisfy herself that everybody was well. Papa had never objected to the pagan practices of decorating the house with holly and ivy and eating roast goose, kindly supplied by Mr Heaton – not the older Heaton who had been so kind at the ill-fated party but his eldest son, another Robert, who was still only a lad – and a plum-pudding.

'I have written to Mr Wordsworth,' Branwell told her.

'What about?' Charlotte asked.

'I have sent him some of my poems,' he told her. 'I begged him to consider them and give me his honest opinion. I reminded him that there is not a living poet worth sixpence—'

'That wasn't very tactful!'

'He will realize that I don't include him – but he is more or less retired now. You should send something to another writer.'

'I have begun a novel,' she confessed. 'I would send it to Mr Southey but he might never read it.'

'He may read it and encourage you. You cannot tell unless you try,' Branwell urged. 'Send it care of his publisher as I did. Tallii, we've been writing stories since we were children. Why should we not become published writers?'

She was swept away by her brother's enthusiasm and went at once to write a fair copy of the two chapters she had scribbled during odd half-hours at Roe Head.

Snow fell steadily during the holidays. Ellen had promised to spend the New Year with them and that prospect spurred on Charlotte's pen.

'Papa has agreed that I should lodge in Bradford and set myself up as a portrait-painter there,' Branwell told her.

'I thought you were going to be a writer.'

'There's no law says that I cannot be both!' he argued. 'My painting shall be for the day when the light's good and the evenings for my writing. I shall very quickly obtain commissions.'

'And how support yourself in the meantime?'

'Aunt has undertaken to lay out a sum on my behalf. She has always had faith in me you know.'

'Yes. Yes, I know.'

A tiny cloud had passed across the Christmas horizon. Aunt had never married or borne children of her own. It was only natural that she should regard Branwell as the lively, mischievous son she had never had.

'The surface of the snow is frozen like glass!' Emily said, coming in and pulling off her wet cloak. 'Keeper and I had a fine slide over the moor! Where's Tabby?'

'She went to the apothecary for some stomach powders for Papa,' Anne said.

'Papa overindulged on the mince-pies,' Charlotte said.

'When did she go?' Emily wanted to know.

'About an hour since. Why?'

'Because I saw the apothecary in the lane not five minutes ago. He said he'd closed the shop for the day because most folk were staying by their firesides.'

'Then Tabby will have gone down to see if her sister has any,' Charlotte said.

'I'll go and look for her!' Emily flung her cloak on again. 'She'll never get up the hill without help.'

'Ems, Tabby's been running up and down Main Street since she was a girl,' Charlotte argued.

'She's nearly sixty-seven years old now and hardly a lass,' Emily said sharply.

'Shall I come with you?' Anne had risen anxiously.

'You'd never be able to keep your balance on this ice,' Emily scolded. 'I won't be long.'

She was less than a couple of minutes. Her voice, shouting for Branwell, could be heard faintly as Anne opened the front door.

'Child! What are you about?' Aunt Branwell emerged from her room majestically. 'You will give us all our deaths of – what's that?'

'Something has happened,' Charlotte began, interrupted by Emily who came flying through the garden gate.

'Tabby has fallen at the top of the road,' she informed them curtly. 'Branwell's gone for the doctor! Anne and Charlotte, you will have to come after all. We must devise a stretcher.'

'A stretcher? Girls, what is all this about?' Papa had emerged from his parlour.

'I think Tabby has broken her leg,' Emily said.

'Dear Lord! Charlotte, Anne, stay here. I will come with you!' Papa was pulling on his coat, wrapping his muffler about his neck.

All was suddenly bustle and confusion. Charlotte, hunting out warm blankets, felt a sickness at the pit of her stomach. If Tabby should die! She had been the fulcrum of their lives ever since Cowan Bridge.

Later that day with Tabby, her leg broken in two places, tucked up in her own room, they sat round the dining room table.

'One thing is certain,' Aunt said. 'Once it is safe to move her then Tabby must be nursed at her sister's.'

'Tabby,' said Emily, compressing her lips, 'will be nursed here.'

'My dear, that's hardly sensible,' Aunt said. 'Mrs Woods will be able to give Tabby the best of care until she is well enough to—'

'Charlotte and Anne have to return to Roe Head and Branwell is going to Bradford so there will be fewer people to feed and fewer beds to make,' Emily returned. 'I'm perfectly capable of seeing to all that but one of the Brown children can help with running errands and washing up. Martha is a good little thing, very quick and willing. I can nurse Tabby myself..'

'Wearing yourself out with going up and down stairs.'

'Papa, I already walk miles on the moor every day,' Emily told him.

'I shall leave the decision in your hands then, ladies,' Papa said, rising with alacrity.

'The decision,' said Aunt Branwell, 'is mine. Tabby will be carried to her sister's and nursed there. You may go down every day, Emily, and spend most of your time with her. It will be better for her in the long run, and naturally I shall contribute to any expenses incurred.'

'Why don't we just shoot her?' Emily flared.

'Don't be ridiculous, Emily!'

Aunt rose and stalked from the room with as much hauteur as a small lady in a large mob-cap could stalk.

'Tabby,' Emily said, 'will stay here! Papa agrees with me though he will not go against Aunt. You are in concord with me I trust?'

'Yes,' said Anne firmly.

'Yes, of course I am,' Charlotte said. 'But Aunt has the final word, love.'

'Not if we stand together!'

'Doing what?' Anne wanted to know.

'We won't eat,' Emily said. 'We won't eat or drink until Aunt agrees to allow Tabby to be nursed here.'

'A hunger-strike?'

'The one way we have of righting what would be an injustice,' Emily said fiercely.

'But if Aunt remains obdurate—'

'She will not. People never do. Anne, what are you doing?'

'Having a last mince-pie,' Anne said meekly.

'The strike,' Emily announced, 'begins now.'

Aunt would yield, Charlotte thought. She meant everybody to fit into their allotted places and she hadn't yet learnt that Emily was almost impossible to fit anywhere.

She went over to her writing-desk and took out paper and a pen. She would have to write and tell Ellen not to come. With Tabby sick in the house – and she had no doubt that Emily would get her way – there would be no time in which to entertain a guest. And Ellen, being Ellen, would insist on helping. She had an invalid sister of her own at home who had been born backward and deformed and already spent much of her life fetching and carrying for her.

She sat down, dipped her pen into the inkwell and began to write, crushing down her disappointment as she explained about

Tabby's accident and the necessity of cancelling the visit.

As she wrote the image of Ellen rose in her mind. Dear, kind, faithful Ellen! If only she had her friend's placid nature, her ability to take life as it came and not prick her heart with longing for things that could never be!

NINE

It was almost ten o'clock. At this hour she and Ellen had vowed to look up into the sky and think of each other.

As if, Charlotte thought, I could confine myself to thinking about Ellen only once in twenty-four hours!

The past year of 1837 had been a long, hard slow one. Tabby had remained at the parsonage to be nursed by a quietly triumphant Emily and she had returned to Roe Head with Anne to resume the tedious round of teaching and sewing and walks in crocodile about the neighbourhood.

In March Robert Southey replied to the two chapters she had sent him. It was a kindly letter but it cast a blight over her hopes. The venerable poet believed that women should confine their imaginations to decorating cakes and embroidering cushions. He phrased the advice with great charm but the message was clear. She had written back to thank him dutifully though here and there her sentences had twisted into sarcasm.

'I confess that sometimes in the evenings I do think but I must learn to deny myself.' She doubted if he would read beneath the surface!

At least she had received an answer. Poor Branwell had had no answer from Mr Wordsworth.

She had visited Ellen but the visit wasn't entirely happy. The Nusseys were finding the expenses of Rydings too excessive and were in the process of moving to a roomy but less handsome dwelling at Brookroyd. Poor Sarah, huddled in her wheelchair, required almost constant attention. And it had seemed to Charlotte that she and Ellen never snatched a moment to themselves before some member of the family came seeking them. It was the harder because Ellen was preparing to pay a long visit to one of her brothers in London.

'I will write to you,' Ellen promised.

'You must! Dearest Ellen, I live only for your letters!'

'Ah, there you are, Ellen! Sarah wishes to be taken for an airing in the garden. Miss Charlotte, have you leisure to help me? These curtains seem to have lost their fringe.'

Ann Nussey, thin and spinsterish, had drawn Charlotte away. Perhaps it was wrong to dote on one person so intensely. It removed one's mind from more important things.

There had been only a couple of brief notes from Ellen since her departure. Her sister-in-law had borne a healthy child and Ellen was enjoying herself taking care of the older children and reading a great many books which was something disapproved of at home. Charlotte had written back frantically, begging Ellen not to neglect her, spattering 'dears' and 'darlings' like ink-blots all through the letters. Ellen didn't reply for almost two months and enclosed a recipe for seedcake.

In the summer there had been a visitor at Haworth. Papa's brother Hugh had arrived without warning from Ireland. It was the first time that any of Papa's relatives had come. Charlotte had been staying with the Taylors for a few days and returned home to find that Papa had whisked his brother off to London to see the preparations for the coronation of the new queen.

'He is even taller than Papa,' Emily said, laughing. 'He and Papa got together over a bottle of whisky and were soon chatting away in the Gaelic! Aunt was quite charmed.'

'But why did he come?' Charlotte asked.

'Probably to charm some money out of Papa!'

'He must resemble Branwell then,' Charlotte said.

She was still smarting from a conversation she had had with Papa earlier in the year when she had bearded him in his parlour.

'Papa, I was twenty-one last week.'

'So you were, my dear!'

'I wondered if – if you had given any thought to granting me an allowance.'

'A – what?' Papa put down his book and stared at her.

'Just a small regular sum of money for my own use, Papa. It is customary. I thought perhaps – a shilling?'

'You already earn fourteen pounds a year plus your keep.'

'The money clothes Anne and myself but there's nothing left. I never have a penny to put in my pocket!'

'My dear child, what do females want with money?' Papa said. 'In any case Branwell still requires some financial support. He has rent to pay in Bradford and until he is fully established there commissions are slow in coming. Perhaps Miss Wooler will see her way to increasing your salary.'

But Miss Wooler had problems of her own.

'The rent of this establishment has risen over the past two or three years,' she told Charlotte. 'I could advertise for more pupils and I am certain to get them for our reputation is very high, but that would mean lowering our standards by crowding more girls into the dormitory and it would be more difficult to give them the individual attention they now enjoy. I have made enquiries and Heald House at Dewsbury is vacant for a most reasonable rent. We shall move there at the beginning of next year.'

Charlotte, who had feared she might lose her post, heaved a sigh of relief.

The autumn had been long and wet with a slow dying of the leaves and flowers. Ellen returned from London too late for Charlotte to visit and though Brookroyd was only a couple of miles off she was constantly occupied with family affairs. The occasional letter, tossed over the school wall by her brother George on his way to the mill, was often the only contact.

She moved from the window and lay down on her bed, closing her eyes. She would not think of Ellen. She would fix her mind upon the psalm she had promised her dearest friend she would commit to memory.

He lay upon a couch piled with vividly embroidered cushions, a loincloth his sole garment. His skin gleamed brownish black and a musky scent emanated from him. He slept, his chest heaving, a lock of curly black hair straying over his broad brow, white teeth gleaming through parted lips. Quashia! His name was Quashia! If she reached out her hand and touched him he would wake, spring from his couch, seize her in a passionate, lustful embrace.

'—and I said to Miss Marriott . . .'

'—absolutely exhausted but Miss Wooler makes the subject so fascinating. . .'

'Hush, you will wake Miss Brontë!'

She wasn't asleep but she couldn't move. She couldn't open her eyes or stir a limb. She couldn't even feel her own body. She floated above it, her eyes on the savage, wonderful Quashia. Was this death? To be suspended between the desire and the act? To be punished for the images that crowded her mind?

She came back into her body with a rush and opened her eyes, feeling her own sweat drying on her skin.

Imagination could be a snare, a vicious enemy, turning one from duty and honour. Charlotte sat up, made her way dizzily into the corridor and sat down in a window seat. Her legs were shaking and she felt sick.

She had best gather her scattered wits together and go down. She stood up, consciously bracing herself and went slowly downstairs.

Anne was coming out of the dining-room. Charlotte heard her breathing before she saw her and was struck by a memory. Maria and Ellie, with heads drooping, every breath a rasping labour, walking along the passage at Cowan Bridge.

'Anne?' she said sharply.

'I have leave to lie down,' Anne said. 'Miss Wooler says that I have a slight cold.'

'Has she sent for the doctor?'

'It isn't a doctor I need,' Anne said in a whisper. 'I need to see a minister.'

'A what? Annie, what's the matter?'

'I don't know,' Anne said, coughing. 'There is such a weight of sin on me, Charlotte, that I can hardly breathe!'

'You? Sin?' Charlotte stared at her sister.

'Not a local clergyman,' Anne said. 'There are the Moravians not too far away, are there not? They are said to understand and deal more gently with such matters. I don't want to die and go to hell.'

She had begun to cry weakly, crying that turned into sobbing gasps as she fought for breath.

'Miss Marriott! Miss Marriott, please help my sister to bed! I must see Miss Wooler immediately!'

Charlotte beckoned the senior pupil urgently and, turning,

ran down the corridor into Miss Wooler's private sitting-room without bothering to knock.

'Charlotte, is something—?' Miss Wooler rose, her face startled.

'My sister is ill, dying!' Charlotte cried. 'Why could you not see it?'

'Your sister has a cold, my dear. I have already had some cough mixture made up for her.'

'It is more than a cold!' Rage swelled in her. 'My little sister is dangerously ill and you have ignored her symptoms! All you care about is your wretched school and the fees you obtain! Of course Anne pays no fees at all so her dying will mean profit for you when you no longer need to feed her!'

'I will send for the doctor but—'

'Do so, Miss Wooler! Do it now if you can bestir yourself so much! As soon as possible we will both be leaving!'

Miss Wooler sat down and burst into tears.

'Crying won't help!' Charlotte shouted. 'She must have been ailing for some time and you never noticed, never told me. I shall write to Papa immediately!'

'Charlotte, please—'

Charlotte slammed the door and ran upstairs to where two of the girls were helping a weeping Anne to climb into the bed reserved for the sick in a side room.

There was no sleeping for her that night. She moved like a restless ghost between sickroom and the front door, rudely shouldering Miss Wooler aside when the doctor arrived and talking volubly of the two older sisters who had already died.

By morning the doctor had gone, diagnosing Anne as having 'a severe attack of gastric influenza, Miss Brontë. The condition often causes severe depression.'

A Moravian clergyman had been summoned. Charlotte wrote a letter to Papa at white-heat speed and chivvied a sleepy-eyed servant to run to the post with it. A dark winter dawn had brought driving rain. It would be at least a fortnight before Anne could be moved. If she was still alive!

Wearily Charlotte sat down and stared bleakly through the window at the rainy garden. It wasn't only Miss Wooler's fault that Anne's condition had gone unremarked, she thought with painful clarity. Anne was always so quiet and dutiful, so uncomplaining. On the verge of eighteen she still looked like a child, scarcely five feet tall with her hair tied back and her figured grey dress emphasising her slenderness.

'Charlotte?' Miss Wooler, eyes dark shadowed, had emerged from her room. 'My dear Charlotte, I do confess that I have been remiss in many respects but nobody could have guessed – your sister never complains. Every care shall be taken, I promise you.'

'It will be,' Charlotte said coldly.

'My dear, please reconsider your decision to leave!'

'I cannot!' Charlotte's voice cracked with weariness and emotion. 'Miss Wooler, soon I shall be twenty-two years old and I have spent my whole life in learning and teaching.'

'As I have,' Miss Wooler said.

'And I honour you for it. I should not have said what I did to you last night. I am as much to blame for Anne's illness. I should have taken more care of her. I should have noticed – in lashing out at you I was also lashing out at myself! But my desire to leave is – it has little to do with you and much to do with myself! I need a change.'

'In Dewsbury, my dear.' Miss Wooler spoke placidly. 'Young people relish a change of scene. Heald House is a well-appointed building and we shall be within walking distance of the town. I shall rely on your help to settle the pupils in. As a friend – I value you, Charlotte.'

'If Anne recovers – after the New Year,' Charlotte said.

'That is all I ask.' Miss Wooler took her hands between her own. 'I too have been at fault. We are all apt to pay more attention to those people who cause us most trouble and forget that the quiet ones may also need our help.'

'Yes,' Charlotte said.

'And as for your own restlessness – we have such moods from time to time. I find that occupying oneself in work for others is the best cure.'

'Yes, Miss Wooler.'

She suddenly had the mad impulse to tell her headmistress about Quashia, but of course she could never do so. She could tell nobody about him except Branwell and possibly Emily.

When the coach arrived a week later, Papa having hired it in a panic after receiving her letter, Anne was well enough to dress and walk downstairs but she was frighteningly pale and her cough sounded hoarse and painful.

Aunt Branwell, taking one look, said briskly,

'Bed at once, my dear Anne! We shall soon have you well again. Charlotte, you have done exactly the right thing in sending for her to come home. Mr Brontë was exceedingly worried.'

'Where is Branwell?' Charlotte asked.

'We expect him in a day or two. He has sold a few paintings which is very gratifying but earned hardly any money which is disappointing. Emily went down to the village to buy some paper. I sometimes think she must eat it all for I know only yourself to whom she ever writes.'

She smiled and bustled upstairs again.

It was good to be at home. No tedious lessons to hear nor exercises to mark, no having to hide her enthusiasms and her temper under a demure façade.

Emily came in with a large packet of paper under her arm. She looked well, Charlotte thought, taking in the slim upright figure, the bright eyes and glossy hair.

'Welcome!' she nodded amicably as she went past. 'Anne is in bed I suppose. Is she—?'

'She is not well but there is no immediate danger,' Charlotte said. 'Her spirits are very low.'

'Being imprisoned in school! Can you wonder at it?' Emily put her packet on the table and ran upstairs.

So Anne would stay at home now, resume her plays of Gondal and their walks on the moors. She had escaped from tedium. Emily had escaped too by making herself ill. She, Charlotte, would be the one still trapped in the endless trawl of duty.

'My dear Charlotte, it is good to have you home again.' Papa looked up from his book when she tapped on the parlour door and went in.

'Have you seen Anne?' she asked.

'I looked in earlier. She will be spared to us for a long time yet. You were right to inform me immediately.'

'I hoped so, Papa.'

'And soon we shall be enlivened by Branwell! He is selling a few paintings here and there and he has made some friends in Bradford. You will be returning to Dewsbury after the New Year?'

'I withdrew my notice,' Charlotte said.

'I recall my time at Dewsbury very well indeed.' He sighed. 'I was engaged in writing for much of the time. I was, though I could not know it, on the verge of meeting your dear mother. They were happy days.'

'And Tabby is quite well again!' Charlotte said.

'Her leg still pains her though she will not admit it. We are none of us getting any younger. You wrote to Mr Franks as I instructed?'

'Yes, of course. I was able to console with him sincerely on the death of his wife. She was always very kind to us.'

'Ah, Miss Firth that was!' Papa chuckled. 'She made us so welcome when we moved to Thornton. Such a pretty young woman and so glad to accompany me on my walks when your dearest mama was with child! This recent outbreak of influenza has been a cruel one.'

'Haworth escaped it,' Charlotte said.

'For which we must give hearty thanks. The air is purer here. I only wish we could persuade the local landowners to contribute to a new water-system and improved drainage which would cut-down the annual epidemics of cholera and typhoid. However they are terrified of a rise in the rates! Tell Tabby that I will have my tea in the parlour but if Branwell arrives he is to join me.'

'Yes, Papa.'

Aunt fussing over Anne, Emily helping Tabby in the warm, friendly, untidy kitchen, Papa welcoming Branwell in the parlour.

Herself alone? She went upstairs to the tiny study bedroom. Emily, who had always shared Tabby's bed during her sister's absence had decided that she was adult enough to sleep alone. Her single bed was by the window, a chest of drawers on the left held her brush and comb.

'I will share Tabby's room while you're home,' Emily said, coming out of Aunt's room.

'There's no need. I can share with you,' Charlotte began.

'No need. You may enjoy your privacy,' Emily said cheerfully going down the stairs.

Herself alone then. Charlotte went over to the bed and knelt on it, gazing through the window. In her mind Ellen's gentle face took shape.

TEN

Sunlight flooded the dining-room and poured through the open front door. The parlour door was also open and Papa sat by the open casement listening with obvious pleasure as Mary Taylor played Irish tunes on the piano. She made a charming picture with her long fair ringlets and dark lashed grey eyes, only the firmness of her jaw saving her from being too perfect.

'Mary Taylor is too pretty to live long!' Miss Wooler had once remarked casually in Charlotte's hearing.

The remark had been a joking one but Charlotte, sealing a letter she had just written to Ellen, found herself watching Mary closely.

Her friend's colour was hectic and sometimes she breathed fast which could mean a pulmonary disease.

Martha, by contrast, was not in the least pretty, her features as irregular and sharp as a pixie's, her hair an untidy mop of toffee-coloured hair and her eyes cat-green, but her gaiety and impertinent remarks made her attractive. She was teasing Branwell now, capping his remarks with comical ones of her own.

'Do you think Mary is quite well?' Charlotte murmured to Emily who had plonked herself on the floor nearby.

'Perfectly well. Why?' Emily enquired.

'Her colour is rather high and her breathing rapid sometimes.'

'Fiddlesticks! Mary Taylor will make old bones,' Emily said robustly. 'You fret too much, Tallii! Put your fears in your pocket and lock them up for the rest of June!'

'That was first rate, Miss Taylor!' Papa was clapping. 'You play beautifully. Branwell, I have a meeting of the trustees to chair. Will you come with me?'

'Ready and willing, kind sir!' Branwell jumped up, ready as usual to be up and away.

Branwell had given up his studio in Bradford and veered back towards literature, though with scant success save for a couple of poems published in the local newspaper.

He went out now with Papa, a short jaunty figure next to the tall grey-haired one.

'Your brother is very clever, isn't he?' Mary said, leaving the piano and coming to sit next to Charlotte.

'Very!' Charlotte said decidedly.

'And at his ease in company.'

'Unlike the rest of us,' Charlotte admitted. 'Oh, we do well enough with people we know but in the presence of strangers—'

'And I relish the company of strangers,' Mary said. 'I am fascinated by the traits of character they reveal without being aware of it. One day I intend to travel and meet dozens of people. I shall collect them like seashells and sort them in my mind! My mother warns me that curiosity is vulgar but if we are never curious how can we advance?'

'And what will you do with all your characters when you have analysed them?' Charlotte enquired.

'I shall write a book and become rich and famous and travel all round the world! Is that your letter to Ellen? Is she still in London with her brothers? Her family cannot do anything unless Ellen is there to help out.'

'I'll post it for you!' Martha came over and took the letter. 'Anne, will you walk with me?'

'Yes, of course.'

Anne, rising placidly and tying on her bonnet, seemed at eighteen-and-a-half to be older than the nineteen-year-old Martha.

'I'll help Tabby with the washing up,' Emily said, scrambling up.

'Tell me about Dewsbury. Is it as bad as you wrote to me?'

'Oh, the actual school building is large enough and well appointed,' Charlotte said, 'but it has no charm, no pleasant garden and it stands low on the moor so that the mist and fog linger longer. The place depresses me.'

'Then find another,' Mary said simply.

'I am happier with the evil that is familiar.'

'Evil? Surely not! You exaggerate.'

'Of course,' Charlotte admitted. 'But I am not happy there despite Miss Wooler's kindness. Let's talk of other things! This is holiday time. Anne is perfectly recovered and Branwell is at home and the sun is shining.'

It continued to shine for the remainder of their stay. She was pleased that Branwell spent a considerable amount of time with them, going ahead with Emily when they rambled on the moors, joking with Martha, debating fiercely with Mary on every subject under the sun.

Watching Mary's lovely face sparkle with amusement and seeing her brother's eyes fixed on her thoughtfully once or twice she found herself wondering. Branwell was attractive with fine features and a frame that though short was graceful and well proportioned; Mary was lively and beautiful. Perhaps . . . ?

She also noticed that Emily had not taken to Mary as she had to Ellen. There had been no suggestions from Emily that she and Mary should take a walk together. She laughed and jested with Martha but she was polite towards Mary. Only once did she display wholehearted approval for the other. As they sat round the fire on a rare cool evening towards the end of the visit Mary said,

'In two days we go home. Joe is coming to fetch us away and I only hope he doesn't follow Joshua's example and have a row of clergymen lined up for mutual inspection when I get home!'

'Don't you like clergymen?' Anne enquired.

'I like those who don't pry into my opinions,' Mary said decidedly. 'Only last month one of the tribe had the impudence to ask me for an account of my religious beliefs. I told him that was between God and myself!'

Emily, looking up from the floor where she was sprawled with a book, lifted her head, fixed her blue eyes on Mary and said with quiet approval:

'That's right.'

Joe Taylor arrived on the appointed day, springing out of the gig he was driving and shaking hands warmly with everybody. Charlotte liked Mary's brother. Indeed it was impossible to dislike him! He was a couple of years older than she and had her features cast in a masculine mould.

'You have heard the news I suppose?' were his words when the first greetings were over.

97

'What news?' Papa enquired.

'Ellen Nussey's brother is dead by his own hand.'

'Not George?' Charlotte said.

'William. He had been suffering from depression for some time, poor fellow. We had the news yesterday.'

'Ellen is staying with him and her brother John in London,' Charlotte said.

'Aye, but my father had it that she has been taken to Bath to recover from the shock. He drowned himself in the Thames.'

They were silent, the pleasures of the holiday overshadowed. Mary said: 'Does Ellen know it was suicide?'

'I imagine so. The balance of his mind had been giving concern for some time. One would have to be in a dreadful state to throw one's life away at the age of thirty-two!'

Poor, poor Ellen! Charlotte's heart yearned towards her.

There was nothing she could do save write a carefully worded letter of condolence and pack her trunk ready for the return to Dewsbury.

Even Miss Wooler's kindly welcome did very little to dispel the gloom that weighed down her spirits when she entered the square, solid, unadorned building and saw that even the fresh paint on the walls and the newly polished floorboards failed to dissipate the barren aspect of many of the rooms.

'We cannot accommodate more than eight or ten pupils,' Miss Wooler confided on the first evening. 'Money is . . . not as plentiful as I could wish. However I have dispensed with the services of the linen-maid for the sorting of linen is a task we can all share and my dear mother, who was, as you know, widowed at Easter, will make her home here. My sister Eliza will take over most of my classes since one day she may wish to take her turn as headmistress. All in all we shall do very nicely!'

On the surface, Charlotte thought privately, her heart sinking further.

As the pupils arrived in ones and twos she was sucked back into the inexorable routine. Rising-bell, prayers, breakfast, tidying of rooms, lessons, walk over the dank moors, dinner, recreation when she was expected to make herself agreeable, music and drawing lessons, tea, supervision of prep, marking of exercises and preparation of the next day's work, and before bed the endless sewing and mending!

At night her brain teemed with images, some clear, some blurred, and her whole being ached for something she found impossible to define. Ellen wrote consolingly but she was still in Bath and likely to remain there for some time. Mary and Martha had gone on holiday into Wales and Branwell had given up the Bradford scheme entirely and was now looking for a job that would bring in a regular salary.

In October a rare letter from Emily fretted her almost beyond bearing. Emily had taken herself off to Halifax to teach in Law Hill School for Young Ladies. The school was run by a Miss Patchett who was a noted horsewoman and part of the place was given over to the breeding of stock. The work, Emily wrote, was hard since there were forty pupils so she was busy from six in the morning until near eleven at night.

Why on earth had Emily gone off to Halifax? Tabby still found it difficult to get around on her crooked leg and Anne wouldn't be able to cope with the washing and cleaning! She would also have to take care of the pets Emily had acquired – the two geese that hissed at Aunt, the hawk that took meat from Emily's fingers, the black cat and Keeper who was her sister's slave and companion!

Papa wrote to inform her that his assistant curate having left he had been greatly occupied with sermons and services and meetings with the trustees. Mr Heaton was well but the young man sired upon his dead aunt by a gypsy from Keighley – and what good ever came out of Keighley? – had stolen a horse and ridden away and was doubtless hanged for piracy by now. Emily would be sorry about that, Charlotte reflected. Young Heaton Bates was one of the few people she ever troubled to greet cordially when they walked over the moors.

Lifting her head one day from her work to check that her pupils were attending to theirs she was horrified to see that every face turned towards her bore the mark of Cain on the forehead. Red tattoos disfigured every brow.

'Is anything wrong, Miss Brontë?' someone asked.

'Nothing. Continue with your work,' she said brusquely, and saw the marks writhe into worms and burrow into the smooth flesh. Sometimes she heard voices calling to her in the wind as it sobbed and wailed around the unprotected walls. Maria and Elizabeth were lonely for company. The dripping shade of Ellen's

99

brother would not satisfy their hungry mouths and empty arms.

Shuddering she closed her eyes and willed Ellen to appear. Ellen remained invisible but Mary Taylor arrived one day in physical fact.

'You look superb!' Charlotte said with appreciation, taking in her friend's riding habit of dark red with its white lace cravat and the tricorne hat with its dashing cockade.

'Actually fashioned out of an old pair of curtains,' Mary said, enveloping Charlotte in a bear hug. 'My boots belong to George! He teased me the last time we met by telling me his feet were smaller than mine but I won the wager and he forfeited his boots!'

Charlotte felt a stab of something perilously close to irritation. Mary who was so bewitchingly pretty and dressed with such flair on so very little money seemed not to appreciate her own beauty nor to make the slightest effort to find a mate, treating the young men of her acquaintance as if they were all her brothers.

'When are you going to behave like a proper lady?' she asked with a smile.

'Never! I leave the fluttering eyelashes and the flirting to Martha,' Mary said, seating herself and giving Charlotte a long look. 'I cannot return the compliment either! You look completely washed out! Is Miss Wooler turned into a tyrant?'

'No indeed! she is very kind,' Charlotte assured her. 'Since our disagreement about Anne she has gone out of her way to be friendly. It's my fault, Mary! I loathe teaching – loathe it with a passion that frightens me. It is not the work – I was never afraid of hard work and the girls are pleasant creatures though I've yet to find a spark of true intelligence or originality among them. What else is there for me? I can't go into a mill or work on a farm, or hire myself out as a servant! The first time I tried to iron when Tabby was sick I scorched Aunt's best lace collar! Yet I must earn a living! Even Emily has gone out teaching and the thought of that fills me with dread.'

'Emily will come and go as it suits her,' Mary said. 'Oh, heavens, Charlotte! You're not going to cry, are you?'

'No,' said Charlotte, who had risen and was pacing the room. 'No, I am going to struggle on, Mary. Branwell has been offered a post as tutor, by the by! It is on the Lancashire borders and he will lodge apart from the family which will give him the chance to continue with his writing and drawing. I don't intend to allow my own stupid discontent to overcome me! Yet there are times when – at night, sometimes during the day – I see shapes that twist into nothingness, am alarmed at the merest thing! There are moments when I fear that my mind is shaking itself into insanity.'

'You probably need a good dose of salts,' Mary said briskly.

Charlotte sat down abruptly and laughed.

'You do me good, Mary,' she said.

'And bring you some books. My father says that you are to keep them for as long as you wish!'

'George Sand's *Indiana and Valentine*!' Charlotte beamed as she undid the string on the parcel.

'And he says to keep them away from the pupils for they are very French and very shocking!'

'My pupils' knowledge of French allows them to enquire the whereabouts of the pen of an aunt, but nothing more taxing to the brain,' Charlotte said. 'Thank you, Mary! And thank your father too.'

'He is not well.' Mary's pretty face had clouded. 'The doctor fears it may be a growth but whether benign or malignant he cannot yet tell. If he should die it will scatter the family for none of us could endure a constant diet of my mother undiluted! None of us can understand how such a pleasant man ever married such a disagreeable woman!'

'Mary! perhaps he loved her,' Charlotte said, shocked by the other's frankness. 'When you marry—'

'Which is highly unlikely.'

'Of course you will! You are so pretty—'

'My tastes do not incline towards men,' Mary said.

'Mary?' Charlotte looked at her.

'At least none that I have met.'

'My brother admired you very much.'

'Branwell? Yes, we both sensed a fellow-feeling. Charlotte, I must go! I would stay talking much longer but since I rode here alone I'd not cause my father anxiety by staying too late. I will go and pay my respects to Miss Wooler. Try to cheer up!'

She gave Charlotte a hug and went out briskly.

She was a dear, Charlotte thought, an original though she expressed her ideas and thoughts that rushed into her head in

101

ways that might lay her open to misinterpretation.

That night she sat down and wrote to Ellen who had returned from Bath and had invited Charlotte to visit. She wrote quickly lest her resolve should weaken that she was far too busy to spare a weekend but that she hoped Ellen would come with the Taylor sisters to spend a few days at the parsonage.

It was months since she had seen Ellen, months since they had sat before a fire curling their hair and giggling over silly puns. The Nusseys always welcomed her very kindly but at Brookroyd she seldom got the chance to be alone with her friend, to exchange confidences. At Haworth they could slip away for long walks or snuggle up beneath the blankets and whisper.

That evening as she lay down for ten minutes before supper she closed her eyes briefly but opened them on the instant as the rustle of a silk petticoat sounded in the room.

'Ellen! What are you doing . . .?'

Her voice faded as Ellen smiled her serene smile and leaned over her. She could smell the musky odour emanating from the browning skin, see the sharp white teeth as the parted lips opened and she was caught up in Quashia's savage embrace.

She heard someone screaming and knew as Quashia/Ellen faded and Miss Wooler hurried in that the screaming came from herself.

ELEVEN

Outside the snowdrops had gone and the first daffodils were springing up. The narrow flower-borders beneath the parsonage windows were alive with March promise and even the weeds that grew between the cracks in the paving stones had a certain jauntiness about them. In the kitchen she could hear Emily teasing Tabby by mimicking her accent as the two prepared dinner. Papa was writing letters in his parlour, looking forward no doubt to the advent of the new curate, a Mr Weightman, who would join them at the end of summer. Anne was upstairs sewing with Aunt and Branwell had already begun work as a tutor and written to assure him that his lodgings were comfortable and his two pupils nice little boys.

'You are on the verge of a complete mental and physical breakdown and must go home at once,' the doctor hastily summoned by Miss Wooler had announced solemnly.

Three months had elapsed since then and the nightmarish visions were gone as if they had never been. She had gained a little weight and there was colour in her cheeks. She slept in Emily's bed, Emily making do with a camp-bed in Tabby's room. She found herself enjoying the food on her plate, laughing at the antics of the two pet geese who seemed to know exactly when Aunt was about to step out of the back door. Life was normal again.

Emily had left Law Hill, though whether of her own accord or not she had never divulged. All that she had said to Charlotte was:

'The pupils were nice enough but the work was tedious and to be honest I thought most favourably of the house dog!'

103

Charlotte looked again at the letter she had just penned. It had been written in response to a letter she had received from Ellen's brother Henry. It had come like a thunderbolt into the peace of her life and astonished her so greatly that she had read it over several times before its sense penetrated her understanding.

Henry Nussey had proposed marriage to her! The fact that any man would ever want to marry her had always struck her as highly unlikely. Henry was twenty-seven and a curate, good looking and amiable, and she had known him almost as long as she had known Ellen. His letter had not only astonished her but pleased her because he hadn't flattered her with empty compliments but made it clear that he liked and respected her, that he hoped to open a small school which she could run as she chose, and that there would be room in his vicarage for Ellen to live with them.

That last presented the greatest inducement. To have her dear Ellen living with them, to sit and talk with her while Henry was out in his parish or writing his sermons would be a joy. Henry was fond of poetry too, and read well. She could picture the three of them seated by a glowing fire and taking it in turns to read from their favourite Cowper – well, perhaps not Ellen! Ellen read very badly indeed, putting emphasis on the wrong words and failing to infuse anything with any passion.

It was no use! Henry deserved a wife who loved him for his own qualities and not because he had a charming sister. And Ellen would be wed herself one day and have to live in her husband's house which would leave Charlotte and Henry with no third person to enliven the fireside.

She had not, of course, in the letter mentioned Ellen at all but had made it clear in the most tactful way she could devise that she was unsuited to him by temperament and could never make him truly happy.

She sealed the letter carefully and addressed it, and put on her shawl and bonnet. As she left the house Anne came hurrying after her with her own bonnet on her head.

'May I walk with you, Charlotte?'

'You don't need to ask permission,' Charlotte said warmly. It was seldom that Anne joined her for a walk or any private conversation.

'You're going to the post office?' Anne asked.

'Yes.'

'Charlotte, I have something to tell you,' Anne said.

'You're not well?'

'I am perfectly well! No, it is something else. I am going away.'

Charlotte stopped dead, gaping up at her slightly taller sister.

'Going where?' she said blankly.

'To be a governess,' Anne said in a rush. 'Mrs Ingham of Blake Hall in Mirfield – you remember she sometimes called upon Miss Wooler? – she is looking for a governess for her two children and when Miss Wooler mentioned this in her last letter I wrote at once to apply for the post. Yesterday I received an answer offering me the post.'

'You're not serious, are you?' Charlotte resumed her walking and slipped her letter into the post box. 'Annie, you couldn't be a governess or a teacher! You're too young.'

'I'm nineteen, Charlotte. I've just spent a year at home and it's high time I made use of the education I received at Roe Head,' Anne said. 'I am resolved to be independent. Mrs Ingham has offered me twenty-five pounds a year which is —'

'More than I received at Roe Head.'

'When you bought my clothes as well as your own. I can begin to pay you back now.'

'You will do nothing of the sort!' Charlotte said. 'What you earn will be your own! But you will never stand it! At least in a school the work is shared out to a certain extent but in a private household – Papa and Emily will agree with me.'

'Papa has consented to my going and Emily thinks I will do very well,' Anne said.

'You've already told them?'

'Yes, and Aunt too. I guessed you might be reluctant so I wished to gain their approval first.'

'I see.' Charlotte turned abruptly and began to walk up the hill again.

'Don't be cross, Charlotte,' Anne said coaxingly. 'You worked at Roe Head and Dewsbury and almost drove yourself into a breakdown and Emily spent six months at Law Hill and now Branwell has steady employment. I want my turn at independence.'

'I shall go with you to Blake Hall to ease you into —'

'Papa has already offered to escort me but I shall go alone and begin as I mean to carry on,' Anne said.

'Annie, you still stutter when you're nervous!'

'Then I shall take good care not to be nervous,' Anne said.

'When do you leave?'

'In two weeks,' Anne said cheerfully. 'To be honest, Charlotte, I am rather looking forward to it. I believe I shall enjoy teaching small children.'

And she herself, Charlotte thought, must now look for a private governess post. It would never do for her youngest sister to be working while she idled at home. Inwardly she sighed. She had recently sent some of her work to Hartley Coleridge, poet son of a greater poet, and had a kind but discouraging letter from him. Branwell had fared better, receiving an invitation to spend a day with Coleridge in the Lakes. It was so hard for a woman to get her work taken seriously by the men who dominated the literary landscape!

Within a month she had, through the good offices of Miss Wooler, obtained a temporary post with a family called Sidgwick who lived at Stonegappe, a large house near Skipton. At least it was something though the five pounds she would earn seemed paltry enough. She wrote to Ellen, asking her if she could visit for a few days, but Ellen was needed at home and sent her regrets.

Swallowing her disappointment Charlotte, having waved Anne off, packed her trunk and took the local gig to the gaunt house buried in a wood on the lower reaches of the moor. Mrs Sidgwick was an acquaintance of the Woolers and Charlotte, having seen her once or twice when she had visited Roe Head, was astonished when, instead of being greeted kindly, she was shown up to a rather shabby bedroom adjoining a schoolroom and informed by a maid with her nose in the air that her duties would commence the next morning and that Mrs Sidgwick would see her when leisure permitted.

'So this is how a private governess is welcomed into a family!' Charlotte exclaimed aloud when the maid had gone.

The Brontës would not have treated any servant with such cavalier disregard for their comfort, she thought bitterly. Even Sally Mosely who came to help out with the washing was greeted by Papa with a kindly enquiry about her family and Branwell tipped his hat to every person he met, even to the barmaid at the Black Bull. Especially to the barmaid at the Black Bull! she thought wryly, and forced herself to smile instead of crying. She had thought herself hard worked as a schoolteacher. She had not, she reflected in the weeks that followed, known what it was like being entirely responsible for a couple of spoilt noisy children who, Mrs Sidgwick informed her when she finally sent for her, were not to be scolded or punished in any way.

'It would not be fitting for a governess to rebuke them so if there is any difficulty you must come to me, Miss Brontë. My children are rather sensitive and would be upset were a stranger to scold them.'

And that, Charlotte thought grimly, put her firmly in her place. In fact the children were spoilt and silly and her hand ached with the desire to spank them which alarmed her because in the Brontë household no child had ever been slapped. Charlotte kept her temper but there were moments when the strain made her temples pound with headache. She left the children to their own devices and went into her room, forcing herself to breathe deeply until the pain was muted.

'Miss Brontë, I did not engage you so that you might have the pleasure of lying abed half the morning! What on earth is the matter with you?'

Charlotte, splashing her face with cold water, reached for a towel and said, voice muffled in its folds,

'I beg your pardon, ma'am, but I have a sick headache. I shall be well very soon.'

'Meanwhile the children are bothering the cook! You seem to imagine that governesses should be treated like fragile ladies! In two days we leave for Swarcliffe where we enjoy our annual vacation. We shall have guests there – important people, Miss Brontë! – and I shall expect you to leave your sick headaches behind!'

Mrs Sidgwick turned and went out, leaving Charlotte shaking with rage. She took a step towards the door and sat down abruptly, tears pouring down her face. She wanted with every fibre to give in her notice but that would be to admit failure after only a few weeks. She would not permit herself to be bullied back to Haworth by a woman who obviously was less well educated than herself!

Swarcliffe was a larger, more cheerful house, with Harrogate Spa near, and grounds thronged with summer flowers. Unfortunately the house was filled with guests – friends of the

Sidgwicks – who spoke in high, affected voices and swished their silk dresses over the carpets with an air of unbearable superiority.

At least there were walks with the children who were actually beginning to behave rather more docilely, and odd half-hours when she could steal away to write to Ellen.

There was one agreeable day when the whole party went over to visit Norton Conyers where an associate of Mr Sidgwick's had rented the huge battlemented house for the summer.

'We shall serve the children their tea, miss.' The plumper of a couple of maidservants whisked her charges away, setting her free to explore for an hour. She wandered upstairs away from the bustle below with some thought of gaining the battlements and seeing the landscape spread out like a tapestry before her. The upper floors were less well carpeted than the lower, the walls bare stone save for tapestries hung at intervals.

Charlotte stopped suddenly as a stream of low laughter issued from a partly opened door set deeply into an alcove. Then the door opened wider and a servant came out with another behind her, both with sewing baskets.

'Art tha lost, miss?' One left off giggling to stare at her.

'I – wondered if there was a way up to the battlements,' Charlotte said.

'Stone's crumbling a lot up there, miss,' the other servant said. 'Stair's blocked off. There were a mad woman held there once.'

'When?'

They looked at each other and shrugged.

'Long years since,' one said at last. 'They say she haunts t'rooms where she were held. We've never heard her, have we, Grace?'

'Nay, but when t'wind blows – I'd not come up here alone,' the other said.

'Thank you.' Charlotte turned back and made her way down to the ground floor again. A side door led into the garden and she slipped through it, suddenly glad to be out in the fresh air beyond the stone walls.

There was a small chapel at the end of the broad walk. She went past a wall against which a pear-tree splayed its branches and pushed open the door. It was cooler here, with a couple of elaborately carved tombs.

108

'Damon de Rochester, slain at Marston Moor,' she read silently and smiled wryly.

That was an excellent name for an Angrian character, married perhaps to the poor mad lady locked beneath the crumbling battlements.

No! She turned away sharply and went out into the sunshine again. The Genii were adults now, the wooden soldiers broken or lost, the secret world part of the magical past. One day she would write and get it into print despite the advice Mr Southey and Mr Hartley Coleridge had given her, but it would be about real people in a workaday world.

The end of the month marked the end of her servitude. She shook hands politely with the Sidgwicks who, she suspected, were as glad to see her leave as she was to go, and reached Haworth to find Papa entertaining his curate Mr Hodgson who had just been appointed to a stipend of his own.

'Welcome home, my dear Charlotte.' He drew her into his parlour. 'You have not forgotten Mr Hodgson? I have just been telling him that he has been sorely missed. I shall be pleased to welcome Mr Weightman when he takes up his duties here as my assistant.'

'May I present my fellow clergyman, Miss Brontë? Mr David Bryce.'

'Delighted to meet you, Miss Brontë.'

Mr Bryce, who had a lively attractive face, also had an Irish accent much stronger than her father's.

'They rode over to see me,' Papa said, looking gratified. 'You will take tea with my daughters, gentlemen? My own digestion is very weak and I require absolute peace and quiet while eating. Mr Hodgson will tell you that I am a martyr to dyspepsia.'

'Indeed he has done so already, sir,' Mr Bryce said. 'Many times.' The corner of his mouth quirked slightly.

'And I must change my dress,' Charlotte said, trying not to laugh. 'I will be down directly, gentlemen.'

She ushered them across the hall into the dining-room where Aunt, wearing her best silk cap, waited to chaperon, and went upstairs.

'Are they still here?' Emily, lank skirts trailing, hair uncoiling, met her on the upper landing.

'Papa has invited them to stay to tea.'

'Which means they'll be here all evening,' Emily grumbled. 'You must do the honours, Tallii. I mean to have my tea with Tabby and put my feet up!'

'Emily! You haven't said you're pleased to see me.'

'Of course I'm pleased! We shall talk later when the clergy have gone.'

The clergy lingered until after dark. Emily stayed out of sight in the kitchen and Aunt Branwell sat at the table, dispensing tea and ham salad graciously.

'They tell me that you have been out as a governess, Miss Brontë.' Mr Bryce leaned to talk to her.

'A temporary position, Mr Bryce. You are from . . . ?'

'From Dublin, ma'am. But you're half-Irish yourself!'

'I have never been there.'

'You should go there, Miss Brontë, to allow the Brontë name for daintiness and charm to be spread.'

Charlotte stared at him in astonishment and laughed.

'No doubt you are come into Yorkshire to allow the Bryce name for blarney to be spread?' she countered.

'You do me an injustice, Miss Brontë!' His eyes sparkled. 'I speak the absolute truth!'

'Hush, Aunt will hear,' Charlotte begged.

'Your aunt cannot place temptation before me and not expect me to respond.'

Charlotte, blushing and flustered, felt a frisson of pleasure. Perhaps she was not so plain after all if a handsome young man was ready to flirt with her! She no longer envied Emily, having her tea in the kitchen with Tabby.

'Have they gone?' Emily enquired a couple of hours later as the front door closed.

'You ought to have joined us.'

'You seemed to be managing very nicely by yourself from the laughter I heard,' Emily said. 'Charlotte, Tabby is speaking of retiring.'

'Retiring where?' Charlotte asked, diverting her thoughts from the visitors with some effort.

'To live with her sister in the village. Aunt and Papa both uphold her wish. She says that she cannot work as well as she used to with her lame leg and nothing I say will alter her mind.'

'Ems, Tabby is close on seventy. Surely she has earned her retirement?'

'Tabby is family!' Emily said fiercely. 'You wouldn't let Aunt or Papa retire into the village. Tabby has been with us since we were children!'

'We're not children now,' Charlotte said. 'Emily, think! Tabby is more or less confined to the house now. She must find it very painful to have to limp up and down stairs. With her sister she can rest more. I agree with Aunt.'

'Oh, there's no arguing with you,' Emily said sullenly.

Charlotte grimaced but didn't follow her. Emily could be obstinate but left to herself she'd probably see sense. Things had to change however much she wanted to retain the old childhood days.

Two days later a letter in an unfamiliar hand arrived with one from Ellen. Charlotte opened the former first and read the contents with a mixture of amusement and excitement. Mr David Bryce, he of the soft Irish voice and handsome face, asked her permission to call upon her with a view to discussing marriage!

She read the letter over in a state of disbelief. She, the smallest and plainest of the sisters, was sought in wedlock again! There was real feeling in the letter, real emotion.

She went to the mirror and peered at herself closely.

She was no longer a very young girl. The following year she would be twenty-four, an age at which many women were married and mothers. Her skin was clearer than it used to be, her eyes sparkling hazel, her brown hair glossy. Nothing to be done about the big nose and the mouth that had a slight twist at the corner, but her hands and nails were beautiful, and her voice, with its faint legacy of an Irish accent, light and pleasing.

Marriage would give her security, the companionship of a young man she had found unexpectedly charming.

Ellen's letter! Going back to her seat she opened it, holding it close to her eyes as she deciphered Ellen's convoluted hand.

Dearest Charlotte,
I write in some haste before you engage yourself to another governess post. You have often told me that you have often longed to see the sea. I believe that I will soon have leisure

to spend a holiday on the coast. Will you come with me there? The expenses would not be high and it would be wonderful to spend time alone together. We have been absent too long one from the other.

Yr devoted friend,
Ellen

To glimpse the sea for the first time in Ellen's company! To spend time with Ellen, walking, talking, cuddling up in the fire-light! She knocked on the parlour door, the words halfway out of her mouth before she had entered the room.

'Papa, Ellen Nussey has asked me to go on holiday with her to the seaside!'

'It would be rather expensive, my dear,' he said doubtfully.

'We could travel by public coach, take cheap lodgings where we could cater for ourselves. '

'Is something wrong, Charlotte?' Aunt came out of the dining room.

'Ellen and I are going to the seaside together,' Charlotte said.

'With her family?'

'By ourselves, Aunt.'

'Unchaperoned?'

'We are not going husband-hunting,' Charlotte said, amused.

'Nevertheless – two young women together? You cannot approve, Mr Brontë?'

'I see no great harm—' he began.

'We shall stay in lodgings.'

'Two unmarried young women in public lodgings together? My dear Mr Brontë, it would look most peculiar! This must be discussed further,' Aunt said.

'I may go, Papa?' Charlotte looked at him.

'I confess I see no harm – but your aunt knows more about such matters as you must agree.'

'We might all take a trip together to Liverpool,' Aunt said.

'Liverpool! I don't want to go to Liverpool! Papa, what harm can there be in Ellen and myself taking a holiday?'

'We must discuss it further.' Aunt stood her ground.

'Discuss it then! I have a letter to write!'

Returning to her writing desk she quickly penned a polite note to Mr Bryce, firmly refusing his offer of marriage.

112

TWELVE

'I cannot believe that we are actually here at last!' Charlotte gave a long contented sigh as she trickled sand through her fingers and looked out over the tossing sea.

'When something is meant to be it generally happens,' Ellen said in her placid manner.

'It would never have happened at all had your brother George not hired a carriage and brought you to Haworth.'

'George is a dear,' Ellen agreed. 'When I told him of the difficulties you were experiencing in getting away he proposed driving to Haworth without warning and abducting you!'

'I had packed and unpacked so many times!' Charlotte laughed at the memory. 'Aunt can be so unreasonable at times! She behaved as if I was proposing to elope instead of taking a holiday with a friend!'

'At least Branwell approved.'

'And most vociferously!'

Branwell, who had been at home for a few days, had greeted Ellen's arrival with glee, insisting that the doubters had been fairly vanquished, and helping Emily to load Charlotte's bags into the vehicle.

'Now we have both had our way,' Ellen said. 'I longed for you to see the sea.'

'It overwhelmed me,' Charlotte said softly. 'Even the memory of it will overwhelm me. Oh Ellen, look! The sun setting on the water makes all the waves look like little dancing flames!'

The holiday had not gone altogether according to their wishes, since Henry Nussey, who evidently shared some of Aunt

113

Branwell's misgivings had arranged for them to be met by friends of his who had whisked them off to their own house, three miles inland, for a month. Yet that had also turned out well since the Eastons were hospitable people who had a delightfully playful little daughter and raised no objection when their guests insisted on walking to the seaside. Only for the final week had they taken lodgings within sight and sound of the sea that had so stirred and thrilled Charlotte that she had burst into tears.

'And tomorrow we go home,' Ellen said now.

'I refuse to be downcast!' Charlotte said robustly. 'When we are old ladies we shall look back at this holiday as—'

'The first of many!' Ellen finished.

'Oh, I do hope so! But by then you will have been married for years with a tribe of children,' Charlotte said.

'I am in no great haste,' Ellen said. 'At present I enjoy not being subject to any man's whims. Of course that will probably alter when I fall in love.'

'You have not yet?'

'No, though I must admit that Joe Taylor has been rather attentive of late,' Ellen admitted, blushing slightly.

'Joe is a very pleasant fellow but not steady enough for your tastes,' Charlotte said firmly.

'But handsome?'

'Handsome enough but you have too much sense to be seduced by a handsome face and a lively manner. Don't be persuaded into it, Nell!'

'He hasn't asked me yet,' Ellen said.

'Think carefully before you accept anyone,' Charlotte said and scrambled to her feet. 'Now let us be done with talk of romance as if we were schoolgirls who didn't know the realities of life! This is our last evening here. Shall we take a moonlight walk across the headland?'

'Arm in arm!' Ellen linked her arm through Charlotte's and kissed her friend on the cheek.

The journey home by carriage and train had a poignant quality as if a bright page had just been turned. Charlotte, stepping off the train at Leeds, found herself wishing that small places could be joined by the long shining lines that diminished the distances between friends.

She reached home before dusk and was slightly taken aback

when a young man who wasn't Branwell opened the side gate
and came to help her down and take charge of her luggage.

'William Weightman, Miss Brontë. We met just before you
went on your holiday.'

'Yes, of course. Forgive me! I haven't put my spectacles on and
so am – I seem to have lost them!' She scrabbled in her handbag.
'Oh dear! I must've left them at the Eastons! They very kindly
gave us breakfast before we set off and —'

'I'll see the coach driver is reimbursed. Your sisters are in the
house, I believe. I persuaded Miss Emily to allow me to give
Keeper his walk so that she would not miss your arrival. Here,
boy!'

He whistled to the massive dog and held open the gate for her.

'Charlotte, we thought you were going to stay away for the rest
of your life!' Anne ran down the steps and relieved her of her
bags. 'You are sunburnt. It suits you very well! Emily is just brew-
ing some tea.'

'And Papa's new curate is walking Keeper. What magic spell
has he cast to cause Emily to relinquish that task?'

'Mr Weightman has made himself useful in many ways,' Anne
said. 'Papa says he doesn't know how he managed without him
before, and Aunt is positively skittish when he calls.'

'He is certainly very handsome,' Charlotte admitted.

'And so jolly! Even Emily remains in the room when he calls
and doesn't dive in to collect a book and dive out again. Papa!
Our Charlotte is home!'

'And looking the better for the break,' Papa said. 'You left Miss
Nussey well?'

'Yes, Papa. We both enjoyed the holiday very much.' Charlotte
went into the kitchen where Emily was pouring tea.

'You look years younger,' she said, coming to take her sister's
bonnet and cloak. 'Before you ask we are all well here. Tabby
moved to her sister's house but one of us goes down to see her
every day though it is not the same as having her here all the
time. Sit down, do, or are you grown too grand to take your tea
in the kitchen?'

'No indeed but I must go up and see Aunt,' Charlotte said.

'She's in high good humour these days,' Emily told her.

Aunt, indeed, looked very well though as usual her room was
far too warm.

'You are done with gadding about then?' She lifted her face for a kiss on the cheek. 'And Miss Ellen?'

'She is very well too and all the better for a change of scene.'

'You have met our new assistant curate?'

'He seems very pleasant,' Charlotte said.

'Indeed he is! So interested in my accounts of Cornwall, and even bringing Emily out of her shell. I am pleased you enjoyed yourselves, my dear. I rather feared that two unchaperoned young women – gossip can spring up very quickly on the most slender of foundations. However it all went very well so no harm is done!'

William Weightman, it seemed, had indeed cast a spell. Ellen must come and stay very soon, Charlotte thought, and Mary and Martha too! A sudden frown creased her brow. She said:

'Why is Anne at home? Is she on holiday?'

'Not exactly.' Aunt Branwell grimaced slightly. 'Poor Anne has found working at Blake Hall very difficult. She found the children not just badly behaved and insolent but cruel – cruel to animals, my dear. She has tried her utmost but Mrs Ingham has informed her that unless this short break will, as she puts it, improve her influence over the children, she intends to dispense with her services after Christmas.'

'Does she indeed! I trust Anne gave in her own notice at once!'

'Anne was paid in advance,' Aunt chided. 'She has far too much integrity to leave before the due time – and it's possible that Mrs Ingham may retain her services after all.'

Mrs Ingham, however, did not. By Christmas time Anne was home with a somewhat lukewarm reference from the Inghams.

'And now you will stay at home where you belong,' Charlotte said.

'Until I find another teaching post,' Anne said. 'I shall study the advertisements in the newspapers closely and apply for a post that promises to be more congenial. I will not allow one failure to deter me from earning my living.'

'You are still far too young to tie yourself to governess slavery full time!' Charlotte argued.

'Charlotte, I am almost twenty years old!' Anne exclaimed. 'I must grow up one day you know!'

'And I shall be twenty-four in April. I must rouse myself to look for a governess post soon myself,' Charlotte said.

116

The truth was that she hadn't the least inclination to go out as a governess or teacher again. With Tabby gone, and Martha Brown too young to do much heavy work, Emily had taken the main household tasks upon herself, with Aunt and Anne doing the sewing and mending. Charlotte had the task of dusting which gave her time in which to write. She had put aside the two chapters of Ashworth she had written and returned to an old theme about two brothers, rivals in business and love, but the figure of a quiet, plain governess hovered on the edges of the pages and refused to come into the light.

'The news seems very grim on the manufacturing front,' Papa remarked one day. 'The Chartists are causing problems again and there's talk of a recession. I understand the Nusseys and the Taylors have lost profits due to industrial unrest.'

'And Mr Taylor is very ill,' Charlotte said. 'The doctor tells him that it is cancer and only a matter of time. I had a letter from Mary last week.'

'Poor fellow!' Papa shook his greying head. 'You have often spoken of his intelligence and his vigorous nature. Mrs Taylor is of a less happy temperament I believe?'

'The Taylors will divide and separate once their father is gone,' Charlotte said. 'None of them will stay with their mother.'

'She must be an unhappy woman then.' Papa took off his spectacles and polished them thoughtfully. 'By the by, my dear, you recall Mr David Bryce who visited us with Mr Hodgson?'

'Yes indeed I do.'

'Mr Hodgson writes to tell me that Mr Bryce has died very suddenly,' Papa said, still polishing his spectacles. 'A burst blood vessel in his brain, quite unsuspected by anyone. I was grieved to hear of it for I liked him very much.'

'Yes,' said Charlotte dully. 'Yes, it is sad news. Mr Bryce made himself very agreeable during his visit. I shall ask Emily to bring in your tea.'

In the hall she stood for a moment, her eyes filling with tears. She had liked David Bryce though she hadn't taken his proposal seriously and the thought that a lively, attractive young man could die without warning made the world seem a little less safe.

Charlotte was greatly cheered when, at the beginning of February, Ellen came to spend three weeks with them. Her brother George brought her over to Haworth but rushed off again so quickly that Charlotte feared he had taken offence at something.

'No indeed!' Ellen assured her. 'George has been most restless of late – cannot sit still for five minutes and cannot keep his attention fixed on anything.'

'He is in love then?'

'I hope it is that,' Ellen said soberly. Her usual serenity seemed ruffled. 'Charlotte, there are moments when I fear for him. We are a large family and not all of us are – healthy. Poor Sarah will never be able to take her place in society and Mercy cannot ever be trusted to take charge of a household – she has no interest in much save reading the Bible from cover to cover once a year and William – he suffered so much from deep depression before he – his drowning was given out as accident but it was not. It was not!'

'Dearest Ellen! In every large family there are always those who are less favoured by nature than others!' Charlotte consoled. 'George is the handsomest and kindest of your brothers and will settle down when he is safely married! Now come down and meet Mr Weightman! Papa already begins to regard him as a second son and Aunt regains her youth when he is present! He is exceedingly handsome and has such a sense of fun.'

Within minutes of meeting William Weightman Ellen had cheered up. Indeed it was impossible to be downcast in his company. Charlotte, eyes sparkling as she exchanged friendly insults with the curate over the tea table, caught her friend's eye, brimful of amusement, and reminded herself to thank Aunt again for suggesting that Ellen come to stay.

It was a mild February, benign enough for them to walk out every day. Branwell who had arrived for a short holiday joined them on their rambles and seemed as taken with Mr Weightman as the rest of them were.

'We shall go shooting in the season, we hope,' he said. 'The Heatons will be glad to accompany us. You shall have plenty of game for your cooking-pot, Emily!'

'The Major is already promised the plumpest of the pheasants!' Mr Weightman said.

'Major?' Emily raised her eyebrows.

'You take care to chaperon the other young ladies when I am

118

present,' Mr Weightman teased. 'You think me a very dangerous fellow where the young ladies are concerned, don't you? Come now, what nickname would you give to me? Lancelot? Don Juan?'

Emily had paused in her walk to look at him. After a moment she said smilingly,

'Celia Amelia!'

'Yes,' said Mr Weightman after the briefest of silences. 'Yes, Miss Emily, you have it exactly!'

'Such a name makes you seem less dangerous to the female sex,' Charlotte said playfully, wondering why she felt impelled to interrupt so quickly. 'Now that you have your graduate robes perhaps you would allow me to paint your portrait?'

'In his full glory for he's a veritable Adonis in his silk gown,' Branwell cried. 'Do we go as far as the waterfall or is that rain I smell?'

'It's probably the dinner I ought to start cooking,' Emily said. 'Come, Keeper!'

She strode away, her hair tumbling from its pins, her boots rimed with mud.

On Valentine's Day four cards, beautifully printed, arrived with a Bradford postmark upon them. Charlotte, opening hers, gave a cry of surprised pleasure.

'It's a valentine card! Someone has sent me a valentine card!'

'I have one too in the same hand,' Ellen said.

'And me.' Anne was gazing with pleasure at the hearts and flowers that adorned her card.

'Ems?' Charlotte looked at her.

'Me too!' Emily laughed, looking pleased. ' "Soul divine" indeed! Celia Amelia walked into Bradford yesterday!'

'And declares his love for us all! He has no favourites,' Charlotte said. 'We must compose a rhyme in reply!'

'I never had a valentine before,' Anne said.

'We none of us did! Better not tell Papa,' Charlotte warned. 'He might not approve.'

'You think Papa hasn't sent a few valentines in his day?' Emily laughed as she reached for pen and paper.

'Mary and Martha must be allowed into the joke,' Charlotte said.

'When do they come next?' Ellen enquired.

'Not soon unless their father improves a little in health. How shall we phrase our reply?'

The fun continued as the days of early spring flew by.

Mr Weightman gave a talk at the Mechanics Institute in Keighley and by some miracle prevailed on Mr Brontë to allow his daughters and Ellen to attend, with Branwell and himself escorting them on the four-mile walk. Charlotte, listening to him expound his argument, glanced at Ellen who was listening intently and found herself idly cogitating. Ellen was young and as the years went by she grew more attractive. If Mr Weightman were to choose Ellen she would make the perfect wife for him. That Ellen would marry some day was inevitable. To have her safely wed to a close friend whom they all liked would salve the wound a little.

They were joined on the walk home by two other clergymen, old college friends of Mr Weightman who had come to hear him speak. As they walked under the starhung sky their chatter and laughter woke the silence of the surrounding moors.

It had also woken Aunt who came to open the door and uttered an exclamation of dismay at the sight of the two strange gentlemen.

'I only prepared coffee and sandwiches for six,' she complained looking thoroughly put out. 'Mr Weightman, you should have given me some notice of our extra guests! And you're so late! It's almost midnight. I began to think you taken by the Chartist mobs!'

'All the Chartist mobs are tucked up in bed, Aunt!'

'It is not a joking matter, Branwell! And I have only my second-best cap on! Excuse me!'

Flustered she made for the stairs, clutching her wrapper about her. Charlotte, lips twitching, glanced at the others and saw they were all, even the docile Anne, convulsed by silent laughter.

THIRTEEN

'What I would really like to do,' Mary Taylor said, 'is to hallock around the world!'

'Hallock?' Charlotte looked an enquiry.

'The word,' said Mary, 'may not exist but it expresses my ambition!'

'But women cannot travel alone,' Charlotte said.

'Don't be so missish! You sound like Ellen who is a dear but will allow herself to be used by her loving family until she either marries or dwindles into spinsterhood.'

'But you stay now because your father is not well,' William Weightman said.

'His illness is mortal but he endures a long-drawn-out dying.' Mary's lovely face had clouded. 'For his sake and my sake I wish its progress was swifter. But in due course I will plough my own furrow! Neither Martha nor I will stay with our mother!'

'Miss Taylor!' Mr Weightman frowned slightly.

'Our mother,' Mary said, 'is one of the most unpleasant women anyone could meet. Would you tell a young man to stay tamely at home with a woman who never stops nagging and complaining?'

'Women have certain duties,' Charlotte said weakly.

'And there are women who defy convention and live as they please! Miss Anne Lister of Shibden Hall manages her estate, travels abroad, wears cravat and top hat with her skirt – you must have met her when you were at Law Hill, Emily? What was she like?'

'I met her very briefly twice. I formed no particular opinion,' Emily said. 'I must go in and take Aunt and Papa their tea.'

She rose from the grass where they were sitting and went into the house.

'Emily,' said Mary, 'is not a great conversationalist!'

'Miss Brontë, how is your sister, Anne?' Mr Weightman enquired.

'She seems to be coping very well,' Charlotte said, glad of the change of subject. 'You know she obtained this post at Thorp Green Hall by answering an advertisement! She writes that the house is lovely and the children not too difficult. She insisted on an annual salary of fifty pounds too!'

'And Branwell plans to work for the railway company?'

'He found tutoring – tedious,' Charlotte said. 'He is wild to be part of this new world of whirling speed and snorting engines.'

'I must seek him out for we arranged to go fishing together.' Mr Weightman rose.

'You are not going to invite me to go fishing?' Mary said.

'I doubt if you will land the fish you crave to catch,' he said.

'In that we are brother and sister I believe,' Mary said.

'Excuse me. Miss Brontë, if you wish a final sitting for my likeness I am available tomorrow. I have some sick visits to make.'

'What on earth is going on between you two?' Charlotte asked when he had gone.

'Nothing whatsoever I promise you!' Mary said airily.

'I must write soon to Ellen. It would be pleasant if she were here too,' Charlotte said.

'Ellen has a new interest,' Martha said slyly.

'What?'

'You should rather ask whom,' Martha said. 'A certain Mr Vincent is sniffing around her at present.'

'Who is he?' Charlotte asked.

'A young clergyman – about your age. We have not met him yet but her brothers approve of him.'

'Does Ellen approve is more pertinent.'

'I believe she does,' Mary said.

'She and Mr Weightman got on very well together when she was here.'

'Mr Weightman scatters his favours too widely among the ladies. I advised her not to become another of his conquests. I must write to her.'

'Ellen is fortunate to have a friend so careful for her love life,' Martha said with a giggle.

'My brother Joe will not welcome Mr Vincent,' Martha said. 'He has long admired Miss Ellen!'

'We had best go in and help Emily with the tea!' Charlotte was on her feet, voice bright. 'Upon my word we talk of nothing but love and lovers these days!'

The parsonage seemed very quiet when the visit was over.

Mr Weightman returned to his parish duties; Branwell went off to Sowerby Bridge to work as a clerk.

'I wonder how long that will last!' Charlotte said.

'There's a great future for young men in the railway industry,' Emily said. 'It looks to me as if he's getting on at last.'

'I shall try to catch your optimism,' Charlotte said, 'but how often has Branny started out on a wonderful career which has come to nothing? First he was going to study art in London, then become a great writer, then a portrait painter in Bradford, then a tutor and now a future railway magnate. He is twenty-three years old and has settled to nothing!'

'Perhaps we expect too much from him. Stop fretting, Tallii.'

'Well, I am resolved not to sit at home for much longer,' Charlotte said firmly. 'A Mrs White at Rawdon has advertised for a governess. I shall apply for the post. It only pays twenty-five pounds a year but I shall be earning something! Will you be able to manage here alone?'

'Of course.' Emily spoke calmly. 'Martha Brown is a useful and willing child. And I often take mending down to Tabby. She likes to feel that she's still needed, still part of the family.'

'I shall go to Rawdon in the New Year,' Charlotte said.

That left the rest of the summer and the autumn to settle to her writing. Her tale of two rival brothers was proceeding too slowly. She missed Branwell's collaboration but he was in high good humour, having been quickly promoted to the rank of station-master and moved to Luddenden Foot from where he could borrow a horse and ride over to Halifax to see his friends there. She was pleased for his sake but felt the lack of his company, of the ideas that had sparked between them. Emily was no substitute since most of her time was spent in the kitchen and for part of every day she set off across the moors with Nero on her shoulder, Keeper bounding ahead, and her portable writing desk under her arm. What, if anything, she wrote she never talked about.

Anne came home for a week at Christmas but there was little satisfaction in that since, having greeted Papa, Aunt and Charlotte and given some account of the Robinsons at Thorp Green Hall, she clung to Emily's side.

'Mrs Robinson is a handsome lady but seldom notices me. Her husband has indifferent health and much of her time is spent with him. The girls are pleasant and mind what I say but the boy Edmund is lazy and does largely what he pleases. I think he needs a male tutor to keep him in line. But the countryside round about is wonderful! And I have some leisure to write.'

So Anne was writing too. Charlotte wondered what about but Anne confided only in Emily.

There were letters from Ellen in which the name of Osman Parke Vincent was occurring rather often. He was evidently courting Ellen and Joe Taylor had given up the chase.

Charlotte, reading over her friend's last letter in which she begged for advice as to what to do for he had made it plain that he meant to propose, felt a sudden illogical fury rising in her.

Ellen was her most beloved friend, in many ways closer than a sister, and now she was actually seriously contemplating marrying a man whom she, Charlotte, had never met! What had happened to the bond they shared? Where was the Ellen who had moved heaven and earth to spend a week alone with her at the seaside?

She took up her pen and answered the letter, confining herself first to the news of Mr Taylor's death, declaring that Mary and Martha would certainly leave home where their unpleasant mother remained and make their own way in the world. When she came to the subject of Ellen's impending betrothal her pen took flight. Had Ellen heard that Mr Vincent was said to be slightly eccentric? Eccentricity was a bad quality in a husband. She signed it formally 'C. Brontë', and then, as if her hand moved of its own volition scrawled savagely in the remaining space:

Ellen Helen Eleonora Helena
Nell Nelly – Mrs Vincent.
Does it sound well Nell? I think it does – I will never come
to see you after you are married.

No answer came. Anne had returned to the Robinsons; Emily

124

was occupied with sorting and mending ready for Charlotte's going to Rawdon. Then a letter came from Henry Nussey. Reading it, Charlotte experienced the most intense relief. Ellen had refused Mr Vincent and stuck to her decision though Henry confided she had cried a little.

Poor silly Ellen to imagine that any husband could ever take the place of a friend! Charlotte seized a pen to write consolingly to her and then laid it down again. It was Henry who had broken the news. Ellen had sent no word. Ellen therefore could wait. When she was settled at Rawdon, she would write as if nobody named Osman Parke Vincent had ever existed.

Upperwood House at Rawdon was, she decided when she arrived, a handsome building with a large garden, and her two pupils seemed, if noisy and too boisterous, friendly enough. Charlotte unpacked her trunk, looked round her plainly furnished bedroom and prepared herself for a season of governessing.

She had meant to delay longer before writing to Ellen but a valentine card from William Weightman altered her mind. No doubt he'd sent a similar card to Ellen and Ellen must be in a fragile emotional state at present. Charlotte wrote to her at once, letting her know that she too had received a valentine again and guessed that Ellen had. The joke was still an excellent one and she was sure nobody would take his protestations in any serious spirit for they all knew that Mr Weightman was the biggest flirt in Yorkshire! When the long-awaited letter from Ellen arrived she opened it eagerly. Dear Ellen! No mention of Mr Vincent who had presumably left the district, no reproaches, only an invitation to visit Brookroyd as soon as possible and the gift of a miniature pair of cuffs, fashioned in silk but sewn together. Ellen's mind must have been elsewhere when she made them!

'A whole day off, Miss Brontë?' Mrs White raised her eyebrows as Charlotte made her request. 'To see the Nusseys? Are you then acquainted with that family?'

'Since my schooldays, ma'am. Ellen is like a sister to me.'

'One of her brothers is a physician I understand?'

'Royal physician to Her Majesty the Queen, ma'am. He has been in London for many years of course but he has always been assiduous in encouraging our friendship.'

'On Saturday? How will you—?'

'Miss Nussey will send a gig for me.'

'And you will be back in time to put the children to bed?'

'Yes, ma'am.'

'Very well.' Mrs White sounded reluctant but resigned.

And on Saturday there was Ellen waiting to greet her and the coldness of the past months dissipated without a word spoken!

The day itself went far too quickly. Ellen wanted to hear all about the Whites and how long Charlotte meant to stay in her post and whether she had heard of Mary Taylor's plans to travel abroad.

'More than plans,' George Nussey put in as he caught part of their conversation. 'I had it from Joe that Martha has already left.'

'Martha? You must be mistaken!' Charlotte exclaimed. 'What on earth would a child like Martha do in a foreign country?'

'Learn the language,' George told her. 'She has gone to a school, what they call a finishing school in Brussels, to learn French and German. Miss Mary is to join her there in a few months' time.'

'And Martha is no child,' Ellen said, laughing. 'She is twenty-two!'

'She seems like a child to me,' George said. 'Her sister means to study mathematics as well as languages when she goes there.'

'Then they mean to teach?'

'Who knows what Mary Taylor will do?' George looked amused. 'Naturally her brothers disapprove of their sisters going out to work.'

'I hadn't thought of work as a degradation before,' Charlotte said tartly.

'Of course it isn't!' Ellen said warmly. 'You do talk great nonsense sometimes, George!'

'To be forced to work because of circumstances is another matter, but where a young lady has brothers she ought to be able to expect them to support her until she marries.'

'Mary will never marry,' Charlotte said. 'She has too much spirit and pride to tie herself down unless she meets a man who is her superior in every way!'

'Which she would never admit anyway! Tell me of Mr Weightman,' Ellen demanded of Charlotte.

'I'll leave you to your conversation,' George said.

'Is George quite well?' Charlotte enquired as he left the room.

'He seems somewhat flushed and abrupt in his manner.'

'His moods are variable,' Ellen said softly. 'Of all my dear brothers he is the one who frets most about us all. William's death hit him very hard and – my brother Joseph – he sometimes imbibes a little too deeply, Charlotte. He settles to nothing though he is past forty and ought to take his responsibilities seriously. As the youngest I see much and can say very little! My sisters too – poor Ann is also in her forties and nobody has ever wanted to marry her. Mercy too is past forty and has no hope of a husband, and Sarah – she has begun to suffer from fits. They alarm us and wear down her strength.'

'Then your presence at home must be invaluable,' Charlotte said bracingly. 'Cheer up, Ellen. The greatest pity is that I was not born a man for I'm convinced that you would have made me a charming wife!'

From the doorway Ann Nussey coughed slightly and said,

'Ellen, our mother says that you must not keep Miss Brontë to yourself. We all desire the pleasure of her conversation.'

'Charlotte was just saying—' Ellen said, laughing. 'Miss Brontë has an unconventional sense of the absurd.'

Ann, an older, sourer version of Ellen, gave Charlotte a tight little smile. The gig was brought round after tea with George in the driving seat.

'When I go home for the holidays, Ellen, you must come and stay,' Charlotte said, hugging her friend. 'We all long to see you again!'

'I shall look forward to it,' Ellen said.

If Mary and Martha were already claiming their independence then she too must follow suit! Going from one uncongenial teaching post to another was no way to waste the years!

During the months that followed she read the letter which Mary sent after the visit of the Taylors to Brussels with keen interest. It would cost money to study abroad but with some form of official qualification they might eventually open a school of their own. To her surprise the Whites proved sympathetic to the notion.

When she went home for her holiday she lost no time in asking Emily and Anne what they thought of the idea.

'To leave home and start our own school? Where would we go?' Emily said.

127

'To Bridlington perhaps?' Charlotte ventured. 'It is not so far away that we could not visit Papa and Aunt very often! Anne, you went to Scarborough with the Robinsons – you liked the sea and the coast there, didn't you?'

'Very much indeed! The air was so pure and fresh that my asthma vanished as if it had never been,' Anne said enthusiastically.

'Have you spoken to Papa?' Emily asked.

'Not yet. I want to find out everything I possibly can very thoroughly before I admit others into my confidence. However Mr White has advised me that before starting a school we must be fluent in at least two foreign languages. To be fluent it's necessary to study abroad.'

'You've heard from the Taylors,' Emily said flatly.

'Their brothers are paying for them both, are they not?' Anne looked doubtful. 'We cannot expect Branny—'

'Aunt!' Charlotte spoke eagerly, her eyes kindling. 'Aunt has money which she could lend to us! If she could be persuaded to lend – say a hundred or a hundred and fifty pounds so that two of us could study abroad then we could pay her back in instalments once we were qualified.'

'Two of us?' Emily looked at her.

'You and me, Emmii! Anne is settled at Thorp Green and doing well, much better than I am doing though the Whites are civil enough! You are not miserable at the Robinsons, are you, Anne?'

'No,' Anne said serenely.

'And you could take your turn once Emily and I were qualified.'

'And who is going to look after Papa?' Emily said.

'Martha Brown could live in and her little sister Tabitha could help her.'

'Tabitha Brown is not yet three years old,' Emily said with a grin. 'Hardly old enough to run errands.'

'Aunt could help Martha Brown then, and Sally Mosely could come in to help out. Papa worked his way from Ireland to make something of his life and we have the right to do the same. I know you hate leaving home, Ems, but you can't spend your entire life washing dishes and cooking and exercising Keeper!'

'Mr Weightman would be willing to walk Keeper and fly Nero

while you were away,' Anne said. 'You know how ready he is to oblige!'

'You don't mind my going then if this scheme ever came to any thing?' Emily looked at Anne.

'I would miss you dreadfully,' Anne said, 'but I miss you now when I'm with the Robinsons. If in the end we were together running our own school a little heartsickness would be justified.'

'Say nothing yet,' Charlotte warned. 'I've asked Ellen to visit so that we can talk it over with her. I wish you had a longer holiday, Anne. You will be sorry to miss her.'

'When duty calls then pleasure must be denied,' Anne said. 'Give Miss Nussey my best love and tell her that I agree with the plan.'

Ellen however never arrived. Having seen Anne off the day before Charlotte stationed herself at the window, straining her ears for the rattle of harness and rumble of wheels in the lane, but the hours passed with no sign of anyone.

'There must have been an accident or she is ill. Emily, what are we to do?' she enquired fearfully.

'There's nothing to be done until we receive word,' Emily said sensibly. 'The weather's calm so an accident is unlikely, and Miss Ellen was well enough when you saw her last. Stop looking at the black side, Tallii! It's wearing on the nerves!'

She patted her sister on the shoulder and began to clear the table.

The message arrived the following afternoon – a short note that made Charlotte flush with anger.

'Apparently Ann Nussey decided at the last moment to invite some friends of her own and insisted that Ellen remain to help entertain them,' she said savagely. 'We are of no account when the nobs threaten to call! Ellen yields to her family in everything as if we were of no matter!'

'Ellen has little choice in when she comes and goes,' Emily said.

'Then she ought to stand up for herself!' Charlotte said fiercely. 'Well, I shall tell her nothing about our scheme until all is arranged! She may whistle for news from me! I shall write to Miss Wooler to ask her opinion and to the Taylors. Miss Wooler knows the ins and outs of running a school. And Mary and Martha will come over and tell us all about their life in Brussels.'

'You are not thinking of hauling me off to that finishing school, I hope?' Emily said.

'It would be far too expensive. No, there is a school in Brussels at the other side of the city – the Heger Pensionnat where higher education is offered to young girls wishing to be teachers.'

'Do we still count as young girls? You will be twenty-six this year and I shall be twenty-four in July.'

'Then the sooner everything is settled,' Charlotte said, her fingers crumpling up the note from Brookroyd, 'the better before we turn into old maids with no independent means of support!'

'So what now?' Emily looked at her.

'I shall return to work out the month's notice I gave to the Whites. I shall write to Aunt from there and when she mentions it to you then you will agree that the idea is a good one. You will agree, Ems?'

'Yes,' Emily said.

'It will be good to be together,' Charlotte said impulsively. 'Sometimes, Emily, I have felt that perhaps I sometimes neglect you for my friends. And you mustn't fret about Anne's not being included at this juncture. Her turn will come, unless – she has always seemed very taken with Mr Weightman. I hope he will not take advantage of our absence to fill her head with nonsense!'

'Anne is in no danger from Celia Amelia,' Emily said. 'I have no fear of that, Tallii!'

FOURTEEN

Charlotte put down her pen and glanced across to where Emily sat, her dark brows contracted into a frown as she studied the book before her. Emily attacked her work as if she were fighting an enemy.

'Emily,' she said abruptly, 'have you written yet to Anne or do you want to include a message in my letter?'

'I wrote to her the moment we received Papa's letter,' Emily said. 'I wrote to Branwell too. He was with Mr Weightman at the end for which I honour him for cholera is highly contagious I believe.'

'Branwell wouldn't have been at home at all had he not been dismissed from the railway,' Charlotte said. 'How could he have been so foolish as to neglect his duties and leave the porter in charge of the booking-office so that the man could help himself to the contents of the till?'

'Had I been stuck in a railway station at the back of nowhere I think I would have dropped a log on the line for the sheer plea-sure of seeing the trains crash,' Emily said.

'When we finally go home it will seem very odd not to see Mr Weightman there, popping in and out, amusing us with his jests.'

'Finally.' Emily repeated the word flatly.

'Emily, you know an extra year here will increase our knowl-edge of French and German!' Charlotte said impatiently. 'We shall be able to charge more for pupils.'

'You're not thinking of taking up Miss Wooler's offer to take over her school?'

'And end up living in Dewsbury in the very place where I was so utterly miserable? No! We shall make for the seaside and rent

131

a good big house there. Anne can join us. Her last letter was subdued.'

'Mr Weightman had just died,' Emily reproved.

'Yes. Poor Anne! She so enjoyed her valentines.'

'We all loved our valentines,' Emily said, smiling slightly.

'At least the rest of the family is well,' Charlotte said. 'I wish you were happier here, Emily. This is such a wonderful chance for us!'

'I survive,' Emily said drily. 'Stop fussing!'

She had indeed endured the nine months they had been in Brussels with a stoicism that had aroused Charlotte's approval. She had even argued with Monsieur Heger himself who came from the boys' school next door to give lessons in French and German literature to the pupils in his wife's establishment.

'If we must read the great writers of France and then write essays in their style we shall lose our own original voices, sir,' Emily had argued when the slim, black-haired, black-eyed professor had begun to expound his teaching methods.

'*Parlez en français, s'il vous plaît, mademoiselle!*' he had snapped.

'I can *parlez le français* when I agree with the methods used to teach the language to me, *monsieur!*' Emily had snapped back.

'*Ç'à suffit! Ç'à suffit! C'est insupportable!*'

He had raged up and down the classroom, reducing some of the pupils to tears and others to nervous giggles. Charlotte had been scarlet with shame.

His rage had subsided as quickly as it had flared forth and at that point Emily had given him one of her rare brilliant smiles and said calmly,

'*D'accord, monsieur. Je suis contente!*'

She had made her point and, apparently happy with that, had applied herself to her studies with ferocious energy, not only in French and German but in the drawing and music classes she had elected to take.

She was also earning herself some pocket money by teaching music to three English girls who had just arrived at the school.

'And since I don't intend to sacrifice my own study hours by teaching beginners their scales then they can come to me during their recreation period,' she had said firmly.

Emily didn't care whether people liked her or not, Charlotte thought wistfully. It seemed to make no difference to her that the other pupils thought her odd with her long lank skirts, and hair bundled back into a couple of Spanish combs. She had even made it clear that she didn't approve of Charlotte's making friends either. At recreation time she stuck to her like a burr and scowled when anyone came near.

On Sundays they walked through the city to the Protestant Church and then went on to spend a couple of hours with Mary and Martha Taylor. Their finishing school was an expensive establishment and the students were less supervised than those in the Heger Pensionnat.

'My real ambition,' Mary told them, 'is to leave England – leave Europe altogether and make my way in the New World.'

'In America?' Charlotte asked.

'Too civilized!' Mary said. 'No, Martha and I have spoken to our youngest brother Waring and he means to emigrate to New Zealand! When he is settled we shall join him. Since our father's death it is quite unbearable at home. We plan to live like human beings on terms of equality with men. Don't we, Martha?'

'I plan to make friends with a few of them too,' Martha said naughtily.

She would too, Charlotte mused, pausing in her letter to bring into her head the image of young Martha Taylor with her bright, sweet face in which every feature was at variance with the others but the whole added up to irresistible charm. The few young men with whom they came into contact admired Mary's beauty and flirted with Martha.

'Are we going over to see Mary and Martha this week?' Emily enquired.

'I think so,' Charlotte decided. 'We haven't seen them except fleetingly since poor Mr Weightman died.'

'It will be good to get out,' Emily said shortly, casting a slightly contemptuous look round the clean, bright classroom with its floors of polished wood and the lilies arranged in a tall vase.

'We go out into the garden,' Charlotte said.

Though the school was in the middle of other buildings and its façade fronted the rue d'Isabelle there was a large, lovingly cultivated garden at the back where rumour had it a nun walked. Charlotte, walking with Emily in the cool of the evening down one of the pleached avenues, had wondered aloud if the rumour was true.

'I shouldn't think so,' Emily had said. 'This place is so boring she'd be an absolute fool not to haunt somewhere else.'

'Mademoiselle Brontë, a letter 'as come for you.' Madame Heger, plumply pretty in black silk, had come in.

'*Merci, Madame.*' Charlotte took the letter and curtsied.

She never saw *Madame* without marvelling that so dainty and feminine a lady could bring up a family, run a large school efficiently and be a model wife without pulling herself into several pieces.

'It's from Mary.' She waited until Madame Heger had departed before opening it. 'Asking us to join her tomorrow in which case I must finish—'

'Charlotte, what is it?'

'Martha Taylor is dead,' Charlotte said blankly.

'Dead! What happened?' Emily came to her side.

' "Dear Charlotte and Emily, A brief note to inform you that Martha died last night. Can you come tomorrow? Mary".'

'Let me see it!' Emily took the letter and read it for herself.

'We would have heard had she been ill,' Charlotte said. 'Oh, poor Mary! we must go to her at once!'

'She says tomorrow,' Emily said. 'The note was sent by hand, so tomorrow must mean tomorrow.'

'I cannot rest until I know—' Charlotte began.

'We must both get a good night's sleep and be fit to give Mary all the support she needs,' Emily countered. 'I shall ask Madame for leave over the weekend.'

They set off the next morning, walking rapidly through the city to the school attended by the Taylors. The portress, opening the door, met them with a shake of the head and the words,

'Mademoiselle Taylor 'as departed to her uncle's 'ome. She tells me you know the address.'

'Is the funeral—?'

'It was yesterday, *mademoiselle.*'

'So soon?' Charlotte exclaimed. 'Then it must have been – was it cholera?'

'The young *mademoiselle* died somewhere at a house in the city,' the woman said. 'The police come to tell us.'

'The police?'

'That is all I know, *mesdemoiselles.*' The door was firmly closed.

'Her uncle – that must be Mr Dixon,' Charlotte said as they

turned away. 'What on earth can have happened?'

'We had best take a cab to Mr Dixon's place,' Emily said. Had she too not been worried she would never have suggested such a thing since on the one occasion they had met the Dixon family who had moved to Belgium for business reasons, she had failed to utter a single word all afternoon.

Mary met them at the door, her manner subdued but her eyes dry.

'It is good of you to come,' she said almost formally. 'I left word at the school.'

'Mary, what happened? Was it – it must've been very sudden,' Charlotte said. 'The portress spoke of the police coming. . .'

'Only to inform me,' Mary said. 'Please, come in and see my uncle. He and my aunt have been very kind to me. They managed everything most prudently.'

Not until they had been greeted by the Dixons and thanked for coming and eaten a light meal during which hardly anyone spoke was Mary free to walk with the two of them in the park opposite the house.

'Martha is laid in the Protestant cemetery a couple of miles away,' Mary said abruptly.

'We would have come to the funeral. You know we would,' Emily said, more warmly than she usually spoke to Mary.

'I know but we felt that a speedy and very private ceremony might attract less attention,' Mary said bleakly. 'My uncle suggests that we give out that she died of cholera should anyone enquire. I will write to Ellen Nussey to that effect.'

'But it wasn't cholera?' Charlotte pressed.

'Martha had left the school about three weeks ago,' Mary said, in a curiously toneless voice. 'She had the right to do so. She was twenty-three. She took a room in the city. We didn't quarrel – I simply made it my business not to interfere. I had not seen her for several days. Two young gentlemen reported her death to the police and left without giving their names. I went to . . . identify her and then sent a note to my uncle. He took charge of all the arrangements and the expense and has been quite wonderfully kind. In a week or two I shall walk with you to her grave. Then it will not be visited by me again. Not because I didn't love her but goodbyes should be final, don't you think?'

Her voice broke slightly but she was instantly controlled again.

'What cause of death was written on her death certificate?' Charlotte asked.

'My uncle persuaded the coroner to leave the space blank,' Mary said.

'Will you go back to England?' Emily asked.

'No, I shall leave for Germany in three weeks,' Mary said. 'I have obtained a post teaching mathematics – to a class of small boys of all things! I shall save sufficient for my passage to New Zealand.'

'If there is anything I can do. . .?' Charlotte said.

'Write to Ellen Nussey,' Mary said unexpectedly. 'There has been a coolness between you for many many months. She was hurt that you never discussed your plans to study in Belgium, that she never met you before you left. '

'She was invited to Haworth!'

'And her family put difficulties in her way. I know that. She ought to stand up to that wretched tribe of hers but she never does, and the cooling of your friendship has deprived her of a great deal. Write to her, Charlotte, in the old affectionate way. Life is so uncertain. Two of our little group are gone and I dread hearing news of a third. They say ill fortune comes in threes.'

'I promise I will write,' Charlotte said soberly. 'Oh, Mary I hope and pray the old superstition is wrong.'

A fortnight later they returned from a sad and silent visit to the isolated corner where bright, flirtatious Martha lay to find a letter waiting for them.

'It's from Branny.' Charlotte lifted a blanched face from the paper.

'It's not Anne?' Emily's voice was sharp.

'Aunt is taken ill. She has an obstruction in the bowel and is in very great pain.'

'We must go home at once!' Emily said. 'Poor Aunt! Branwell cannot possibly be expected to nurse her all by himself. Is Anne not there?'

'She is still at Thorp Green. Emily, perhaps Aunt will get well?'

'I am going home whether or not you come with me,' Emily said stubbornly. 'We must go and find *Madame* at once and tell her that we are leaving.'

'Yes. Yes, of course we must,' Charlotte said. 'We can hire a diligence to take us to the railway station and then there is the boat and the train at the other end to Keighley and perhaps we could hire a gig to Haworth.'

'Then let us do it instead of talking about it!' Emily said.

They had just finished explaining the situation to the Hegers when a second letter arrived.

'Aunt is dead,' Charlotte said. 'Emily, we cannot possibly get home before the funeral. Do we need . . . ?'

'This makes it all the more imperative that we travel as soon as possible,' Emily insisted. 'Papa will have no housekeeper and poor Anne will have had to organize everything alone.'

'Yes, I will finish packing at once,' Charlotte said.

Her eyes, moving slowly round the classroom where a fire had been lit to warm the pupils against the winter chill, vowed what her tongue refused to utter.

Come hell or high water I will return here!

FIFTEEN

It had been stifling all day even with the windows open. Charlotte opened the french doors going into the garden where there was the promise of shade under the trees, but even the trees were heavy with heat, their laden branches drooping limply, the grass borders dry and brown. Behind her the building was silent. Even to whisper within its walls would rouse an echo that might waken the dead.

The year of 1843 had begun so differently! Ellen had at last come to stay for a long weekend and, after the endless months apart, any small awkwardness was forgotten in the warm embrace of their reunion.

'Everything is settled,' Charlotte said excitedly. 'Anne has prevailed upon the Robinsons to engage Branwell as a tutor for their son Edmund. They left together for Thorp Green. And Monsieur Heger has sent a most courteous letter to Papa regretting our leaving so quickly but offering one of us a place there as English mistress. The salary is low but I shall have use of the family sitting room and—'

'So you are the one going back?' Ellen said.

'Emily refuses to be dragged from home again. She has already appointed herself as housekeeper in Aunt's stead and brought Tabby back to live here and take what share she can of the housework.'

'You spoke of starting a school,' Ellen reminded her.

'And will do so eventually, but Anne will wish to save a little more from her salary at Thorp Green and another two or three years in Belgium will benefit me enormously! Of course Mary has already gone into Germany to teach. I believe she was glad to leave Belgium behind her.'

'Poor Martha,' Ellen said softly. 'You will be solitary in Brussels without the Taylors or Emily.'

'But I don't mean to be lonely!' Charlotte said with energy. 'Ellen, why don't you come with me to perfect your command of French?'

'Me? Go to Brussels?' Ellen looked at her.

'Why not? We would be together and company for each other and you could improve your French, study music.'

'I wish I could come,' Ellen said, 'but at present it would be quite impossible. The family—'

'Do what you want to do for once!'

'I cannot,' Ellen said sadly. 'Charlotte, Sarah is dying. It will be a merciful release for she never enjoyed any quality of life but my mother is deeply distressed and – no, I could not come.'

'Don't dismiss the idea out of hand,' Charlotte urged. 'Think about it!'

'I will – and I will write you long gossipy letters,' Ellen promised.

They had left it at that and after Ellen had gone home there had been the bustle of packing and travelling alone down to London to catch the Channel ferry. The journey ought to have warned her of troubles ahead for the train didn't arrive until after ten at night and Charlotte, shy of rousing the hotel porter at so late an hour took a cab straight to the dockside where she endured the embarrassment at being mocked by a couple of watermen before she found a boat to row her out to the ship where in a quavering but determined voice she demanded to be allowed aboard early.

The crossing itself had been rough and the journey across France towards Brussels cold and tedious but the welcome afforded her by the Hegers made up for that. Madame Heger who was, Charlotte noticed, in the first stages of pregnancy, had embraced her and *Monsieur*, black eyes sparkling, had held both her hands and smiled at her as he assured her in his fractured English that he was *enchanté* to greet her home again, and that his home was her home!

He had even signed up for private English lessons from her. And it had been almost like coming home, though she had a lot of work to do.

Being a teacher was different from being a pupil, she reflected wryly. She had almost forgotten how tiring it was to prepare and mark lessons, to keep order in a class of boisterous girls and to do so in a foreign tongue as she was doing now made the task more exhausting.

She looked forward eagerly to the lessons she gave Monsieur Heger, amused by his efforts to pronounce some of the harder words and by his delight when he got an exercise perfectly correct.

'You are a slave-driver, *mademoiselle!*' he would exclaim. ''ow can one speak a language when the spelling is of the eccentric most extreme!'

Monsieur Heger was kind and not only kind with his gifts of books and an occasional cake wrapped in tissue and placed as a surprise in her desk. He had lost his first wife and child to a cholera epidemic before meeting and marrying his present wife but that had been when he was a very young man. Yet he was only in his thirties now, she had realized, with Madame several years older than himself though the marriage seemed happy enough. Though Charlotte seldom availed herself of the freedom to use their private sitting-room in the evenings he was kind in the way he often sought her out, the scent of the cigars he smoked betraying his presence before she saw his spare, dark figure, the glint of mischief in his eyes as he turned from her desk with his small gift ready to be left there.

More valuable than cakes and books was the encouragement he gave her when she confided that she had always longed to write.

'Harness your imagination to your technique, *mademoiselle,* and write about what lies closest to your heart,' he advised.

'I try, *monsieur,* but may not imagination soar on wings?'

'Of course! Provided your readers can fly so high themselves,' he teased. '*Mon Dieu!* but your tales leave me breathless on the earth!'

'Then I must trim my pen to fly a little closer,' Charlotte said playfully.

And then it all began to sour so gradually that she could not afterwards recall how it had begun as one cannot tell the exact moment when milk begins to curdle.

Suddenly Madame Heger began to put her head round the

door when *Monsieur* was chatting with her to remind him that the children were ready for their story or their romp. Charlotte fancied that someone besides *Monsieur* looked through her desk when she was absent, trod softly along the passages in velvet slippers when Charlotte was talking to him.

'We leave on vacation in a few days, to the seaside,' *Monsieur* remarked. 'The other teachers also return to their families. You will be content here, alone in the pensionnat?'

'*Zut!* she will enjoy the peace and the quiet,' Madame said.

'Your friend, Mademoiselle Taylor, is not here though,' *Monsieur* remembered.

'But there will be the cook and the cleaners to take care of Miss Brontë's needs,' his wife said, 'and with no lessons she will be free to visit many of our fine galleries and parks without the distraction of others to annoy her.'

The vacation lasted through most of August and nearly all of September. What Charlotte had not anticipated was the silence and the emptiness of the large rooms, the queer creaking noises that sounded so loud in the dormitory where she was the sole occupant. She wrote to Ellen and Ellen replied sympathetically but her friend was still mourning the death of her sister Sarah. She wrote to Mary but Mary was full of her own plans for emigrating to join her brother in New Zealand.

Now, turning into the covered walk known as l'Allée Défendue since it was forbidden to the pupils for what Charlotte considered the rather silly reason that the boys in the school next door could see the *demoiselles* strolling there from their upper windows. But today everybody was away save for herself as she walked beneath the arching roof of branches and paused briefly at the grey stone set into the soil which, legend held, was the entrance through which the rebel nun had been thrust, still alive, to suffocate in the dark wormy earth. Charlotte shivered, thinking of fingers tapping on the wall of a crypt – Mama, Maria, Elizabeth, Aunt – and then she was hurrying back to the schoolroom, opening the lid of her desk to sniff the faintest memory of *Monsieur*'s cigar.

That night an owl hooted outside the window. Charlotte sat up and pushed back the covers, padded across to the window and looked down into the quiet lamplit street. A figure stood beside one flaring sconce, cloak half-concealing his face. Monsieur had stolen back to find out if she was all right. She opened her mouth to call but the figure was gone, a shadow melting into darker shadow. She turned to face the moonlit room and saw the skulls crowning the beds grinning at her. Not skulls but the white hangings on the half-tester beds tied up out of the way! She shook her head, turned to her own bed and saw, lying there, Quashia in all his naked and splendid barbarity!

A few days later, trudging through the streets, empty save for an occasional road-sweeper or a beggar, she could sense Quashia following her but when she dared to look round the street was deserted, and in the air she heard Ellen laughing.

She turned abruptly and went up the steps of the nearest church. There might be peace here from her tormented imagination and the sick rage that oozed through her pores. Like every Papist church it had its vacant-eyed statues, its vases of heavily scented lilies, its red sanctuary-lamp and high carved altar glinting with ivory and gold. Nothing here of the simplicity of home but a few people were going into the row of confessionals near the door. Presumably they found a kind of peace here.

A woman, coming out, crossing herself, touched Charlotte on the arm and indicated the empty coffinlike kiosk where the hidden penitent knelt. Her turn apparently. As if in a dream she found herself going into the confessional, as her Irish grandmother must once have done.

She would tell nobody about it save Emily and to her she would make light of it. Coming out, her Protestantism confessed, an empty promise given that she would come again to learn the true faith she felt only shame though the unseen priest had been very kind.

Suddenly afraid he might have followed her she hastened her step and went down the steps into the rue d'Isabelle with little dancing demons laughing at her all the way.

Emily wrote back to say that there were rumours in the village that Papa was drinking a little too much though he had visited Thorp Green and seen how highly valued Branwell and Anne were there. She made no mention of Charlotte's visit to the church.

Ellen wrote to say that George was not well. He seemed very restless, though he had no fever, and often contradicted himself

143

in the middle of his sentence or set out somewhere but forgot where he was going.

Mary wrote to tell her that she had stayed long enough in Brussels and ought to go home.

The Hegers returned from holiday with the children and the assorted nursemaids and the other teachers and pupils drifted back, filling the skull-headed beds, clattering their desk lids as they stowed their books away.

Everything had changed. Waiting for *Monsieur* to arrive for his English lesson she was confronted by *Madame*, big-bellied in her black-silk robe, every curl in place, her lips smiling.

'Hélas! my husband regrets that he cannot take the lessons you so kindly gave him last term for he has extra duties at the Boys' Academy. He will miss them very much but when circumstances demand we must submit.'

Smiling still she left the classroom. Charlotte felt angry tears rise into her eyes and trickle slowly down her cheeks. She had so looked forward to their lessons with herself in control as she scolded him for his abominable accent and felt her face glow when he teased her.

Autumn became winter and the heat froze into icicles that hurt the heart. If there had been an open quarrel then she might have defended herself but there was no quarrel, no disagreement, not a single complaint.

She sat down at her desk one day and scribbled in the old ways with her eyes half-shut, in the margins of an exercise book.

I am very cold – there is no fire – I wish I were at home with Papa, Branwell – Emily – Anne and Tabby – I am tired of being among foreigners it is a dreary life – especially as there is only one person in this house worthy of being liked – also another who seems a rosy sugar-plum but I know her to be coloured chalk.'

Yet when she told *Madame* that she was thinking of going home *Monsieur* stormed in and told her that her work was too valuable, her company too precious and her will too strong for her to be permitted to give way to homesickness!

Struggling on she saw the faces of her pupils blur into masks,

144

each mask like the skull-mask they had worn in turn as children while Papa asked them questions. Going along the corridor after supper one evening she strayed unthinkingly into the quarter of the building reserved for the Hegers' private sleeping quarters, heard the murmuring of voices and a low laugh, smelled the fragrance of the familiar cigar, and saw the gleam of scarlet curtains through the half-open door.

It was no longer possible to endure it! Stealing back to her own part of the house she lit a lamp with trembling fingers and sat down to reread Mary Taylor's latest letter.

If you value your health and your sanity then either come to me here or go home.
You have lost your rudder, Charlotte. Find it in your own will and leave Brussels! Ellen is still there for you.'

Dearest Ellen, who had relinquished her suitor to please her! A few days later she wrote to Emily, announcing her intention of returning to Haworth the day after the New Year and then told *Monsieur* and *Madame* together.

'My father's health is not good and Emily has only an old servant to help her and a very young girl. It is my duty to go.'

'And you are right to do your duty, Miss Brontë,' *Madame* said, 'though we will be sorry to lose you. Your pupils also will miss you sadly but the call of family is very strong and must take precedence.'

'Yes, *Madame*.'

'You will write to us of course,' *Monsieur* said. 'I shall look forward one day to reading a book with your name inscribed as the author.'

'Dedicated to you, *monsieur*,' Charlotte said. 'To you both of course!'

'Mademoiselle Charlotte must get on with her packing, my dear,' *Madame* said.

All a bustle at the last moment. The other teachers giving her small gifts she knew she didn't deserve for she had never troubled to try to make friends with them, her pupils declaring they would miss her, the driver carrying her trunk down the staircase into the waiting diligence, *monsieur*'s hands holding hers.

'We shall not say goodbye, *mademoiselle*, but *au revoir*, for we shall meet again one day?'

'Yes, *monsieur.* Oh yes!'

The plump smiling figure in a furred cloak.

'Are you quite ready, my dear?'

'Yes. Yes, *madame.* Good bye . . .'

'That can be delayed a little longer, my dear. I shall be coming with you to the boat myself to see you safely launched.'

Bitch! She had never been a threat to her. She had wanted only a small part of his attention, his affection. She turned but he had gone already through an inner door, his footsteps receding.

'One day, *madame,*' Charlotte thought savagely. 'One day I will be revenged!'

SIXTEEN

If I were to make a ledger that detailed the good and the bad of these last months, Charlotte thought, how would it look?

Certainly there would be happy items to record. After the journey home she had wanted only to sleep, to sink into the comfort of Emily's cooking, Papa's anxious enquiries as to her health and Tabby's awe at the certificate of proficiency that she had brought with her from Brussels. There had been the plea- sure of arranging her things in the larger bedroom that had been Aunt's and was now hers and Anne's when the latter was home. There was the satisfaction of knowing that Branwell and Anne were both doing so well at Thorp Green Hall.

'The Robinsons gave Anne a spaniel,' Emily told her. 'I regret to say that she whelped over Christmas and now we have Flossy and Little Flossy! Keeper is vastly put out!'

There had been the knowledge that Aunt's will had left each of them, except Branwell, £350 better off.

'I put the money in railway shares,' Emily informed her. 'They are holding steady at the moment but I keep a sharp eye on them!'

'They will be needed when I establish our school,' Charlotte nodded.

'As to that . . .' Emily hesitated, then hurried on. 'Tallii, I know you had your heart set on the seaside but there is Papa to think about. His sight is growing weaker and he relies more heavily upon his curate who, by the by, is a sad contrast to Mr Weightman. A florid Dubliner who thinks himself a riot with

147

the ladies! The point is that we cannot just waltz off to the seaside and open a school and leave Papa here.'

'But we set our hearts on a school,' Charlotte said.

'I know.' Emily paused an instant, then went on eagerly, 'Had you thought of starting a school here in the parsonage?'

'Where on earth would we put the pupils?'

'I've thought about that too! The loft over the back kitchen could be converted into a dormitory without too much trouble and the dining-room could double as a schoolroom or we might build on to the barn eventually and give some lessons there. We could certainly take a couple of pupils.'

'A couple of pupils isn't exactly a school,' Charlotte said.

'It would be a start!' Emily argued. 'You could give each one individual attention.'

'Me?'

'You and Anne can share the teaching between you,' Emily said, 'and I will see to the cooking and washing and sewing.'

'Surely you don't intend to waste your education on that!'

'Education is never wasted,' Emily said placidly.

That would be a negative mark in the ledger, Charlotte thought. On the other hand Emily managed the household very well and had never liked teaching.

The brightest marks would be due to the reunions with Ellen and Mary! Ellen had come to Haworth, still wearing black for her sister Sarah but as pretty as ever, her smile as warm and her embrace as loving and after the initial slight constraint had worn off they had talked their heads off, whispering together in the big bed where Aunt had slept.

'You have a very high opinion of Monsieur Heger,' Ellen said slyly. 'Is he so handsome?'

'Not in the least but he has flashing black eyes and he has presence. You cannot be five minutes in his company without being filled with enthusiasm! He is a most gifted teacher!'

'And you write to him?'

'We agreed that I should write every six months giving details of the progress of our school but I doubt if we shall stick to that for I always have so much to say in my letters. We hope that one day he will send us one of his own children.'

'When you advertise for pupils I will distribute the prospectuses for you,' Ellen said. 'You will come to Brookroyd very soon, won't you?'

'Yes, of course! I look forward to seeing your family.'

She had spent three weeks in Brookroyd – a mixed three weeks for it was clear that George was far from well. Charlotte noted with real concern his frequent pauses in the conversation when he would repeat himself or use the wrong word. Once she and Ellen, out for a walk, came upon him seated on the grass verge, confusion in his face as he looked up and said,

'You will think me foolish but I cannot remember how to get home.'

The good side of the ledger would have to include Mary who was back from Germany for a spell and rode over to spend the day at Brookroyd.

'I shall return to Germany after the vacation and continue teaching my tribe of small boys!' she informed them. 'Next year I shall go to New Zealand and join Waring out there.'

'Will you teach there?' Ellen asked.

'Lord, no! I intend to farm and open a shop,' Mary said.

'You don't know anything about farming!' Charlotte exclaimed.

'I've been reading books and for the rest I shall rely on trial and error.'

'Women can't farm,' Ellen said.

'Women,' said Mary, pushing back a long flaxen ringlet, 'can do anything! One day they will be doctors and lawyers and judges and go into the city and—'

'Have the vote?' Charlotte said.

'That too! Why not? A clever woman can use her good sense in political affairs as well as a man,' Mary said vigorously.

'You won't find many men to agree with you,' Ellen said.

'If we waited for men to agree with us,' Mary said, 'we would never stir out of our houses.'

'I believe that Monsieur Heger would agree with you.'

'And how is the *Professor*?' Mary darted her a glance.

'He writes that he is well and asks how our plans are going. His encouragement is most stimulating. His eloquence could hold a class spellbound!'

'And his wife?'

'What about her?' Charlotte said, confused.

'*Madame.* She has a new baby I understand.'

'A son. She has called it Victor. I believe. I sent my meed of congratulations.'

'Are you in love with him?' Mary asked bluntly.

'In . . . ? Whatever put that into your head? No, I respect him for his talents as a teacher; I admire his intellectual abilities.'

'And he has flashing dark eyes,' Mary said.

'Mainly in temper! Emily caused them to flash continually when she was in Brussels. She and *Monsieur* didn't draw together well at all!'

'Does Emily draw well with anyone?' Mary asked.

'Of course she does!' Charlotte said indignantly. 'She gets on well with you, doesn't she, Ellen?'

'Emily is very lovable,' Ellen said.

'She wasn't so friendly in Brussels,' Mary said with a chuckle. 'Do you recall, Charlotte, how we would be laughing and talking together and then some young Jenkins or Dixon would join us and she would freeze them out with a glance!'

'Emily is a law unto herself,' Charlotte admitted.

Yes, it had been a good year on the whole, with Papa giving Ellen the new puppy when she came for a brief second visit, and George feeling well enough to drive the gig himself when he took Ellen home.

Only the letters from Brussels secretly disappointed her. They were fewer and shorter than she had hoped and they said nothing that was personal but talked instead of her school plans, advised her about the best curriculum to follow and always, always sent greetings from *Madame.*

Charlotte returned the greetings punctiliously but sometimes her pen took flight and ran away into protestations of longing, the vow that one day she would return and see him again if only for a moment.

She gave Mary a letter to deliver when the latter passed through Brussels *en route* for Germany.

'Perhaps *Monsieur* will give your brother Joe a letter to bring back to me?' she said hopefully.

'I thought you were only supposed to write every six months.'

'It is merely a chance to send a letter without paying the postage. You will deliver it?'

'Of course I will. But Charlotte, after I've gone to New Zealand you must find another postman,' Mary said.

'You met *Monsieur* once or twice in passing. Surely you felt the inherent power of his personality?'

'I saw an attractive intelligent man who was very well aware of his power to inspire hero worship in the bosoms of romantic young girls.'

'Then I cannot be counted among their number for I am twenty-eight years old and impervious.'

'What a liar you are, Charlotte!' Mary said admiringly.

But she took the letter and unexpectedly kissed Charlotte on the cheek.

Ellen came back to Haworth for a second visit which was made more pleasurable because Anne and Branwell were at home for a week. He, she had to confess, seemed moody and out of sorts and Anne looked tired, but they walked on the moors as far as the waterfall and made plans for the school though Emily persisted in her refusal to teach.

There was a fifth person often present when they were indoors.

Papa's new curate had taken a decided fancy to Ellen and went out of his way to drop in at odd hours, to stay for tea and to spend his time gazing at her, listening intently to everything she said, and paying her neat little compliments in his beguiling southern accent. And Ellen seemed not to mind, Charlotte mused, for she chatted with him quite freely and even blushed prettily when he picked up a dropped shawl.

'You seem to like Mr Smith,' she commented casually as they curled their hair that evening.

'He is vastly amusing,' Ellen said, carefully placing a hairpin.

'He has a certain amount of Dublin bravado.'

'And not unhandsome.'

'I grant you that but you are not one to be swayed by looks, are you?' Charlotte said.

'Mr Vincent was very nice-looking though he did wear spectacles for reading.'

'Mr Weightman didn't wear spectacles at all. Do you remember how keen his eyesight was?'

'Mr Weightman is dead, Charlotte. Don't you think we must move on?'

151

'Well, I shall let you know if he asks after you when you are at Brookroyd again,' Charlotte said. 'I mean Mr Smith of course, for poor Willie Weightman is in heaven and Mr Vincent has left the district.'

'And there are no more valentines,' Ellen said softly.

Romantic nonsense long since outgrown, Charlotte thought. She was relieved when, after Ellen's departure, Papa came to her with a serious expression to say;

'James Smith seems rather too interested in Miss Nussey. He has asked me if she has a dowry.'

'Mr Smith would do well to keep his questions to himself!'

'I said she was a nice girl but he repeated the query.'

'Tell him that it is none of his affair! Certainly he has no right to try to gossip to you about her circumstances,' Charlotte said. 'Papa, I am going to draw up prospectuses for our school here. Ellen has promised to distribute them. You don't disapprove?'

'Of course not! A little hustle and bustle won't disturb me in the least,' he assured her.

Losing his sight, for there was no doubt that he was suffering from cataracts, had its advantages in that much simply evaded his notice, she thought. He read and wrote with the help of a large magnifying glass; his meals were ready on time; Mr Smith for all his faults took many of the services, and he knew the village and the moors so well that he was still able to take solitary walks with only Keeper and Flossy, Anne's dog, as his companions. Papa didn't have to go into the kitchen where Tabby presided like a genial witch over chaos as Emily moved around among half-made meals, unwashed dishes, bowls of dough set to rise by the fire, and bits of paper covered with her indecipherable scribbles which she shoved into the cutlery drawer when Charlotte popped her head in.

There were no long friendly letters from *Monsieur*, only a brief stiff note advising her not to write so frequently or express herself so vehemently. She had written back at once, apologising for her emotional tone but telling him that she could only survive on the crumbs of friendship she gleaned from his bountiful table.

It was *Madame*, of course, who was behind it. *Madame* with her plump pregnant figure and soft footsteps as she moved up and down the shining corridors of her school. It was *Madame* who

152

whispered and laughed with him in the room where, beyond the partly open door, a red lamp cast fire on scarlet hangings.

'If Monsieur Heger does not write,' Emily said on one occasion when she and Charlotte were walking the dogs, 'it is because he is occupied with his own work and his own family.'

'I appreciate that, but it would not cost him much in time or effort to correspond with an ex-pupil,' Charlotte argued. 'It is so hard to wait day after day for letters that never come.'

'Then don't wait around for the post,' Emily said briskly.

It was useless to make Emily understand. Charlotte resolved to say nothing more to her about the Hegers. Instead she would write to *Monsieur* telling him how she denied herself the pleasure of speaking his name even to her sister.

The prospectuses had been drawn up and looked handsome, and Ellen was sending them out to all her acquaintances but so far not one pupil had appeared on the horizon.

'If any loving parent came here she would snatch up her child and run away again,' Charlotte said.

'What's wrong with the place?' Emily demanded.

'We haven't even begun on the alterations and the rest of the house is – it's bleak, Ems! Grey walls, stone floors, no curtains, the garden full of weeds, the churchyard so near. . . .'

'Simplicity isn't poverty,' Emily demurred. 'We can give the walls a lick of paint and shine up the floors when we get a sniff of a pupil, and it's not worth starting on alterations until that happens. And the children will benefit from healthful walks on the moors. There's so much beauty there that it would last for a lifetime!'

It was useless to talk to Emily! Charlotte asked Ellen to send out more prospectuses and returned to the story she had begun to write many times before. Rival brothers, one the abuser, the other the victim, moving now from a Yorkshire mill-town to Belgium and a school where the younger brother becomes a teacher. She could see the Belgian school clearly in her head with its shining, echoing classrooms and dormitories, could see the sly, sensual Madame Zoraïde who moved on soft shoes through the dusk, tempting the teacher away from the pale slim girl who sat in his class day after day but paid for her own lessons by mending lace. She wrote in the first person, in the character of the male, seeing aspects of Ellen's serenity in the quiet

Frances Henri, gave a little start when, seeking a phrase, she rose to walk up and down the dining-room and felt the full skirts she was wearing drag across the floor when she could have sworn a moment before that she had been wearing breeches.

There were bright moments. Mr Smith took himself off to Ireland and a Mr Grant arrived who was dull and snobbish and safely betrothed. At Christmas Mary Taylor returned from Germany and came to stay, as full of plans and projects as ever. She brought news that George Nussey was worse in health.

'Confused and irritable and with his short-term memory clouded! He is the best-looking and the nicest of all the Nussey men so I count it a great pity,' Mary said. 'They hope a water cure will allieviate the symptoms but one is doubtful! William suffered from a similar depression and confusion and we all remember poor Sarah! You know George is betrothed?'

'To Amelia Ringrose. Ellen has mentioned her in passing.'

Rather too often Charlotte privately considered. She was rather tired of having to wade through long paragraphs in Ellen's letters about the fascinating and pretty Ringrose sisters whose family had settled near Brookroyd!

'One hopes that he will recover quickly,' Mary said. 'So far news of his illness has been kept from her.'

'Then I hope she is not too much in love with him,' Charlotte said sombrely.

'Charlotte! Have you thought any more of coming out to New Zealand with me?' Mary asked. 'You have found no pupils for your school and you hated governessing. You have the money to buy a passage out to Wellington. We would get along very well together.'

To escape to a beautiful half-tamed land where the wonders of nature threw up hot springs and enormous trees and the people were not bound by habit or convention. To begin afresh in the year that saw her own thirtieth birthday draw threateningly near.

'I cannot,' she said at last. 'Anne and Branwell are both well settled but Papa is losing his sight quite rapidly now. Emily already does most of the household tasks and reads to Papa and plays the piano for him. I help where possible and take all the Sunday-school classes, for Emily flatly refuses to teach anyone anything anywhere! I couldn't leave her here to manage everything alone! I truly wish that I could.'

It would be, she thought, like dividing herself into three, with her body in New Zealand, her conscience in Haworth and her heart rent between Brookroyd and Brussels from where no more letters came.

SEVENTEEN

'This has been such a pleasant time together,' Charlotte said with a little sigh of contentment as she and Ellen sat together in the green shade of Hathersage parsonage.

'God bless Henry for getting married and being offered the living here!' Ellen said with a chuckle. 'I knew I would never be able to make everything ready for their return from honeymoon without your help.'

'You know that you could've managed everything beautifully without any help from me!'

'Does it trouble you – that my brother has wed another lady? He wanted to marry you once,' Ellen said tentatively.

'Nell, that was years ago! I give him credit for waiting so long before turning his attentions elsewhere though,' Charlotte said. 'No, I shall never marry. I heard rumour that Joe Taylor was sniffing round you again though.'

'Not me.' Ellen looked uncomfortable. 'Charlotte, Joe has begun to pay particular attention to Amelia Ringrose.'

'Who is engaged to your brother George!'

'Who is still in the sanatorium at York. I know! We shall have to tell Amelia the truth about George's condition very soon. The doctor holds out little hope of his regaining his sanity. The worst of it is that George is aware of his condition and it distresses him beyond bounds.'

'Is he kindly treated?'

'Oh yes! Each patient has his own room and is free to walk about in the town when they are well enough,' Ellen said thankfully. 'The doctor relies very much on simply talking to the sufferer, on the use of herbs and music. It costs a great deal but we don't grudge it.'

'Then Joe may chase Amelia once she is told the truth. How is it, Nell, that when we're together, even here among the glories of Derbyshire, we end up gossiping about marriage?'

'Because we are female. Charlotte, has there been any word of Mr Smith recently?'

'Not a line. He is presumably still in Dublin. The new curate is also Irish – Ireland breeds them like rabbits.'

'But you like Mr Nicholls?'

'I can't say that I've ever wasted a thought upon him,' Charlotte said in surprise. 'He reads well in church and Papa says he is very conscientious. I believe he is seeing a girl in Keighley.'

'Being here like this – do you remember how much we once wished to share a cottage and grow old together?'

'Once wished it? Nell, I still wish it! One day you and I will be together somewhere and we shall wag along in perfect harmony.'

'And your family?'

'Is not as demanding as yours! Branwell seems fairly ensconced at Thorp Green and is to join them at Scarborough in a few days. Anne has decided not to return. That pleases Emily immensely for they've always been close. You know they went off for a few days to York together. Emily who cannot be persuaded by me to set foot outside the village, whirls off to see the minster because Anne expresses the desire to show it to her!'

'But you were pleased for them?'

'Of course, yes! It meant that I could come and stay here with you without being accused of dereliction of duty. I do wish our school plan had been a success but you did your best.'

They had visited the great house at Chatsworth and toured the caves at Castleton, and Charlotte had visited North Lees Hall with its battlements and the madwoman's chambers up in the attics. The current owners, Mr and Mrs Eyre, had been kind enough to offer herself and Ellen tea and to give them a guided tour of the property.

'And tomorrow I go home,' Charlotte said. 'And you go home and we shall look forward to our next holiday together.'

'Oh yes!' Ellen beamed at her friend.

'And I must seek another governess post,' Charlotte said with a grimace. 'I have delayed because of Papa's poor sight. I can at least make myself useful by reading the newspapers to him and taking the Sunday-school classes. That is my only excuse for delay.'

And not an entirely true one, she admitted to herself as she travelled home to Haworth. Papa was coping well with his loss of sight, and it was usually Emily who went with him to exercise the dogs and played the piano for him after tea.

It was dark when she arrived, paid the driver and opened the gate. A figure glided towards her along the path and Anne said in a slightly breathless voice:

'We heard the wheels! Have you everything with you, dear?'

'Is my reputation for losing gloves and umbrellas so fixed?' Charlotte said, laughing. 'Yes, I am back with all my belongings. Ellen sends her love to you and Emily. Is Papa well?'

'Yes, yes, quite well,' Anne said, something hurried in her tone causing Charlotte to stop and peer at her in the gloom.

'What's wrong, Anne?' she said sharply.

'Branwell is – he has been dismissed from Thorp Green and Mr Robinson has sent a letter threatening to shoot him if he goes near any member of the family or even shows his face in the district again,' Anne said in a rush.

'Oh no! And he was getting on so splendidly! Almost two and a half years in the same post! What on earth has he done? Can it be set right? Where's Branwell now?'

'Emily's getting him up to bed. He is very drunk. No, leave them to get on with it!'

'But what led to this? Anne, can you shed any light on the affair?' Charlotte sat down abruptly on the steps leading up to the front door. 'You were at Thorp Green. When you gave in your notice had you no inkling of anything wrong?'

'Branwell declares himself in love with Mrs Robinson,' Anne said in a choked voice. 'He affirms that she has returned his passion in every possible way.'

'Branny and Mrs . . .? She's years older than he is, surely!'

'Seventeen years older but she looks well for her age. She is generally considered to be a very handsome woman.'

'Since when did Branwell show any interest in handsome women whether young or old?' Charlotte demanded. 'Why, when Mary Taylor was here as lovely as spring itself he preferred to go out shooting and hunting with Mr Weightman!'

'Mr Robinson says that unless Branwell breaks off all contact with the Robinsons he will expose him.'

'And by so doing expose his own wife to social denigration? Anne, there must be more to this than you've told me! Has Branwell been stealing? No, he would never stoop to that! Anne?'

'I must turn down the bed and put the kettle on for a cup of tea,' Anne said, picking up one of Charlotte's bags. 'Papa has been persuaded to retire to bed. He is, as we all are, very shocked.'

The arched hall was candlelit and through the half-open door of the kitchen she could see the glow of the fire.

'I'm glad you're safe home, Tallii.' Emily came down the stairs. 'Branwell is asleep at last, so leave him. Anne has told you so there's no point in talking about it.'

'No point?' Charlotte's shock boiled into rage though she kept her voice low. 'Ever since we were children Branwell was the one who was going to make a great name in the world, going to support us all on his earnings! We all three of us went out teaching so that Aunt and Papa could aid him in his training. And what's his record? A bare fortnight in London. If he ever went there at all which I seriously doubt! Months spent idling his time away in the boxing club, the Black Bull, the King's Head, the White Lion – name any tavern between here and Leeds and Branny has drunk in it! Months spent setting himself up as a painter in Bradford when he came home owing rent and having neglected to varnish several of the paintings he was commissioned to do! A few months as a tutor and we never did learn why that post came to an end, and a spell as railway clerk from which he was dismissed for drunkenness and neglect of duty! And now after over two years at Thorp Green he lets us all down again and shames the family with his immoral conduct!'

'Papa has asked John Brown to go with Branwell for a holiday,' Emily said. 'He believes a few weeks in Liverpool and perhaps a sea trip along the coast of North Wales will raise his spirits.'

'A holiday?' Charlotte sat down abruptly on a stool and began to laugh. 'He is twenty-eight years old and has disgraced himself over and over and so he gets a holiday! Emily, it isn't fair! Cannot you see that it isn't fair?'

'Tallii, why not go up to bed?' Emily said. 'I'll make some toast and brew the tea and you shall tell us how Miss Nussey is and if the house at Hathersage is likely to please Mr Nussey and his bride.'

'I'll have it by the fire down here,' Charlotte said. 'You look fagged out yourself.'

'The news was a shock,' Emily admitted. 'But people are what they are. One cannot change them, love!'

She patted Charlotte's shoulder and went out.

Charlotte gazed into the heart of the fire, her face clouded. Why did her sisters not fully confide in her? They knew more than they were saying. She was certain of that! They had always clung together, gone about like twins when both were at home. Anne was sweet and gentle but Emily had the more interesting mind, the more fugitive personality. Yet Emily never told her anything private, never passed a strong opinion, had never asked her to share in their secret world of Gondal.

Branwell diverted their thoughts from anything but himself until arrangements were made to send him away in the company of John Brown. John Brown of all people! Charlotte wanted to laugh at the idea of the burly, good-looking sexton who had caroused with her brother on more than one night, being appointed to get him back into a state of sobriety! And John Brown had sired at least one bastard in addition to his large legitimate family of daughters!

'Papa, was it wise to send Branwell to Liverpool and Wales in the company of John Brown?' she asked one afternoon when Emily and Anne had taken the dogs out on the moors.

'I trust John implicitly,' Papa said, blinking rapidly to try to bring her into focus.

'You think he will help?' she said doubtfully.

'Truly, Charlotte, I cannot tell,' he said wearily. 'You and the girls have lived your lives as I might have wished, working hard and making full use of your education, but Branwell – it is possible there is an inherent weakness in him that cannot be helped. But he professes the utmost remorse for his recent folly and has sworn to improve when he comes home.'

'He always does,' Charlotte said bleakly and went silently out of the parlour where her father sat, his long talonlike fingers endlessly tapping his knee as if, no longer able to see himself, he needed to make certain of his own identity.

She went across the hall into the dining-room. Their portable writing-desks were on the table. Her own held the almost completed book, *The Master.* It needed lengthening and a new title.

She picked up a scarf that Emily had left on the floor and folded it, her small fingers nervously smoothing the folds.

Anne's writing-desk was unlocked. Charlotte lifted the lid but there was nothing to tidy except a couple of sketches of babies – why was Anne drawing babies when they were never likely to have any?

Emily's desk was unlocked too, which was unusual. Emily had a habit of locking her drawers and desk as if she wanted to keep parts of herself locked away too. Charlotte picked up the small exercise-book lying on top of the clutter within and opened it, holding it close to her eyes as she deciphered her sister's tiny writing.

Then dawns the invisible
The Unseen its truth reveals
My outward essence flees
My inward essence feels.

She read on with increasing excitement. These were – the only word that leapt into her mind was magnificent! They were unlike anything she had ever read before. No rich, brilliant phrases, no complicated rhythms or baroque images, only simple, strong phrases that made the heart sing.

'What are you doing? What've you got there?'

Emily's question scythed the quietness in the room. She stood at the door, cloak hanging limply from her shoulders, skirt smeared with grass stains.

'I was tidying up, Emmii.' She used the old childish nickname as if it were a shield. 'These poems are – they are wonderful!'

'How dare you pry into my work? How dare you rummage among my belongings?'

'Emily, I didn't mean to pry! But these ought to be published! They ought to be shown to the world!'

'No!' Emily had lunged forward and snatched the book out of Charlotte's hands, pushing it back into the desk, frantically feeling for the small key.

'What is it? What's happened?'

Anne came in, her own dog, Flossy, at her heels.

'I was reading Emily's poems,' Charlotte said tremblingly. 'I came upon them by chance and I merely glanced but I could not stop reading them! I could not stop, Anne! They ought to be published.'

'Those dribbling rhymes?' Emily had turned, her face white and set. 'I write for my own amusement. Anne knows that. She would never even enquire into them much less snoop and pry!'

'I write verses myself,' Anne said. 'You are welcome to read mine if you think you might gain some pleasure from them.'

'Why not display them in the Black Bull?' Emily said, bitterly sarcastic. 'Branwell would!'

'Emily, this might be our chance!' Charlotte faced her taller sister. 'Please think about it, Ems! Please! If we were to collect our poems together – yes, I write verse too sometimes though it comes nowhere near your own standard – we might publish. Papa published both verse and prose in his youth and is still proud of the fact. Please think about it, Emily!'

'No!' Emily had turned towards the door.

'Aunt left us money,' Charlotte persisted. 'We could use some of it to publish our poems – under pseudonyms of course! Nobody must know what we're doing! Not even Papa! Emily—'

'Go to hell,' Emily said tonelessly and walked out of the room.

'Do you think we could – publish?' Anne asked. 'How would one go about it?'

'We could write to a publisher and make some enquiries. First we must persuade Emily to take part. Her poems are – have you read any of them?'

'Only some of the Gondal ones we make up together. Emily would never agree to Gondal's being made known.'

'Of course not. Anne, make her agree. Make her see that we are adults now and we cannot live in our childhood imaginings for ever. I gave up Angria when I went to Brussels and – do you still play at your secret world?'

'Emily does but for my own part I don't feel they've been in first-rate playing condition for a long time,' Anne said.

'We could write stories – novels – send them out if the poems are a success. I have almost completed a novel. It isn't very long but I believe that it is – not unreadable. Anne?'

'I have a kind of diary which could be adapted,' Anne said reluctantly.

'And Emily?'

'I know she and Branwell were discussing a story but I don't know if anything ever came of it.'

'Branwell must never find out,' Charlotte said low and tense. 'It would be abominable to have him trying to take over . . .'

'Of course not. I'll talk to Emily,' Anne said.

She went out, leaving Charlotte alone – though not for long, she thought with dawning triumph – for soon she would be close to her two sisters again, directing them, advising them, recapturing something she was only just beginning to realize had slipped away during the advancing years.

EIGHTEEN

Charlotte stood at the window and looked out into the dark street. It was raining. When, she thought wryly, didn't it rain in Manchester? The house they had rented was small with a tiny back-garden no bigger than a yard and it was one of dozens of exactly similar houses marching along both sides of mean streets under a sky coloured dung by the smoke from the surrounding cotton-mills.

At least the operation was over and done! Papa had been very nervous about it beforehand for which she could hardly blame him since the process of extracting the cataract from a fully-conscious patient was a very painful one. She had remained in the room during the entire fifteen minutes it took, forcing herself to silence and stillness. Now Papa must lie in a darkened room in absolute quietness for about a month and she perforce must stay with him.

'Do you need anything, Miss Brontë?' The nurse had come into the room, voice respectful.

'No thank you,' Charlotte said.

'Then I'll say good night. Mr Brontë is sleeping soundly.'

'Good night.'

Did she need anything? Dear God, did she not! She imagined the expression on the nurse's face had she answered:

'I need this wretched toothache to cease; I need my brother to stop making us all miserable at home by drinking and dosing himself with laudanum; I need the *Poems* on which I spent so much time and money to sell more than the two copies that have been sold already; I need my novel *The Professor* to be accepted; I need a letter from Monsieur Heger to tell me that he still thinks

165

of me, still admires my intelligence; I need Ellen and Mary with me, the one with her affection, the other with her bracing common sense; I need to feel happy that Emily and Anne have both had their novels provisionally accepted – I need to find the red room and not stay locked in the attic of my own smallness and plainness and insignificance!'

A sleepless night lay ahead, during which the wretched craving ate at her loins and the secret places she had never dared investigate. Once she had summoned the beings of Angria to come to her and sometimes they had come to her unbidden. But Branwell had lived in Angria too long and no longer coped with the real world.

The Professor was too quiet and dull, the publishers said. Yet she knew it was well written, that the plot held no loose ends, that it reflected real life. But readers didn't want real life. They wanted passion and action and a touch of the supernatural. They wanted men like Heathcliff sprung from some depths of her sister she shrank from, for if Emily had created him and his *alter ego* Catherine out of herself then she had never known her sister at all. Even Anne's gentle little tale of a governess had occasioned her some unease. Why had Anne called her heroine Agnes, the name of Mr Weightman's onetime sweetheart? Did Anne under her quiet face think thoughts of what might have been?

A whole month stuck here with nothing to do but worry as to how Emily and Anne were managing Branwell! An Irish uncle, James Brontë, had paid a brief visit. A neat, respectable yeoman she had labelled him and been grateful that he had agreed to stay on for a little while. Papa had been visited only twice by two of his younger brothers and they hadn't been the illiterate peasants she had feared, but she had no wish for any more to turn up.

Suddenly without warning she thought of Nancy and Sarah Garrs, of their rough kind hands and loud laughter and the timbre of their voices. They still wrote once or twice a year and she had met Sarah once quite by chance in Bradford. She was still the same handsome girl with the wide eyes and mouth recalled from childhood.

'But wedded now, Miss Charlotty, and with three childer! My husband's gone ahead to mek a home for us in America! Aye! there's a great adventure waiting out there! Tha'll give my respects to t'maister and love to thy brother and sisters? Aye, tha's not long out on my mind, Miss, even now! Thee and Miss Maria and Miss Elizabeth, bless them!'

And when Sarah had gone and she herself was old who then would remember Maria and speak out for the children bullied by men who used faith as a weapon? Who would know about Zamorna who had been born in her own mind and would die from the world's memory unless she captured him in print? She moved to the table where the stack of paper she had brought with her lay and sat down, lifted a newly sharpened pen and dipped it in the inkwell and wrote in her neatly slanting hand across the top page the name that had arisen in her mind: *Jane Eyre*, without fully realizing that she had borrowed Emily's second name for the child locked in the red room and employed as surname the pleasant name of the couple who lived at North Lees Hall where a madwoman had once been shut up, just as in Norton Conyers a similar legend was bound with an ancient tablet in the little private church dedicated to Damon de Rochester.

Within the month, toothache forgotten, writing at top speed she finished relating her heroine's bleak childhood and had sent her off to Thornfield Hall with its saturnine owner and Miss Wooler-like housekeeper and the nameless threat in the locked room under the eaves which was the more terrible because it exuded the passion and the craving she had tried so hard to crush down in herself.

And then they were together again as the new year of 1847 came in with ice and snow. Papa's sight was daily improving. He preached twice on most Sundays, tested his strength by taking longer walks each day despite the weather. Even Branwell had pulled himself together to a small degree and was apparently looking about him for some kind of employment though without much enthusiasm and certainly with no result. At least he slept for most of the morning, went into the village in the late afternoon and staggered home too drunk to do anything more than utter a few threats and complain loudly as Emily dragged him up the stairs to bed. He slept now in Papa's room since almost burning his own bed with himself in it to ashes by overturning a candle lit too close to the tester.

'I smelled the smoke and Emily put out the flames,' Anne confided to Charlotte. 'Emily made me promise to say nothing to

Papa but of course Branwell must needs tell him the moment you returned from Manchester!'

'It means Papa gets little sleep,' Charlotte frowned.

'But Papa can rest during the day and the elderly are often wakeful at night,' Anne said. 'Mr Nicholls has returned from his holiday in Ireland and can take the Sunday-school classes and other services.'

'Is Mr Nicholls back? I didn't even notice he'd been away,' Charlotte said in faint surprise.

'I wish I could go to Ireland,' Anne said wistfully.

'You! What on earth put that idea into your head?'

'If my second novel is a success I might take a holiday there. Uncle James talked so vigorously about the green of the land and the lakes and the soft calling of the birds through the reeds.'

'The Brontës are still peasants, Annie! Surely we have moved beyond that?'

'It would be somewhere to belong,' Anne said wistfully.

'You belong here with me and Emily and Papa!'

'Emily and I are not so close as we once were,' Anne said. 'I know I have no right to criticize her work for her talents are far above mine but I cannot approve of *Wuthering Heights*, I cannot!'

'It is powerful.'

'It isn't true!' Anne said heatedly. 'People in real life do not behave like Heathcliff and Catherine Earnshaw. She has been busy in adding a happier, more hopeful ending but even the second generation she has created snarl and snipe at one another and – it reads as if the soul of evil breathes through every page. I must show in my new book the reality of wrongdoing and the misery it brings! When men drink too much they do not become more attractive. They stagger and vomit and make fools of themselves. Those who commit adultery cause great suffering to their partners!'

'My dear child, you are the last person fitted to write about such things!' Charlotte cried.

'I am twenty-seven years old,' Anne said quietly, 'and I have seen more than you know. I regard it as my duty and I mean to continue with it though it hurts me to stand against Emily.'

'Anne, what really happened at Thorp Green?' Charlotte asked sharply. 'Was Branwell dismissed for his adultery with Mrs Robinson?'

Anne gave a slight shake of the head, put her hand to her mouth and left the room.

By spring *Wuthering Heights* was ready, and Emily sent it off, having agreed like Anne to pay part of the costs of publishing.

By spring Charlotte was so well advanced in her novel that she felt able to invite Ellen to stay. Poor Ellen had been burdened with numerous cares through the winter and early spring, having to deal with the aftermath of her brother Joseph's death from alcoholism the previous year, having to tell Amelia Ringrose that there was no hope of George's ever fully regaining his sanity, having to support her mother and her sister Mercy who was definitely becoming slightly peculiar in her moods of high delight followed by depression. Ellen had mentioned several visits from Joe Taylor as well. Her feelings were flattered by his visits and kind little notes.

Joe was attractive and flirtatious and adored making young women fall in love with him. Ellen must be shielded from his nonsense.

A warm invitation was sent and accepted. Branwell had gone to spend a few days with his Halifax friends and would likely stay longer. The weather was fine and warm and they all felt the need of a respite from the constant writing.

'We could all go and meet Miss Nussey at Keighley and have a jolly tea at the Devonshire Arms before walking home in the twilight,' Emily suggested.

Emily was in high good humour having sent off her finished novel and begun upon another which she worked at in the privacy of her small bedroom.

'It is such a long time since the four of us were together,' Anne said.

The next morning Charlotte, reading a short note from Ellen cancelling her visit because her sister Ann had suddenly decided to take a holiday and so Ellen would be needed at home, felt cold, bitter anger.

Ellen, she thought, no longer cared as she once had done. She allowed her family to dictate her movements and dominate her life, and though the Nusseys had always welcomed Charlotte kindly she had never failed to notice how somehow or other they contrived to keep Ellen and herself apart when they wanted to talk or walk together. And now Ellen colluded in the plot – no doubt because her new friend, Amelia Ringrose, was become more dear to her or Joe Taylor was expected to tea!

She seized a pen and paper and wrote back coldly, signing the curt note merely with her initials and sending it off without rereading it. Turning for home she changed direction and went into the church.

It was deserted and her footsteps echoed hollowly on the stone. She went up to the altar and stood, looking down at the slab under which her mother, her aunt and her sisters lay. They too had left her, died, gone away. Now the living turned their backs – Branwell too sodden on most occasions to hold a sensible conversation, Emily and Anne writing their books without mending the rift between them or turning to her for consolation, Mary Taylor sending breezy letters from New Zealand where she was leading a most unfeminine life in a log cabin, Monsieur Heger silent as the stone.

'Miss Brontë? May I assist you?' Mr Nicholls, large, dark and tweedy, had come in.

'Thank you, no,' she said curtly and walked past him, her small hands clenched into fists at the unwarranted intrusion.

Then everything was thrown out of her head by the arrival of *The Professor*, returned for the umpteenth time, but with a letter from the publishers Smith and Elder offering to consider seriously a book of more varied interest in three volumes.

She had almost finished her fair copy and sat down at once to the task of completing it, half glad that Ellen hadn't been able to come after all. And by the time the neatly bound parcel containing *Jane Eyre* had been sent off her quarrel with Ellen was over, blown away like the seeds of a dandelion. Ellen could come at the end of July and would do so!

The weather joined in her mood, flinging warm sunshine over the moors. For a brief season their work was put away and even Branwell with consummate tact absented himself a second time in Halifax with his friends, Francis Grundy and the Leyland brothers.

'I wore a pink dress,' Ellen said, looking shy. 'Do you think it too young for me now that I am thirty?'

'I think you look at least ten years younger,' Charlotte said truthfully. 'How is it that you retain your girlish bloom when I never really had any? At this rate I shall soon begin to be mistaken for your mother when we appear in public!'

'Are we going into public?' Ellen enquired.

'Emily has a fancy to take a trip into Bradford to buy some material for dresses,' Charlotte told her.

'Emily wants to buy dresses?' Ellen looked astonished.

'Emily wants to buy material for dresses! She is not so blind to her appearance as you might imagine.'

'She reminds me of a gypsy queen,' Ellen said, her eyes on the tall slender figure ahead, dark hair tumbling from its Spanish combs.

'Since when have you seen a gypsy queen?' Charlotte said. 'I suppose I look like a stunted dwarf to you!'

'You look like my own dear Charlotte,' Ellen said, 'let us have no more lovers' quarrels, please!'

'No more lovers' quarrels!' Charlotte vowed.

They went to Bradford together, taking the coach from Keighley, joking and teasing as they picked over materials in the draper's shop. Charlotte chose a soft green patterned with tiny black leaves, Anne a pale grey, Ellen a creamy white. Emily, draping herself in purple silk patterned with white lightning flashes, struck a dramatic pose.

'Ems, you can't! We're a clergyman's daughters!' Charlotte cried.

'There's no law says we have to look dull and spinsterish,' Emily retorted. 'I shall buy this. One word, Tallii, and I shall buy a purple bonnet with a curling white feather!'

It was the first of many bright days. Ellen's coming cast a glow that not even Mary or Martha's presence had ever evoked. They went out on the moors with picnic baskets and Ellen cried out in delight as she noticed how the sun reflected in the sky seemed to hover over the heads of her friends. They teased Tabby who from her seat in the kitchen still had a fund of stories about the doings of the folk who had once lived on the moor.

'You will come to Brookroyd soon?' Ellen asked as they sat in the room where Charlotte and Anne slept, Anne having just announced that she intended to share with Emily so that Charlotte and Ellen could gossip until dawn.

'I shall be happy to come,' Charlotte said.

'I may have news for you then.'

'George is better?' Charlotte guessed.

'No, my poor brother will never recover,' Ellen said sadly. 'No, it is only that – Mr Vincent has written to me renewing his suit.'

Charlotte carefully rolled her hair round a curling pin.

'So he is back bothering you again?' she said, smiling. 'I daresay he has grown even more eccentric in the time since you met.'

'He was open and spontaneous,' Ellen protested. 'He was never the eccentric you fancied.'

'Of course I never met him,' Charlotte said with a light laugh, 'so I must have gleaned some idea of his being eccentric from your own impression. Your first impressions are very sound, my love.'

'He is really most amiable,' Ellen faltered.

'And you are wild with desire for him?'

'No, but – Charlotte, I am not a person who falls madly in love as you term it, but the years seem to be flying by,' Ellen said. 'I am thirty years old and – I would so like to have children and—'

'Then you must marry him and take the risks that come when a woman past thirty weds,' Charlotte said briskly. 'If you are fathoms deep in love then marry him by all means, but think how dreadful it will be if after marriage you discover your first impression is right and he is so odd that you find his company insupportable. And your own feelings change so often! You were rather flattered by the attentions of that clergyman we met at Hathersage – Mr . . . ?'

'Mr Rooker.'

'The one with the rather common accent. Yes. And then Joe Taylor has been calling rather often, has he not, though if I had a guinea for every girl Joe has called upon I'd be a very rich woman by now!'

'I am not yet so old that I need to rush into marriage,' Ellen said.

'Of course you are not!' Charlotte took the comb from Ellen and began to pin up her friend's dark hair. 'Send Mr Vincent a polite but unenthusiastic letter. You are a mistress at that! You know I have not lost hope that one day you and I might set up a homestead together.'

The next day Ellen went back to Brookroyd with Charlotte's promise to stay with her before summer was done.

The day afterwards a letter from Messrs Smith, Elder & Co. accepted *Jane Eyre* by Currer Bell and enclosed a bank draft for one hundred pounds with the promise of more to follow.

'Five hundred in all,' Charlotte said to Emily and Anne. 'I want to shout it from the housetops!'

'But you will say nothing, tell nobody!' Emily said.

'I swear,' Charlotte said.

'Not even Ellen. I like her immensely but she would never be able to keep the secret. You may write to Mary Taylor if you wish. She will say nothing to anyone.'

Telling Mary in strict confidence was something, Charlotte told herself. The best thing of all was that she was going to be a published author!

NINETEEN

'It begins to look,' Charlotte said, carefully casual, 'that *Jane Eyre* is becoming what they call a bestseller.'

'And the reviews of it are splendid!' Anne said.

'Your own *Agnes Grey* was praised by some,' Charlotte said. 'It is a tale exactly suited to your personality and cast of mind.'

'And *The Tenant of Wildfell Hall* is not? It is selling well.'

'And is well written,' Charlotte allowed, 'but the subject matter is so utterly distasteful! I believe the writing of it has done you harm.'

'I felt it was my duty to write it,' Anne said earnestly. 'I needed to show that vice is not attractive and adultery not a little thing to be shrugged aside by society. Emily isn't pleased because she sees my novel as a parody of her own, but I can't help that!'

'Her book is most powerfully written.'

'It is false glamour,' Anne said obstinately. 'Charlotte, you ought to tell Papa that you've published a book. His sight is much stronger now and the letters addressed to Messrs Currer, Ellis and Acton Bell must attract his attention.'

'Yes. I'll take in a copy of the book when I take his coffee in,' Charlotte said. 'And your novels?'

'Let him get over the shock of learning that one of us is published first!' Anne said, laughing.

Charlotte tapped at the parlour door and carried in the tray on which the cup of weak coffee and two wafer biscuits shared the space with a copy of her book and half a dozen review cuttings.

'Thank you, my dear.' Papa glanced up at her smilingly. 'Is Branwell up yet?'

175

'No, Papa. He hardly ever is,' Charlotte said.

'I still cherish hopes that he will pull himself together,' Papa said. 'You know had that wretched woman married Branwell after a suitable interval had elapsed following the death of her husband then one might have been able to accept the situation to some degree, but he tells me that she is prevented from communicating with him under the terms of her husband's will. I no longer know what to believe. What's this?'

'Papa, I've written a book,' Charlotte said.

'Have you, dear? The writing of prose or poetry is a most delightful occupation. I well remember—'

'Will you read it?'

'My sight is vastly improved but I couldn't decipher your tiny script.'

'The book is published,' Charlotte said.

'My dear girl, surely you haven't wasted your dear aunt's legacy on getting one of your stories into print! '

'Messrs Smith and Elder, the publishers, have paid me for it and the London newspapers are reviewing it. The publishers have paid me five hundred pounds in total.'

Now he would be proud of her! Now he would admit that it was not only sons who could bring honour to a family!

'You haven't told Branwell? It would be a terrible blow to his self-esteem!'

'We have told nobody, not even Ellen,' Charlotte said stiffly.

'Very wise. A woman ought never to seek notoriety. You have used a pseudonym I see.'

'Yes, Papa.'

'I'll look through it and give you my opinion later,' he said, laying the book down and sipping his coffee. 'Tell Emily to take some breakfast up to Branwell. He ought to eat a little something.'

'Of course, Papa.'

She went out, hands balled into fists.

It was mid-afternoon before he emerged from the parlour, coming into the dining-room where they sat.

'What d'ye think, girls? Our Charlotte has written a book!' His eyes gleamed reluctant pride behind his spectacles. 'I've read a good part of it and it's much better than likely!'

'Thank you, Papa!' Gratitude blossomed like a flower.

176

'Not a word to Branwell!' He put his fingers to his lips and went back across the hall.

'So now you will continue with *Hollows Mill*?' Anne looked at her.

'Yes I will! I want to say something about the condition of women,' Charlotte said. 'All the stories that Miss Wooler used to tell us at Roe Head about the Luddites! They fired my imagination then and with the Chartists on the march again the topic is contemporary.'

She had already decided on two heroines – one sweet and gentle and the other vibrant, rich and beautiful, and two heroes, brothers who were rivals in love and Belgian immigrants. And she would put the Taylor family into the book, the strong-minded Mary and the impetuous, ill-fated Martha.

'I am planning a comedy of manners,' Anne confided. 'After the style of Miss Austen, though I lack her wit.'

'From what I hear of Miss Austen's work I am not attracted to it sufficiently to read it,' Charlotte averred.

'But you included a passage from *Mansfield Park* in *Jane Eyre*,' Anne said.

'How could I have done when I never troubled to read it? Emily, are you going to tell us what you are working on?'

'No,' Emily said serenely.

Impossible to capture Emily, to make her part of oneself. When they perambulated round and round the dining-room after Papa had retired Emily had little to say these days and nothing she would read aloud though she was working steadily at something which she kept carefully locked up.

A few days later, looking up from a letter she had just received from Mr George Smith she exclaimed in alarm.

'You are not going to believe this! Your publisher, Anne, is advertising your next book as being by the author of *Jane Eyre*, and as my next book has been promised to Smith and Elder they have written to me to ask for an explanation! They are too polite to say so but they clearly suspect me of double dealing! We shall have to go to London immediately to prove to the publishers that we are three separate individuals!'

'We shall do no such thing!' Emily said vigorously.

'I refuse to be suspected of double dealing!' Charlotte said indignantly.

'Who cares what people think?' Emily retorted.

'Where my professional integrity is at stake—'

'Oh my, aren't we grand!' Emily mocked. 'Professional integrity, forsooth! Well, if you go to London you don't say one word about me! You don't even hint at my existence! Swear it!'

'We shall say nothing,' Anne said.

'We? Ah, I see! you are going with Charlotte! Very well, you must do as you please but I place the same embargo on your tongue as I do on Charlotte's.'

'If we pack a small trunk we could carry it between us and catch the early evening train from Keighley to London,' Charlotte said.

'Don't be ridiculous! It's starting to rain!' Emily said.

'It will clear later,' Charlotte persisted. 'We shall reach London early in the morning so we can register at the Chapter Coffee House and tidy ourselves before we set out for Smith and Elder.'

'If you both catch pneumonia don't come coughing to me!' Emily snapped.

The rain began in earnest when they were half-way to Keighley, the trunk being carried between them. Overhead the clouds swirled low and black, lit by the frequent crack of lightning as it sawed the sky.

'If you want my opinion,' Charlotte said darkly, pulling her hood further over her brow, 'Emily called the storm up!'

Anne giggled, a sound that heartened Charlotte as they went on steadily through the downpour.

At ten the next morning, having spent a night sitting up in wet clothes and having contrived to tidy themselves and register at the Chapter Coffee House they reached the Cornhill offices, having spent an hour finding out where to cross the wide road without being trampled by the horses trotting and cantering up and down with various vehicles bumping along behind them.

'Do publishers work on a Saturday morning?' Anne enquired.

'I never thought of that! We shall just have to hold our breaths and – yes, the door is open!'

She dived into the reception area with its long counter and piles of books ready for despatch and asked the lad busily packing them up to tell Mr Smith that two ladies wished to see him urgently and in privacy.

Ten slow minutes elapsed before they were ushered upstairs into an office also piled high with books and manuscripts.

'Ladies?' A tall, good-looking young man had come round from his desk to greet them.

Charlotte fumbled in her pocket and handed him the letter she had received the previous day.

'Where did you get this?' He stared at them.

'It came in the post,' Charlotte said, suddenly enjoying the look of bewilderment on his face. 'You are Mr George Smith? Well, I am Currer Bell and this is Acton Bell. We are three . . .'

Anne's elbow dug her sharply in the ribs.

'We are Charlotte Brontë and Anne Brontë,' she hurriedly said. 'We are here so that you may have oracular proof that there are at least two of us.'

'You wrote *Jane Eyre?*'

'Also *The Professor* which you refused to publish. My sister has published *Agnes Grey* and *The Tenant of Wildfell Hall.* My other—'

'We wish to remain entirely anonymous – save yourself and your partners should know,' Anne said.

'My business manager Mr James Taylor and my reader Mr Williams must be informed at once. Do please sit down! Are you aware that all of literary London is speculating about the identity of the Bells? The latest theory is that you are three brothers who work in the weaving industry. Mr Taylor! Mr Williams! A moment please!'

He strode into the passage, one hand still on the door handle as if he feared they might vanish.

'You should not have mentioned Emily,' Anne whispered.

'I won't again.'

She would worry about that later when she reached home. In any case if two of the Bells were revealed as sisters it didn't require a genius to deduce the existence of a third sister. Suddenly Charlotte was enjoying herself as she was swept into introductions to a short, red-haired Scot who was James Taylor and a tall, prematurely grey gentleman with a gentle voice who must be Mr Williams.

'Where are you staying? Of course you must stay at my house! My mother and sisters will be honoured—'

'We are staying at the Chapter Coffee House,' Charlotte said hastily. 'Nobody must learn our identities. We are the Misses Brown! We do insist upon that.'

'The Misses Brown. Yes, of course.' He looked puzzled.

'We wish to remain completely unknown,' Anne said.

'Publicity of any kind would be anathema to us,' Charlotte said firmly. 'You cannot imagine the chagrin I felt when I discovered that my dedication to Mr Thackeray for the second edition of *Jane Eyre* led many people to assume that Mr Thackeray was the original of Mr Rochester and the novel itself written by his governess! Of course I had not the least idea that Mrs Thackeray was not in her right mind!'

'Neither did we, else we would have pointed it out to you before the dedication appeared,' Mr Williams said.

'Were we to become known as published authors similar mistakes might well occur in the future,' Charlotte said. 'We shall stay over the weekend and visit Mr Newby who has not dealt fairly with my fellow authors, nor indeed been honest in deliberately muddling us together.'

'Well, the matter is clear now.' Mr Smith looked as if he wasn't quite sure it was.

The visit had begun well. It continued in a rash of engagements, a visit to the opera that same evening when George Smith accompanied by his mother and two of his sisters arrived to take them to the theatre.

'I really am not used to this kind of thing,' Charlotte whispered to him as they went up the red-carpeted staircase into the gold and white of the box he had ordered.

The other ladies wore crinolines that swept the floor with low-cut bodices and flowers in their hair. Charlotte was in the green dress with the pattern of black leaves on it that she had made up out of the material bought in Bradford. It had a neat white collar and elbow-length sleeves. Anne, in the dress of pale grey, seemed completely at ease as she gazed about her.

The opera began with a burst of music that nearly shot her out of her seat. The scene was brilliant, the singing superb, but something a trifle quieter would not have exacerbated her headache quite so much, and she was quite sure that Mr Smith had already whispered her identity to his mother!

The next morning being Sunday they made their way to church and returned to find Mr Williams in the hotel lobby waiting to take them to tea at his comfortable but crowded house and then on to George Smith's house for dinner. The next morning

180

they found their way to Messrs Newby & Sons where, to her surprise, Anne abruptly said:

'I will see Mr Newby alone if you don't object, Tallii. I have a great deal to say to him concerning unpaid advances and the most untruthful advertising.'

'You know you will become upset and confused and stammer,' Charlotte said.

'I outgrew my stutter years ago,' Anne said placidly. 'I will meet you afterwards for coffee. I would very much like to see the Royal Academy and St Paul's Cathedral this afternoon, and then we are due to dine with the Smiths again, aren't we?'

'But Annie —'

'I intend to offer my next book to Mr Smith,' Anne said. 'Emily, I know, intends to continue with Mr Newby. I will see you later at the hotel.'

She went in through the glass-windowed door, back straight, head high. Anne, thought Charlotte as she reluctantly turned away, was no longer a child.

By Tuesday, with more rich dinners under their sashes and gifts of books for Papa and Emily, they caught the train home. The weather had swung towards the wet again and when they reached Leeds they left the train and took a cab to the nearest hotel where they booked in for the night and sank thankfully into bed.

'We shall have so much to tell Emily when we reach home,' was Anne's last sleepy comment.

Charlotte, lying awake for a little, decided to send an account of their adventure to Mary Taylor who could be trusted to keep the secret. Her last thought as she fell asleep was that she must write to Ellen soon with news that her old friend might gossip freely about with her friend Amelia Ringrose. Ellen had already written to Charlotte, hinting strongly that she had read *Jane Eyre* and guessed the author, and Charlotte, in a panic, had sent a furious letter back telling Ellen in no uncertain terms that she had granted nobody the right to speculate about her doings! Her next letter would be a kinder one, full of the trivial news that dear Ellen relished so much.

'You both look fagged out,' was Emily's greeting.

'We have so much to tell you!' Charlotte began.

'Give me your cloak. I hope you dried it properly before you wore it again or —'

'What's that on your arm?' Anne interrupted.

'Nothing of any consequence.'

'It looks like a burn. Surely Branny. . .?' Charlotte peered at the livid scar.

'Branwell has been practically comatose since you left. No, I was giving a stray dog a drink of water in the lane when it snapped at me and ran off. Some farm lads running after it shouted that it was rabid, so I came straight into the kitchen and cauterised it with one of the hot irons.'

'Have you been to the doctor?'

'No, and there's no need for it,' Emily said stolidly. 'I have never noticed any doctor doing Branwell much good and I prefer to treat myself anyway.'

'Branwell isn't as ill as he makes out,' Charlotte said. 'He usually manages to recover in time to get across to the Black Bull! I still think you ought—'

'I shall tell Martha to get the tea brewed. You must both be parched!' Emily said briskly, on her way out.

'I am glad we went to London,' Anne said placatingly. 'Your Mr Smith is a gentleman I shall be happy to have deal with my future works.'

'He is hardly my Mr Smith,' Charlotte said, amused. 'He is some years younger than I in any case.'

'He admired you,' Anne said. 'I mean as a woman – I could tell he admired you very much.'

'Then he must have a penchant for dwarfs!'

'I think he has a penchant for dainty little ladies with beautiful hazel eyes,' Anne said, giving her a kiss before she followed Emily down to the kitchen.

Life, Charlotte thought with a smile, was becoming rosier. They were at last published authors and Anne and she would soon be sharing the same publisher. Her new novel, which she had retitled *Shirley*, was racing along. *Shirley* was Emily in outer aspects but also a little like Mary Taylor, and Caroline Helstone looked like Anne, wore pink and white like Ellen, but was in other things besides her name a version of herself.

Papa's sight was almost as strong as it had ever been and Mr Nicholls was proving hard-working even if he was stiff and narrow-minded. There was no doing anything for Branwell but even he might soon pull himself together and cease pining over an affair that she was becoming more and more certain had largely existed in his own imagination.

She would write a pleasant note to dearest Ellen and send her good wishes to Amelia and which ever young puppy might now be sniffing round their skirts!

TWENTY

From the window of her bedroom she could see them wending their way to the church. Her legs shook and she held on to the back of the chair, determined to remain standing until the last of the cortège had entered the grey stone building where one more relative now went to join his mother, aunt and sisters.

He had been in the village the day before, staggering up the street, his clothes hanging loosely on him. William Brown had come and helped him up the steps and Emily had armed him up the stairs with Anne hovering anxiously below.

'Is Branwell not well again?' Papa's voice had quavered with concern.

'Probably drunk,' Charlotte had said and gone back into the dining-room and closed the door.

Why had she done that? Why hadn't she offered to help? Why hadn't she asked Branwell to contribute some of his own poetry to the book they had published? Branwell had talked of a novel he was trying to write. She could have told him about their novels, made three into four again. Her sisters wouldn't have minded. Emily had pronounced Branwell a hopeless being but it had been said with a smile and a shrug. Anne had never ceased to hope that one day the old Branny with his wild enthusiasm and his energy would come back to them.

At the very end she had stood with Emily and Anne and the weeping Martha and heard him gasp out,

'I am thirty-one years old and in all my life have done nothing great or good!'

'My son!' Papa's anguished cry had rung through the silent room. 'My best beloved!'

Aye, that was it! Papa had always loved Branwell best, his only son, his Benjamin! Little King he had called him and laughed at his antics. Mama had loved him best too, playing with him in the firelight while she had watched from the door. He had been Maria's favourite. Maria would not have stayed silent about the cruelties of Cowan Bridge had Branny been the one to suffer them!

The howling of the wind down the chimney brought with it a shower of black soot. After the wind came the first flash of lightning and the first long grumble of thunder.

She pulled her shawl about her and crept back to bed, turning her face to the wall, crying silently for Chief Genius Brannii, for all the wooden soldiers he had sent into battle, for the lad who had sung in the morning years.

'I have written to Miss Nussey to give her the sad news,' Anne said, coming in later. 'Mr Morgan preached a beautiful eulogy. Now you must get well as soon as you can, Tallii! Dr Wheelhouse says it is a disordered liver that has laid you low.'

'Where's Emily?' Charlotte asked.

'Talking to John Brown. Poor John is so upset for he and Branny have been close since Branwell was a little boy. He had so many friends!'

'I cannot lie here and leave the work to you and Ems,' she protested.

'There is hardly anything to do,' Anne said. 'I will bring you something to eat very soon. Emily is coming in so we shall have the tea brewed soon. Only think, Charlotte, at this moment Branwell is being greeted by Mama and Maria and Ellie and Aunt, all as happy to see him as we are sad to have him gone.'

But she wasn't sad, Charlotte thought. His going would remove an intolerable burden from their lives. And that was the saddest thing of all!

She hunched her shoulders and turned away, knowing she should say something nice but unable to utter a word.

By the time she was well enough to go downstairs autumn was leaping towards winter. Nothing had changed though Emily still tensed when she heard a door slam or a window blow wide.

She didn't look well, Charlotte thought, shocked into noticing that Emily was losing weight she could ill afford to lose, that her usual pallor was greyish and her eyes dark-rimmed.

'Are you all right?' she asked sharply.

'I have a bit of a cold,' Emily said indifferently. 'I must have caught it at Branny's funeral. It doesn't signify.'

'You ought to take things easy. I am perfectly well again and can do my share of the work!'

'There will be a little more work soon,' Emily said. 'Papa has received a letter from his brother Hugh. He is coming here soon to pay his respects.'

'And hold a wake if he gets half a chance!'

'With the singing and the drinking and all the people saying nice things about the deceased? Branwell would have liked that,' Emily said.

'It will cheer Papa at any rate,' Charlotte allowed.

'He can sleep in Branny's old room.'

Emily went out, pausing briefly in the hall to cough. A deep, hoarse, painful cough that brought alarm into Charlotte's face. She had heard Emily coughing before and thought nothing of it.

Suddenly the minutes and hours rushed into days and the days turned into nights and she lay wakeful, listening to Emily coughing in her tiny bedroom where they had once snuggled together in the canvas beds that were taken down in the mornings.

'Emily, you must see a doctor! Your cough is worse and you're not eating anything!' she expostulated one day.

'I'm eating as much as I want and I don't want any poisoning quack near me,' Emily said obstinately.

'Emily, Dr Wheelhouse did his best for Branwell.'

'Too little, too late! Best if he'd never begun at all! Let me alone, Charlotte!'

Charlotte tried to work at her new book. She had researched the Luddite period assiduously, had the characters clear in her mind. Yet it seemed to her that the more vivid and lively the character of Shirley became, the thinner and paler grew Emily as if the imagined image sucked the life-blood from her.

'Shall I invite Ellen to stay for a while?' she suggested one evening as they took their customary walk round the dining-room table.

'No visitors!' Emily said harshly.

'Emily, you like Ellen Nussey! Why not enjoy her company for a little while?'

187

'I won't have anyone here! Not until spring. Don't talk of it again,' Emily said.

Charlotte opened her mouth to argue, glimpsed the shake of Anne's head, and was silent.

A few days later she came in from the church where she had been helping Anne to arrange a few late-blooming flowers for the altar and was met as she opened the front door by a sight that chilled her.

At the foot of the stairs Emily, her face hidden by her long hair, was beating Keeper with her fists, her arms striking out over and over, while Keeper, blood streaming from eyes and muzzle, cowered.

'Emily!' Her voice died in her throat as Emily rose, turned to reveal a set white face in which only the eyes seemed alive, and said in a strangled voice,

'Out! Get out!'

Charlotte opened the dining-room door and stepped inside, her hands over her ears, her body vibrating with shock and revulsion. That Emily who of them all cherished animals the most should strike Keeper!

Papa had taken Tabby down into the village to see her sister, thank God! After a long time she heard Anne come in, heard low voices – Anne and Martha – whispering in the hall.

'Charlotte, are you all right?' Anne came into the dining-room.

'Did you – Annie, what's happening?' Charlotte said.

'Keeper went upstairs and lay on Emily's bed, on the clean white coverlet. You know she has tried to break him of the habit,' Anne said. 'She – lost her temper. Martha dared not interfere until her rage was spent.'

'And now?'

'She took Keeper out into the yard to bathe his head. Let her alone, Tallii! She is best left alone.'

'But why? Emily has never . . . ?'

'The bite she received from the rabid dog,' Anne said, her hands twisting together. 'Charlotte, I think she fears that she didn't burn out the infection entirely. Hydrophobia takes six months to develop.'

'And is characterized by headache, fits of violent rage – no, Anne! No, I'll not believe it! Emily has a chest cold, a bad cough! I will write to Mr George Smith who will surely know of a reputable doctor who will send advice? She is fearing something that will never happen! Why, Miss Rooker, an acquaintance of Ellen's, was bitten not long since by a rabid dog and suffered no ill effects.'

'Say nothing about it to her or Papa,' Anne begged.

'I promise. Anne, you look chilled to the bone! I'll make you some tea. Sit by the fire for a while. Where's Martha?'

'I sent her across to her father's house for an hour.'

Anne sat down by the fire, holding her hands to the small blaze.

Charlotte went through to the kitchen and picked up the kettle. When she went into the back kitchen to fill the kettle from the pump she could see the first flakes of snow whirling beyond the small window.

She set down the full kettle and opened the back door. She could see Emily, kneeling by the kennel with both arms around the huge mastiff. Above the wind she could hear her sister's wild remorseful sobbing that seemed to be carried on the rising wind across to the moors where the snows were slowly settling. Quietly she closed the door again and went through to make the tea.

She had begun to write frantically to George Smith, to Mr Williams, most of all to Ellen, pouring out the fears she dare not express to her sisters or even to Papa.

Uncle Hugh Brontë arrived, a black band round his arm, his red hair greying rapidly, but his frame still upright and tall.

Emily had gone to her room, though both Anne and Charlotte had begged her to share their room where a fire might be lit, but she had shaken her head and gone doggedly up the stairs, pausing on each one to catch her breath.

'So you are my niece Charlotte! You were not here when I first came into Yorkshire.'

He took her hand and looked down at her kindly.

'I met Uncle James,' Charlotte said.

'Indeed you did! when you took your father to have his eyes operated upon! Patrick seems in good health!'

'Yes, he does indeed!'

His Irish brogue had a lilting melody in it. 'The loss of your brother was a blow to you. We held a wake in Ireland when we heard.'

'Branwell would have liked that,' Charlotte said softly.

'Aye! he would've liked Ireland too,' Hugh Brontë said. 'We are all poets and minstrels there.'

'And drunkards?' she asked sharply.

'Ah, your poor brother couldn't hold his liquor,' her uncle said with a grin. 'Sure but James was telling me that after a couple of whiskies he had to carry Branny home to bed! Your little sister was eager to see the old country too. And she seems not so spry! Shall I take her home with me for a visit?'

'I could not possibly spare her – though it's kind of you to suggest it,' Charlotte said quickly. 'I beg you won't put the idea into her head again!'

'I must talk to your other sister.'

He turned and went up the stairs. Charlotte heard him tap on Emily's door and then enter. She went into the dining-room and stood looking out of the window where the snow was whirling now. Victims of hydrophobia were generally put out of their misery by being smothered between two feather mattresses. Was that why her uncle had stayed? No, surely not! Emily had a bad cold, an infection in her lungs, perhaps a touch of consumption.

'Charlotte?'

She must have been standing there for a long time, her mind making angels and devils out of the snowflakes as they shaped themselves into faces.

'Uncle Hugh?'

'Is there a plentiful supply of laudanum in the house?'

'Yes. Branwell practically bathed in the stuff,' she said.

'If the worst came to the worst then it would be a mercy,' Hugh said soberly. 'I will stay a while longer if it's no great trouble?'

'It is no trouble at all,' she said tonelessly.

He was sleeping in Branwell's old room and had already charmed Tabby and Martha out of their wits.

'Then what's necessary, if it's necessary, God help and save us all I will do,' he said.

The phrase had a Popish ring, an echo of the Catholic grand-mother she had never known.

In Brussels they would be preparing now for the *lecture pieuse* which *Monsieur* had given after supper once a week. When the lecture had centred upon some Catholic saint she and Emily had absented themselves.

She had written to him three years before to tell him that they were preparing some poems for the publisher, but there had been no reply. *Madame* had probably intercepted the letter!

190

That evening the sound of a cry of pain sent her and Anne into the back passage where they found that Emily, her apron filled with scraps for the dogs, had fallen heavily against the wall. As Anne rushed to close the back door, blown open by the wind, Charlotte hurried to Emily's side.

'Let me be! Let me alone!' Emily struggled upright, her face set in the skeleton mask of their childhood.

In the morning, Martha came, voice choked with sobs.

'Miss Emily dropped t'comb in't fire and was too shaky t'pick it up,' she quavered, showing the half-burnt comb.

'Say nothing, Martha! Don't cry!'

Charlotte stood in the hall, watched her sister coming down the stairs, eyes faded to ice-grey, only her unbound hair still glossy and thick.

She went past without a word, seeming not to see her, the breath rattling in her throat.

She had to get out for a while! Charlotte snatched up her cloak and took the back way on to the moors, feeling the wind tug the hood from her head, her feet sinking into the drifts. One harsh gust brought her to her knees and her hands, scrabbling for a handhold, tugged at dried grass, stiffening into spears. Among them was a sprig of pale heather, the faded blossom still holding the memory of its perfume.

'Look, Emily!' Entering the dining-room where Emily sat with a piece of sewing in her lap, her fingers plucking idly at the air, she laid the withered spray on the small table. 'Your favourite flower!'

Emily turned her head slightly and stared indifferently in the wrong direction.

'Go and change your boots, love!' Anne's anxious voice came from a great distance.

A little later she sat writing to Ellen, dashing down words on paper: 'moments as dark as this I have never known!'

Emily had moved, felt her way to the sofa, Keeper at her heels. Her voice was threadlike in the silent room.

'If you send for a doctor I'll see him now.'

Uncle Hugh stood by the door, something in his hand. Charlotte heard a cry stronger than could have been expected from where Emily sat, as if in this moment life battled with death.

'No! No!'

It rang like a clarion call through the dining-room.

191

TWENTY-ONE

Branwell and Emily had died suddenly and dramatically. Anne edged her way out quietly, the cold she had developed lingering as her cough grew worse and her appetite failed.

'If I could only get to the seaside,' she said wistfully, 'I know that I would get well again. The specialist said the disease has not yet advanced beyond the possibility of complete remission. Charlotte, if you cannot come with me perhaps Miss Nussey would agree to accompany me? I shall write and suggest it to her.'

Anne and Ellen together as once Emily and Anne had been? The first volume of *Shirley* had been duly dispatched to Smith, Elder & Co. A second edition of *The Tenant of Wildfell Hall* had been published and was receiving some favourable notices. With Emily gone there was nothing now to stop Acton Bell rivalling Currer Bell in popularity.

She wrote to Ellen warning her that she ought not to consider going with Anne to the seaside for Anne was sicker than she knew. When the weather was warmer they might consider it. Meanwhile she was carrying on with *Shirley*, exchanging long letters with George Smith, Mr Taylor and Mr Williams. Sooner or later she must go to London again, taste a spoonful of the fame they had all dreamed about as children. It would be almost impossible to go if she were burdened with a delicate sister who had also written two novels and was embarked upon her third, which she kept locked away as Emily had locked her last book away.

'Once I am strong and well again,' Anne said hopefully, 'I shall be able to visit London once more. I am going to give my book to Smith and Elder, Charlotte. We shall be under the same imprint.'

It wasn't going to happen, Charlotte thought. Anne was not destined to make old bones. The angel had told her that long ago.

She was writing the second volume of *Shirley* now, and the Anne-like heroine was beginning to fade away, gently and beautifully.

In the end it had been impossible to delay any longer even though on the day finally settled for leaving, Anne had been too sick to move. Before a note could be sent to Ellen cancelling the journey, however, Ellen herself had arrived.

The train journey to Scarborough, broken by a night in York, had passed more pleasantly than Charlotte could have hoped. People had been very helpful along the way and Anne was in high spirits, eager to appreciate the beauties of the minster and insisting on treating them all to new bonnets.

In Scarborough they settled into the rooms they had rented and the next day, as they watched Anne walking slowly along the sands, Ellen had murmured,

'She is much better than I was led to believe. Perhaps this is the turning-point of her illness?'

'I believe it is only a temporary remission,' Charlotte said.

If she had brought Anne to the seaside she loved so much would it have made any real difference? Had she been selfish in insisting on delay? But Anne was destined to die young! She had always known it deep within herself.

And Anne, with the perfect timing that had marked her life, had died very peacefully the following day, closing her eyes and drifting away as gently as a butterfly hovering over a stream.

'She was glad to die!' Charlotte said fiercely as they turned from the newly made grave high on the hill by St Mary's Church. 'Life was always a burden for her dear soul.'

She had to believe that! It would be unbearable to entertain the thought that Anne had loved life and wanted to live. She thrust out of her mind memories of her youngest sister fording the moorland streams, joking with Emily, happily declaring that her second novel was starting to make her some money. She didn't want to recall how Anne had twice obtained teaching posts that were better paid than the ones she herself had had, had flushed and giggled when Mr Weightman had made eyes at her in church, had clung steadily to her own notion that in the end everybody went to heaven.

Anne had left instructions that the headstone was to be as plain and brief as possible, with no mention on it of the books she had had published. Then Charlotte fled with a bewildered Ellen to Bridlington where the two of them could enjoy again that first precious holiday they had spent together.

In the end, of course, after three weeks away Ellen's family began to agitate for her return.

Haworth had to be faced alone some time! Charlotte left Ellen at Birstall and travelled home, girding herself for the inevitable questions that Papa would want her to answer.

'Had you delayed a day or two I would have travelled to the funeral,' Papa said when the first muted greetings were over.

'Dear Papa, you could never have endured it!' Charlotte said.

'I am not quite decrepit yet, Charlotte.' His expression softened as he saw her face. 'I'm sure you did what you thought right. Mr Nicholls has been walking the dogs and taking many of the services. His personality is not an attractive one but he is a hard worker and makes himself useful at least.'

He patted her shoulder, turned and walked into his parlour. In the kitchen Tabby, voice quivering, said,

'Tha should've brung our Annie home, Miss Charlotty! Tha had no right leaving her alone out there!'

'It was her wish to spare Papa the pain of another funeral,' Charlotte said. 'Martha, do stop crying! Miss Anne was so good that she is in heaven now and that's cause for joy!'

'Mebbe I'll see it that road later on,' Martha sniffed.

There were prayers as there had always been in the parlour and then Tabby shuffled out with Martha at her heels. Charlotte, waiting to bid Papa good-night, said in surprise,

'What happened to the piano?'

'I told John Brown to shift it upstairs into the study room.'

'Why? It's a handsome piece and in perfect tune?' she queried.

'There is nobody here now to play it for me after tea,' he said. 'You were never musical, Charlotte.'

'No. No, I never was. Good-night, Papa.'

She turned and went across the hall into the dining-room and closed the door. The room looked exactly as she had left it, the books at each side of the fireplace, the square table with the four upright chairs set about it and the oil-lamp in the centre illuminating the black sofa and the two high-backed armchairs set in the window. The shutters had been closed and fastened, a small fire burned in the grate. On a side table was her writing-desk.

She jumped violently as a scratching came at the door. When she opened it Keeper and Flossy trotted in, sniffing about her skirts, pacing to the corners and sniffing there, then returning to look with mute and puzzled questioning into her face.

'They won't come again,' she said aloud. 'They are dead.'

But the dogs went on pacing, sniffing, ears pricked up, whining now and then as if longing could bring back the past.

Once in Angria she and Branny had killed off people and then made them come alive again.

She lifted her writing-desk and put it on the table. The third volume of *Shirley* remained to be written. Shirley would be tortured by the fear of rabies after being bitten by a mad dog and gentle Caroline was dying of a broken heart. At least she could remove the threat of death from them both!

She wrote without pausing until only red ashes glowed in the grate and the flame in the oil-lamp was low. Then she rose and began the slow habitual perambulation round the table, longing and fearing to hear the soft footsteps of the dead following her.

'Papa, I have accepted an invitation to go to London.'

With the advance copies of *Shirley* in her hands, she faced Papa.

'From whom?' He looked at her over his spectacles.

'Mrs Smith, my publisher's mother, has invited me to go. I am to have the opportunity of meeting Mr Thackeray, Papa. You know how I admire his work.'

'Then you must certainly go, my dear. It will set you up for the winter and the writing of your next novel,' Papa said.

'Thank you, Papa.'

She had not intended her statement to sound like a request for permission to go anywhere at all, she thought with a stab of irritation.

In the following spring she would be thirty-four years old, for heaven's sake! On the other hand Papa had the habit of authority and it did no harm to indulge him a little.

If only Ellen or Mary Taylor could have accompanied her! But

Ellen was making preparations for the wedding of her eldest sister Ann who, at the age of fifty-three – God save the mark! – was going to marry a local widower, and besides, Ellen was much occupied with the Ringrose sisters, Rosy who was pretty and sensitive and Amelia who had at last been brought to accept that poor George's mental balance would never improve sufficiently for wedlock. Charlotte had paid a brief visit to Brookroyd in the late summer but there had been little opportunity for any private time with her friend. Sometimes she had the uncomfortable feeling that Ellen was being drawn away from her by new friendships and the constant demands of her family.

They had managed one short conversation when Charlotte, looking at Ellen's clear, pale complexion and the glossy bands of her hair had said:

'How is it that you don't age, Ellen? There isn't a line on your face and your step is as light as a fairy's and yet you are always being summoned hither and thither as if you had no life of your own!'

'I take pleasure in small things,' Ellen said.

'You know, Nell, if you should take it into your head to marry,' Charlotte said playfully, 'I will dance at your wedding with a happy heart. You would be charming in silver and white.'

There was a tiny pause and then Ellen had said very softly, 'Mr Vincent is married, Charlotte. I heard about it some months since and Joe Taylor is paying court to Amelia. Would you have me advertise?'

No, perhaps Ellen wasn't the one to accompany her to London! And Mary Taylor was still in New Zealand, sending the occasional breezy letter full of news about cattle and buying material and a typhoon and calling *Wuthering Heights* a strange thing.

'I'm afraid I agree with her,' Ellen said. 'I think it is a dreadful book, Charlotte. It pains me to say so because I liked Emily so much but – it never should have been written!'

But it was better than her own books, Charlotte thought, holding back her rage. Ellen was the last person to pronounce on literary excellence.

The short red-haired James Taylor had collected the last few chapters of *Shirley* on his way south from his native Scotland. Papa had not only greeted him with his usual courtesy but actually drunk tea with him and invited him not to stand on cere-mony another time.

'You liked Mr Taylor then?' she had remarked.

'He struck me as a man of good sense,' Papa said. 'Did you not think that if Branwell had lived – the resemblance seemed to me to be quite marked. It was strange to think that had that wretched woman not tempted him Branwell might have been with us today, earning himself a place among the great.'

'And I was never your son,' Charlotte thought even as Papa said:

'You mustn't imagine that I don't take both pride and pleasure in your own success, my love, but – sons are different.'

So she would go to London alone and she would lighten her mourning clothes with a dress of pale-grey silk and a cloak of grey velvet edged with grey fur. She would be the quiet, modest girl stepping out of the deep shadow to take her rightful place on the brilliant stage of public admiration. She padded the child-sized bodice she wore to give herself the illusion of a more womanly shape and fastened her corsets more tightly to achieve the fashionable sixteen-inch waist, carefully polished her nails and coiled up her hair and shortened her skirts by an inch so that her feet, impossibly narrow and dainty, could be the more clearly seen in her new patent-leather shoes.

London was a revelation. The Smiths had a large handsome house, and her bedroom was luxuriously furnished with hot water for washing and a brilliant shining of candles. More than once she found herself outside a door wondering if she'd taken a wrong turning in one of the corridors. The visit passed like a dream. She felt as if she had entered the lost universe of Angria when she was armed into dinner by the tall man with the ugly sarcastic face and knew she was with Mr Thackeray whose books she had always revered. She heard him say teasingly,

'Were you led hither by the scent of my cigar, ma'am? I refer of course to the scene in *Jane Eyre* . . .'

'The book has nothing to do with me,' she said teasingly. 'My name is Charlotte Brontë, sir.'

This then was the role she would play – not an eager, showy female hungry for public notice but someone thrust against her will into society, speaking her mind frankly when it was necessary, but otherwise lingering in the shadow.

She visited Harriet Martineau whose novel *Deerbrook* had cheered many an hour when she had longed for someone with whom to talk.

'A strong plain face,' she told Papa on her return, 'and very deaf but with fine expressive grey eyes. Slightly masculine in her manner.'

There had been an odd moment when, glancing at the other's plain features, she had been reminded for no good reason of Mary Taylor, which was ridiculous since Mary's loveliness surely could never fade!

Shirley was being well received in most quarters. Papa had read it with interest but warned her that her characters were so close to the originals that her identity as Currer Bell would very quickly be known.

'I suspect that it's an open secret already, Papa,' she told him. 'Happily we live in too isolated a spot to be bothered with people come to sniff out the author!'

'But if any do come we must receive them politely, my dear!'

Papa, she thought, relished the notion of dwelling a little in the limelight earned by her efforts.

Mr Nicholls, meeting her in the lane one morning, said in his ponderous manner,

'Miss Brontë, forgive my temerity but there is rumour that you are the author of two published books which have achieved much public notice. I would be grateful for some advice as to how to respond should I be asked about the matter.'

'Tell them you know nothing about it, Mr Nicholls! Good-day.'

She went past him through the gate, her cheeks burning with embarrassment. Mr Nicholls had some excellent qualities but no right to be poking into her affairs.

Martha, rushing into the kitchen, said excitedly,

'My father says as how tha's written two grand books and the Mechanics Institutes's going for to order them.'

'Martha, you talk too much,' Charlotte said.

'Yes, Miss Charlotty, and Mr Nicholls got one of the books and was reading it and slapping his leg and laughing fit to burst my mother says!'

'Get on with your work, Martha. The step needs a good scrub,' Charlotte said.

As Martha rushed out again, intent on anything except scrubbing, Tabby said from her fireside chair,

'It's t'be hoped Mr Nicholls were chortling at the comic bits!'

Now people she had known since childhood would know! It was one thing to play the role of the reluctant celebrity in London, quite another to be aware that everything she had written – would write – would be read over by people she saw nearly every day! She had used bits and pieces of real people for her characters – large bits and pieces, she admitted privately. Would the Taylors be insulted at finding themselves portrayed as the Yorkes? Ellen would be flattered at finding herself in the outward aspects of Caroline Helstone.

She had made several attempts at a new novel and given up after a chapter here, a couple of chapters there. She had reread *The Professor* and wished that George Smith would agree to publish it, but he remained adamant. Perhaps she could rework the themes in that unwanted novel into something more passionate, more exciting.

For the moment she could write nothing save letters to the people now writing to her in increasing numbers. Neither ought she to neglect Ellen, though she certainly couldn't discuss literary matters with her! Ellen would soon be thirty-three years old! Yet she still wore white and pink and curled her hair and fancied, not unjustifiably, admiring glances from the gentlemen.

What gave Charlotte the keenest pleasure as the year of 1850 wore on were the letters from Cornhill. Mr Williams, who had written to her with such delicate feeling after her sisters' deaths, had a pleasant wife and a family of young daughters and wrote to her on both literary matters and his own problems. Mr Taylor wrote also, brief businesslike epistles in which Papa took a keen interest.

'A Scot with a good business head and an appreciation of your talents, my dear.'

He shot her a thoughtful look as if he were weighing something in his mind.

Did he think that she might be considering marrying James Taylor? Certainly the latter had gone to some trouble to visit Haworth the year before. Charlotte found herself grimacing – there was nothing in his short, thickset figure or hard face to attract her. It was much more agreeable to think of George Smith who so plainly admired her. His letters came often, demanding that she visit London again soon for he had many other sights to show to her and people for her to meet, and he was personally attractive with an easy courtesy that banished the last vestiges of her shyness.

Then a letter arrived from him that sent her into a fever of excitement and trepidation. In the summer he was bound for a trip to Scotland. Could she not come to London and then travel with him up into the Highlands?

The two of them alone together? He was eight years her junior and unattached. What would people say? Such an unchaperoned holiday would surely be regarded as shocking even in London circles!

She wrote to refuse and received by return a letter from Mrs Smith. George's mother thought that there could be no harm at all in her son's travelling with one of his authors to a place which might give her the inspiration for a third successful novel.

'I can see nothing against the expedition, my dear,' Papa said, when she broached the subject with him. 'It is not as if you were a young lady who might have cause to fear scandal. A few days in the north cannot possibly be misinterpreted.'

What Papa meant was that she wasn't pretty enough to attract scandal! Charlotte took a long look at herself in the mirror up in her bedroom and frowned slightly. The fashion now was for plaits of hair worn coiled high on the head. Her own brown hair was glossy but fine. She hurried downstairs to write to Ellen that she needed a plait of false hair and some brown satin ribbon with which to trim her straw bonnet and light wrap.

'You will call upon the Kay Shuttleworths, my dear?' Papa said.

'Yes, Papa, if his health permits but he is very far from well,' Charlotte reminded him, her heart sinking slightly for Sir James Kay Shuttleworth and his wife had descended upon the parsonage some months before, eager to meet the famous Currer Bell. Sir James with his large white teeth and half-pompous, half-fawning manner had irritated her but Papa had been most gratified that a member of the gentry had called.

'You will write and tell me everything you have seen, all the people you have met?' Papa insisted.

'Yes, of course. Of course I will, Papa!'

Suddenly stricken with compunction she spoke warmly. Papa was seventy-three now and suffered intermittently from bronchial attacks. In his youth he too had craved fame and now must taste it vicariously through his last surviving child.

201

'And do call upon the Wheelwrights. They are in London too.' The Wheelwrights! They had been kind enough to her on the rare occasions that they had seen her in Brussels, but she wanted to forget that part of her life. Emily had taught music unwillingly to the Wheelwright girls. She wanted to forget how she had dragged Emily away from her moors to learn and teach in a Catholic country. Papa had been insensitive to remind her of it.

'I have been thinking, Papa,' she said sweetly, 'that while I am away would be an ideal time in which to have the roof reslated and the undertimbers replaced. You have often mentioned how badly they are rotting. And the dining-room ought to be enlarged. If the wall could be moved about three feet into the hall and my bedroom above enlarged to the same degree the house would be much more commodious.'

'The expense—'

'I am sure the Church Commissioners would defray part of the costs and what remained – don't you feel that Emily and Anne would be happy to have their money put to such good use?'

Her sisters had died intestate and the money they had invested from their share of Aunt's legacy, the money they had earned from their novels and Anne's small bequest from her godmother had reverted to Papa.

'I suppose you are right, my dear. Certainly we cannot have the building falling down about our ears,' he admitted.

'And Gawthorpe Hall where the Kay Shuttleworths reside is said to be the last word in elegance.'

'You are perfectly right, Charlotte! I ought to have had the repairs attended to long since! Do you think that it might also be an idea to make inner doors for Tabby and Martha's room and the downstairs store? It would be much more convenient in the winter especially now that Tabby is so lame?'

'That is an excellent idea, Papa. All must be done according to your wishes of course.'

When her bedroom had been enlarged the little study room which Emily had made her own would be useless as a bedroom in future. No longer would she go past at night with her candle and see the faint outline of the tall slender figure in the long lank skirt beckoning her – a trick of the light which elongated her own shadow on the wall but never failed to make her shiver.

By the time the workmen were in the house she was safely in

London from where she wrote long letters to Papa describing the view she had had of the old Duke of Wellington as he walked from church – he was still tall and distinguished and reminded her, after all the long years, that she had named her wooden soldier in his honour; she wrote an account of the grotesque animals she had seen in the Zoological Gardens and the day she had sat to hear a debate in the Ladies' Gallery in the House of Commons. She told him of the opera she had attended and of another visit from Mr Thackeray. She said nothing of the way in which George Smith held her hand as she negotiated a steep staircase, nothing of the teasing looks exchanged between them when at a dinner party some bore held forth for too long on a subject of which he was ignorant.

George Smith, she wrote to Ellen, was becoming like a brother to her! There was nothing more to it than that! Absolutely nothing more!

TWENTY-TWO

'So Edinburgh lived up to your expectations?'

'More than lived up to them, Papa! The city seemed to me to be steeped in its own past and when we climbed to Arthur's Seat and looked down at the roofs and towers then I felt myself to be in a kind of dream,' Charlotte told him.

'And you enjoyed Mr Smith's company?'

'Very much!' She bent to pour more tea as she went on, 'And in the end there was nothing in the least shocking about it at all! As it happened Mr Smith's young sister, Eliza, elected to join us and during our weekend there he brought his young brother Alick from school. So it was all very proper!'

'Tell me again about your evening at Mr Thackeray's house.'

'Papa, there is nothing more to tell! Mr Thackeray had invited a crowd of ladies to meet me – I'm sure he meant it kindly but it was clear to me that I was expected to shine and sparkle. Of course I refused to do any such thing – you know how I detest public notice! I sat mute the whole evening save for a brief conversation with the governess. The gaiety of the evening dwindled into an occasional remark; the fire smoked; and Mr Thackeray sneaked out to his club.'

'You will have to be a little more sociable when you stay with Sir James,' he observed.

'I wish you had not accepted on my behalf, Papa,' she said irritably. 'Two weeks in his company is going to be very trying on the nerves! And I have agreed that a new edition of *Wuthering Heights* and *Agnes Grey* with some selected poems should be brought out by Smith and Elder for which I must write a biographical notice.'

'Not *The Tenant of Wildfell Hall?*'

'No, Papa! That book should in my view be forgotten as soon as possible. Anyone reading it would gain a completely erroneous idea of dear Anne's character!'

'And you will go to Brierly Close.'

'Yes, Papa, and then I will settle down for the winter. Geo – Mr Smith expects a new novel from me soon and I cannot make a start on anything that holds my attention. Oh, there is talk of Mr Taylor going out to Bombay to open a foreign branch of Smith and Elder.'

'I liked that man,' Papa said. 'He reminded me of —'

'Papa, your tea is getting cold!'

In a moment he would begin to tell her all over again that she was fortunate to be going to stay near Lake Windermere because she would see places on which Branwell's eyes had rested.

The fortnight's visit proved more congenial than she had envisaged. Lady Kay Shuttleworth was confined to her room with the illness which incapacitated her from time to time and Sir James himself was tied up with business matters for part of the time but another lady had been invited and Charlotte found herself immediately drawn to the tall, rather stately woman who arrived a day after her own arrival.

'Miss Brontë and I have already exchanged letters,' Elizabeth Gaskell said, shaking hands cordially. 'I am very happy to meet you in person at last, Miss Brontë.'

'And I you, Mrs Gaskell.'

Charlotte retreated to her seat near the fire and watched the newcomer narrowly.

'Happily married to a Unitarian minister and does a deal of charity work among the Manchester poor,' George Smith had told her. 'She lost a child – a little lad – and her husband advised her to write some stories to alleviate her sorrow. She is already quite a rising star and having four young daughters already she divides her days between them, her charity work and her writing.'

She was also skilled at drawing people out, Charlotte thought.

There was something warm and so motherly about her that Charlotte found herself chatting away as if they had known each other for years.

'You must come and stay with us in Manchester.' Mrs Gaskell spoke impulsively, her eyes large with sympathy. 'My husband will be very happy to meet you, and I know my four girls will be delighted. I am exceedingly proud of them all – you heard that I lost a little boy?'

'And was desperately sorry,' Charlotte said.

'And you too have known great sorrow. You lost your dear siblings in a very short space of time, did you not?'

'Within seven months. Happily I still have Papa.'

'He must cherish your company,' Mrs Gaskell said.

Charlotte smiled faintly. 'Papa is not a sociable being,' she said. 'He was devoted to my brother of course and he is proud of my having published but the books themselves are not mentioned between us for months at a time.'

Yet he had enjoyed *Shirley* very much and often asked when she meant to begin her new novel.

As if writing a book was the same as baking a cake! she thought irritably.

'We must keep in touch,' Charlotte surprised herself by saying when they parted.

'I warn you that I am an inveterate gossip!' her new friend said lightly. 'Not that I would ever divulge —'

'I shall rely on your discretion,' Charlotte promised.

Making a new friend gave her a little thrill of pleasure. It would be like knowing an older, more literary Ellen who knew how hard it was to juggle household duties with the work of authorship.

'We writers must band together, Miss Brontë! We cannot allow the gentlemen critics to have it all their own way!'

'No indeed,' Charlotte agreed fervently. 'Mr Lewes penned a most savage critique of *Jane Eyre*. It made me feel so cold and sick for he judged me as a female first and a woman afterwards and last of all as a writer. As a female I was, in his opinion, less intelligent by nature than a man, as a woman I ought to be fulfilling all the duties of an angel in the house and as a writer I had described things that were unsuitable for me to know anything about!'

'Have you met Mr Lewes?'

'Yes, and I was prepared to have a few sharp, short words with him but – you may think me fanciful but he resembles my poor sister Emily. The arrangement of the features, the full mouth and the blue eyes – cast in a more masculine mould, of course, but the resemblance was mystical.'

'Your carriage is come, Miss Brontë.' One of the servants had approached.

The two women embraced and Charlotte climbed within. The visit had after all been a success and she had made a new friend.

At home again she satisfied Papa with a full account of her visit and wrote to Ellen to tell her that Mrs Gaskell was a good, maybe even a great woman, of whom Ellen herself would approve.

Ellen wrote back to tell her that Amelia Ringrose was at last to marry Joe Taylor.

Charlotte sat down to answer it, pen racing over the paper.

She believed the marriage would be miserable unless Amelia got herself with child at once for Joe, despite his many attractive qualities, could be moody and the fact that Amelia had only a tiny dowry must make her less in his eyes once the first flush of romance had faded.

Then, her bread-and-butter letters written, she settled herself to read her sisters' novels and poems in readiness for the new edition of them that George Smith intended to publish.

Reading them as the year of 1850 drew into winter, she was back in the days when they had written their stories together, had perambulated round the table, reading portions of their tales, arguing and laughing and imagining how they would spend their fortune when they were rich authors.

But all that had changed. The writing that had bound them had in the end torn them apart. Emily had shocked Anne with her novel of a passion that could only be satisfied beyond the grave, with her depiction of a man who might be ghoul or goblin and a girl who killed her own soul out of the longing to be with him. She herself had begged Anne in vain to put aside her second novel and write something more suited to her gentle nature. In the end they had worked separately and alone, each sister with secrets behind her eyes.

Papa had retired to bed as had Tabby and Martha, the two latter chatting cheerfully as they made their way upstairs to the door that now gave them access to their bedroom without the necessity of going outside.

Their writing-desks and a box filled with their unpublished work were still up in the tiny study. Charlotte went upstairs and brought down Emily's desk, conscious that it was heavier than she had expected.

Outside a late autumn wind moaned softly through the cracks in the stone. She unlocked the desk and took out the pile of manuscripts, placed it on the table and stood up. The top page lifted and fluttered to the carpet as if some invisible hand had gently dropped it there.

A draught from the half-open door – no more than that! She stepped across the hall and into the parlour, took up Papa's big magnifying glass and came back into the dining-room, stirring the coals into a blaze, turning up the flame of the oil-lamp. With her spectacles set firmly on her nose she seated herself and drew the sheaf of closely written pages towards her.

This then was the novel Emily had penned in silence: sparse, unadorned by fine phrases, its sentences wounds to the heart. Here, in words that seemed burned into her brain as she read them, were the secrets laid bare – the red room, the games in the cellar, the secrets that a frightened child was constrained to keep.

This must never be seen and yet to destroy it would be a crime against the truth. Perhaps in some future age someone might read it with compassion and lift this heavy burden from her conscience because she ought to have understood, ought to have known, ought to have protected her sister.

It was almost dawn when the task was done. Down in the cellar, her lamp flickering as the last of the oil was consumed, she stood by the wall that divided crypt from cellar and leaned her head against the stone.

Behind her sounded the soft padding of feet and a breathing that was irregular and harsh. Slowly as she turned old Keeper settled himself at her feet, licked her shoe, and laid down his head with a last upward look as if he thanked her for a job well done.

'We shall lay him in the garden,' Papa said. 'I'll have John Brown dig a grave for him in the far corner. Poor old lad! Poor old boy! Flossy will be dull now without him for they were great companions.'

'Flossy is getting fat and sluggish,' Charlotte said, trying to smile. 'I must bestir myself to go out more often on the moors.'

'How is the biographical notice coming?' Papa enquired.

'I am making a start on it, Papa.'

Her sisters had never sought fame and she would write about them as she imagined they would wish her to write. Emily, that sullen, difficult individual who had once been the prettiest of them all, would emerge as a mythic figure – stronger than a man, simpler than a child. Anne would remain almost unnoticed in the shadows, cloaked in innocence and ignorance. People would understand that their books had been written by two almost uneducated young women who had little idea of what they had created. People would learn only that they were plain and shy, their noble natures apparent only to her. As she wrote feverishly during the days that stretched towards winter, Emily and Anne became characters in a play of her own devising.

When the task was finished she took out *Monsieur's* letters, the few he had written to her in response to her pleas for answers.

They were kindly, sober letters, full of sound advice about running a school, not one of them free of a certain slight impatience. He had urged her more than once to moderate her enthusiasms and to damp down her too emotional responses.

Was that what *Monsieur* had really wanted? She didn't believe it for a moment! It was *Madame* who had made it impossible for him to show how greatly he esteemed her mind, appreciated her talents, relished her company.

Ought she to have hidden her own esteem, her own affection? Had she responded too eagerly to his charm, made cheap what he would have valued more highly had it been hidden?

In her mind a new character was taking shape – a plain, still young woman with none of Jane Eyre's charm; a cold young woman whom life had almost battered into submission; a young woman whose heart was a furnace under ice and in whose veins flames and not blood danced unseen.

Her name was Lucy Snowe. She would be befriended by a handsome young doctor and his mother who lived in a house very similar to the one where the Smiths lived. There would be a journey to Belgium – she would call the town Villette – Little Town because Brussels had, after all, proved but a narrow place for the heart to flourish.

She wrote at white heat for whole days together and then sometimes in the middle of a sentence broke off abruptly and stared at the words she had just composed as if they had flooded from some part of her brain with which she was unfamiliar.

Spring came and the flowers that Emily and Anne had loved waved their heads in the inchcape grass. The last frost was gone from the hills and the breeze was warmer. To walk with Flossy on the lower reaches of the moors should have been a pleasure but when she ventured on them now she could only recall Emily, hands stuck in her pockets, whistling cheerfully as she forded the streams and when she turned for home the sky itself held Anne's yellow ringlets and quiet face.

James Taylor called again on his way back from Scotland.

'To bid you farewell, Miss Brontë.' His hard determined face repelled her. 'I leave for Bombay in May. I hoped that – may I write to you?'

'Yes, Mr Taylor. I shall be pleased to hear from you,' Charlotte told him.

How odd, she reflected when he had taken his leave, that now she should be in a position to answer or not someone who esteemed her.

'I believe Mr Taylor might propose when he returns in four or five years' time,' Papa said genially.

'Nonsense, Papa!'

'I believe he will, given a little encouragement.'

'When he is away I like him better,' Charlotte said and went into the dining-room to write to Ellen whose soothing company she suddenly desired above all things!

TWENTY-THREE

Charlotte leaned back against the sofa and closed her eyes. From the chair where she sat sewing Ellen said anxiously,

'Are you feeling ill again? Shall I get —?'

'I am feeling so much better since you came that I could almost dance a jig,' Charlotte said, opening her eyes and sitting up. 'When you are here, love, life becomes easeful again. The last two years have seen me trapped on a merry-go-round.'

'But you must've gained some pleasure from your fame,' Ellen said mildly. 'You have met so many important people and stayed in so many grand houses that surely —'

'That surely I have to consult an almanac to discover where I am at any particular moment!' Charlotte said. 'Oh, it is ungrateful of me to grumble when I'm kept too busy because the alternative is the silence and solitude here at Haworth, but this junketing around, as Papa calls it, interferes with my writing and if I don't send *Villette* to George very soon he will conclude that I have written nothing at all!'

'Mr Smith is still very attentive then?'

'More than that! There is a mutual attraction there, Ellen! Looking back I believe it was present from the first time we met. My last visit to London was full of pleasant things. At first I convinced myself that we thought of each other as quasi-brother and sister, but his desire for my company is – significant. He devoted himself to me, Nell, when I was last in London with such kindness, such delicate attentions!'

'And the new bonnet helped?' Ellen said slyly.

'Black silk lined with pink and a white lace mantle to wear over my black dress. Yes, your advice in all matters of fashion ought always to be followed by any woman who wishes to become a social success.'

'Tell me about London again.'

'You have heard it ten times already,' Charlotte said. 'It was a world of brilliance, of outings, of Thackeray lectures – that man is more concerned with flattering his coterie of aristocratic ladies than in giving the world the splendid fruits of his mind – of visits to the opera and the theatre – I shall never forget the impression the performance of *Rachel* made upon me! It wrung me to the depths.'

'It sounds very tiring,' Ellen said with a smile.

'That is exactly what George said. I turned to him at the end, my whole soul fired up by her towering performance, and he said that her performance had exhausted him just watching it. But unless we are fired and stimulated we shall dwindle away to nothing! Harriet Martineau knows that! When I stayed with her I was so impressed by her tireless energy and her charitable works! I admire her tremendously, Ellen, for making her own way through life with such single-minded determination!'

'Like Mary Taylor.'

'I wish she would come home.' Charlotte frowned slightly. 'I cannot help feeling that life in New Zealand has – coarsened her a little. She writes with a kind of careless jauntiness which grates somewhat.'

'Amelia is safely delivered,' Ellen remarked.

'Aye, something tumbled into the bassinet at last and Joe acts as if he was responsible for the whole affair!'

'He was partly.'

'Having children isn't a possibility I've often considered,' Charlotte told her. 'If one might do it spontaneously without the invasion of a man then the possibility becomes more attractive.'

'Charlotte!'

'On the other hand, the example of Mrs Gaskell leads one to alter that opinion,' Charlotte said thoughtfully. 'She and her husband are very happy and there is a glow over her domestic life which cheers the heart. Her house is so large and airy, quite out of the Manchester smoke, and her girls are charming. I loved little Julia. She is sweet!'

'I would like to meet Mrs Gaskell,' Ellen said, laying her work aside. 'Charlotte, if Mr Smith proposes will you accept him?'

'I have thought about it from every angle,' Charlotte told her. 'I know that he is going to do so and for many months I have been on the seesaw of indecision! I am older than he is and more vehement in my feeling but we get on so well together, laugh at the same things – no, Nell, it would never do! George ought to marry a young, pliable, beautiful girl who shines in society and can give him a large family. Then again if I wed him, since his business is in London, I would have to move south and what would then happen to Papa? He frets when I go away for a visit and his routine is so set and unvarying that to alter it would cause great harm.'

'Like my mother,' Ellen said with a sigh. 'She wants her days to follow the same pattern at the same hours. Mercy would help me but she is so forgetful and her housekeeping skills were never very great. She is a good soul though for she frequently visits poor George who is happily settled at the Nursing Home save that his short-term memory is impaired. We have never told him of Amelia's marriage though Mercy says that he seems to have forgotten her entirely.'

'Which is a blessing in disguise,' Charlotte said. 'You and I are in much the same situation, Nell, with parents who cannot be left. I shall complete *Villette* and then go to London where I shall refuse the proposal of marriage George Smith was clearly working up to the last time I saw him, and you will stay with your mother. And one day – Nell, one day we shall live in that cottage together and that will be the truest happiness of all!'

'Dear Charlotte!' Ellen rose from her seat, came over and gave her a warm embrace.

'Charles Thunder if you please!'

Charlotte returned the hug.

When Ellen had returned to Birstall Charlotte took out the manuscript of *Villette* and read it over. There was still half of the third volume to complete and she knew that the struggle between her own wishes and her artistic integrity would be a fierce one. Lucy Snowe could not be permitted to marry the charming Dr John. Lucy was the soul mate of Monsieur Paul Emmanuel, the Belgian professor, but were soul mates ever destined for union?

'I hope your new book will have a happy ending,' Papa said when she took tea with him later that day.

'It's a novel, not a fairy story, Papa.'

'You ought to take a little holiday, my dear.' He regarded her worriedly. 'Your health and spirits have been very low for months.'

'It was a liver complaint, Papa. Dr Ruddock told me that I had a bad reaction to the mercury and quinine he prescribed.'

'Well, I shall be happy to see you bright and cheerful again. I don't suppose – you have had no letter from Bombay?'

'Not recently, Papa. James Taylor has a great deal on his mind.'

'When he returns – an engagement lasting for about four or five years might be very suitable, though I'd not interfere, my dear girl. Young ladies generally manage these matters for themselves these days.'

She wanted to scream at him: *Look at me, Papa! I'm in my mid-thirties and it is a long time since I was a girl!*

Aloud she said placidly,

'Once *Villette* is accepted I shall go to London and stay with Mrs Smith who has invited me to return several times. I rather think that I will be paid seven hundred pounds for the book. Publishers do increase their remuneration to authors year on year.'

'You are investing wisely?'

'Yes indeed, Papa, but I intend to buy a few things for the house. I thought that curtains might be —'

'My dear child! The risk of fire —'

'Papa, that was when we were all small children toddling around and falling over things!' Charlotte cried. 'As it was, not one of us ever did actually fall into the fireplace! I thought red curtains for the dining room and parlour and white ones for our bedrooms. If Mrs Gaskell comes to stay here – and you will enjoy her company exceedingly – her own house has the most elegant drapes.'

'If your heart is set upon them then I see no serious objection,' he said reluctantly.

'Thank you, Papa.'

She went back across the hall and sat down at the table. From now on she would allow herself no respite until the last chapters were complete. She dipped her pen into the inkwell and within moments was back in the shining classroom with the french windows leading into the garden, had her hands enclosed in *Monsieur's* hands, felt the sinking of her heart as *Madame* entered, slippers felt-soled and silent.

Why had he turned and walked away? Why hadn't he remained, her hands in his and told his wife that he reserved the right to have a friend, an intellectual friend with whom he could exchange letters? Why had *Madame* won?

Her pen raced on, turning herself into Lucy Snowe, *Monsieur* into Paul Emmanuel and Madame Heger into the treacherous Madame Beck.

When she had finished it was dark. Martha had brought in the lamp and gone out again unnoticed. Charlotte blotted the page and sat back, suddenly empty of all emotion save relief that it was done. Now she would parcel it up and send it to Cornhill and wait for the payment.

It came before the end of the month, with only a short note of acceptance and no personal message at all. They had paid her £500, just as they had for the other two! Other writers to whom she had talked earned more from Smith, Elder & Co. Charlotte felt the bitter disappointment corrode her veins. George Smith was taking advantage of her good manners and her pride to pay her less than she was worth. He had not liked the book and chose this way to tell her so.

The next morning the personal note arrived, inviting her to visit London again and telling her that a further edition of *Jane Eyre* had just been arranged and would yield her another hundred pounds. The admiring friend was not, then, submerged in the hard-headed business man.

Greatly cheered she went to tell Papa the news and then sat down to write a warm acceptance to Mrs Smith.

The closing of the parlour door told her that Mr Nicholls, whom she had glimpsed earlier, passing the window, was on his way back to his lodging at John Brown's house. The front door didn't open or close. Instead there came a tap on the dining-room door.

'Come in?'

She raised her head as Mr Nicholls, solid and tweed-clad, came in and stood before her, heavy shoulders hunched, his long pale face solemn as usual.

'Mr Nicholls?' She stared at him in perplexity.

'Miss Brontë, may I have a few words?'

Charlotte, carefully folding her hands together under her

chin, knew immediately what was coming next. There was no time to say anything more. He took a step towards her and said in his rich Dublin accent,

'Miss Brontë, for many years I have followed your progress with great interest and sympathy, have admired the manner in which you have met with sorrow and calamity – I now ask that you consider my suit. . . .'

He stammered to a halt.

'Have you spoken to my father?' she asked lamely.

'I have not. I wished to know your mind first.'

'I can give you no answer until I have talked with Papa,' she said quickly.

'Yes, of course, Miss Brontë.'

He turned and went out, fumbling for the door handle.

Charlotte stared bemusedly at the door panels, listening to the front door open and close, to the crunching of his boots along the path.

Arthur Bell Nicholls had proposed. She gave him credit at least for asking her personally and not writing a letter as Henry Nussey and poor David Bryce had done.

She wondered why she was not more surprised. Mr Nicholls had been curate for eight years; he had done his work conscientiously, had been unobtrusively helpful and sympathetic when her siblings had died, walked Flossy in bad weather, went on holiday to Ireland every year. She had never considered him as a matrimonial prospect, had indeed been angry with Ellen when her friend had teased her about the possibility. Yet more than once she had caught him looking at her thoughtfully. More than once he had been hanging about in the lane when she passed with a polite enquiry as to her well-being.

She must certainly inform Papa and they could have a shared smile about it.

Rising, going across the hall, she tapped on the parlour door.

'Is it time for prayers?' Papa looked up at her.

'Not quite yet, Papa. I – Mr Nicholls just spoke to me.'

'He seemed abstracted this evening. What's on his mind?'

'He – wishes to pay court to me, Papa. I said I would —'

'He – what?'

'He wants to marry me, Papa. I said —'

'Was he drunk? I've never known him drunk before.'

'Papa, he was perfectly sober as he always is. He wishes to marry me, Papa.'

'A jumped-up Irish nobody!' Papa was on his feet, looming over her, eyes bulging in his congested face. 'A nobody from Ireland! A Mick on the make! You must've dreamed it, my dear girl!'

'No, Papa! I told him that I would speak to you and —'

'Lacked the courage himself, did he? That doesn't surprise me! No money, no background, no personality – the parishioners cannot stand his high-handed ways, you know! He's after your money of course. That can be the only reason for daring to – of course you will refuse him.'

'Yes, Papa, of course I will. I have no thought of —'

'I shall write to him immediately forbidding him to raise the subject again! If he were not so competent I would complain to the bishop! What on earth was he thinking about? Leave me to deal with it, Charlotte. I will ensure he doesn't come sniffing round you again!'

'Please don't excite yourself so!' Charlotte begged in panic.

'I – am – not – excited!' He thumped the table with each word, the veins in his forehead pulsating.

'I have no intention of marrying him, Papa!'

'No indeed! You are past the age of marriage, an independent woman able to support yourself, welcome in the best houses in the land! Get me pen and paper and I will make certain he never troubles you again. You can take it across to John Brown's directly!'

'Yes, Papa.'

She stood motionless, hardly knowing whether to laugh or cry, as he wrote, his pen digging into the paper viciously.

'Seal it, will you, and take it across to John's. If Mr Nicholls is there snub him. I need not tell you how to do that! You know it very well!'

He signed with a flourish, threw down the pen, and held out the letter to her.

'Read it!' he ordered. 'If I have not expressed myself plainly enough then strengthen it with your own message!'

'Yes, Papa.'

Taking the note she fled back into the dining-room.

It was a letter that would have devastated her had she received it. It was not, she thought uneasily, a letter that anyone ought to receive.

Taking up her own pen she wrote neatly at the foot of the page,

'While I cannot agree with the manner in which my father has expressed himself nevertheless I must reiterate my refusal to your suit.
Yours faithfully,
C. Brontë.'

She sealed it, and put on her cloak. She hesitated in the hall. It would be better for Martha to deliver it save that both Martha and Tabby must have heard Papa's loud and furious tones. Better to slip it over herself and that would be an end of the matter.

She went down the lane past the school house to the sexton's lodge. John Brown was seated on the wall, coughing over his pipe.

'Is owt wrong, Miss Charlotty?' he demanded.

'Papa wishes this note to be delivered to Mr Nicholls,' Charlotte said.

'I'll give it him when he gets back,' John Brown said. 'He's away up on't moors.'

'In the dark?'

'Aye, he often walks at all hours to let off steam I reckon,' John Brown said gloomily. 'Queer sort of fellow he is! The missus were on t'other day because he went and cut holes in his bedroom door.'

'Whatever for?' Charlotte asked in astonishment.

'To let in th'air so he said. He's a rum un!'

'Why doesn't he just open the window?'

'Says night air's unhealthy! Branny would've laughed at that.'

'You still miss my brother, don't you?' Charlotte said.

'I do, Miss Charlotty! Every day! He were like the son I always wanted but never had, though I love my girls dearly, mind! Branny was a real lad was Branny! Red-headed young devil!'

'He caused great unhappiness,' Charlotte said.

'Maybe too much were expected of him,' John Brown said.

'Aye, maybe so. Good night, John.'

'Good night, Miss Charlotty.'

She turned and walked back up the lane, head bent and cloak

wrapped tightly about her. She must go to prayers and afterwards, when the long lonely hours began, she would write to Ellen, presenting the day's events in their most dramatic form. Ellen would be amused and interested.

Then she must prepare for her visit to London. She would wear the grey fur tippets and a dress of light green with lace collar and cuffs that she had been persuaded by Ellen to have made up.

TWENTY-FOUR

'Where would you like to go today?'

George Smith asked her the question as they walked along Gloucester Terrace on a bright clear morning.

'I feel guilty at taking you away from the office,' Charlotte admitted, 'but I thought another visit to Bethlehem Hospital might prove instructive,'

'Instructive!' He looked down at her, his mouth curling with amusement. 'My dear Charlotte, during your visit to us we have tramped round two prisons, the Stock Exchange, and we have already been to Bedlam once. Your next novel is going to be intensely gloomy I suspect!'

'I have no book in my head,' Charlotte said. 'I can write very little unless it is related to my experience and my experiences have been limited. No, I wished to see something of real life this time. Glitter is very beautiful but the heart of the city must be the commercial area, the great merchant banks and the insurance companies, Threadneedle Street, the hospital of St Bartholomew – these places inform the mind.'

'But walking round looking at poor wretches out of their senses . . .'

'Then I will excuse you a second visit to the hospital! George, may I ask you to tell me frankly – what troubled you about *Villette*. I can sense that something did.'

'It is powerfully and sensitively written and the critics are going to be as divided over it as usual.'

'But you didn't like it,' Charlotte said bluntly.

'There were sections in the first part that – stuck in my throat,' he said.

'Yes. I thought they might.'

She had guessed even as she wrote about the half-suffocating affection between Dr John and his mother that he would catch some hint of how she had incorporated echoes of the teasing exchanges between his mother and himself.

'I use bits of people to form a character. They are not photographic representations,' she said defensively.

'And the abrupt shift of Lucy Snowe's affection from Dr John to Paul Emmanuel – I hesitate to question you about it but —'

'I don't want *Villette* to be translated into French,' she said abruptly.

'I think I see.' He had paused to look into her face, his own eyes searching.

'You see nothing,' she said flatly. 'What happens in novels need not be reproduced in reality. There events can go quite the opposite direction!'

'Is that your hope?'

'The ending of the tale is inconclusive,' Charlotte said. 'I wait to see whether nature imitates art or proceeds on her own irrelevant way.'

'Have you heard from India recently?' he asked.

'Nothing for many months. Mr Taylor and I – his absence is, I confess, more pleasant to me than his presence.'

'His quick temper and harsh voice alienate people but he is an extremely able businessman. He has no intention of returning to this country for many years. Miss Brontë —'

'What happened to Charlotte?' she queried playfully.

'I have a great deal of business to transact these days,' he said. 'The next time you come to London we shall have more time together.'

'Is that an invitation?' she said with a swift upward look.

'Surely you need no formal summons! Come when you can. My mother is always pleased to see you – as am I.'

He pressed her hand and they walked on through the bright spring.

Had she made her meaning clear? She stole a glance at him as they strolled along, tracing with her eyes the outline of his features. Though he was still handsome it struck her that he had aged since their last meeting, the contours of his face hardening, his bearing less lively than before. The eight-year difference in their ages was less apparent now. She left with feelings that were part hope and part a gnawing sense of frustration since nothing definite had been settled between them. 'Write to me,' she said at the last as he escorted her to the train, 'if you have time. I'd not have it become a chore when you have so little free time.'

'Writing to you is never a chore, my dear Charlotte! Give my regards to your father.'

'I will indeed. He looks forward to meeting you one day.'

'*Au revoir* then, Charlotte.'

He pressed her hand as she mounted up into the railway carriage. She had a sudden urge to step down on to the platform and announce her wish to stay for another week but she had arranged to meet Ellen at Leeds so they could travel on to Haworth together. With Ellen in the house there would be no danger of Mr Nicholls renewing his unwelcome suit.

Ellen, punctual as ever, was waiting, her face beaming as Charlotte stepped down and signalled a porter.

'I have ordered tea before we journey on,' she said. 'Did you enjoy your visit? Is the friendship between yourself and Mr Smith grown warmer? How does his mother view your friendship?'

'Our friendship is – I believe it is warmer than mere friendship,' Charlotte confessed. 'His mother entertained me with her usual kindness but . . . I fancy she watches me more narrowly than before. She wonders how soon George will declare himself and what I will say.'

'Surely you will refuse him?' Ellen said. 'You could not go and live in London and leave Mr Brontë alone?'

'Of course not!' Charlotte seated herself at the small table in the station restaurant. 'Surely you and I agreed that it was our duty to stay with our respective parents? They cared for us when we were young and we must care for them as they grow old!'

'And Mr Nicholls?'

'Behaved very sullenly before I went to London and has gone on behaving in the same fashion since I left according to Papa,' Charlotte told her. 'Apparently he resigned his curacy, then rescinded it, then told Papa he had applied for missionary work and then excused himself on the grounds he was suffering from rheumatism! Papa remains utterly opposed to any idea of his ever marrying me. He distrusts his motives.'

'So do I!' Ellen said. 'He took no interest in you until he discovered you were a successful author and suddenly he wishes for an alliance. As you do not,' she added.

'No. No, of course not, but I cannot help feeling sorry for him.'

'Pity makes a bad bedfellow,' Ellen said.

'I'm sure you're right, Ellen dear. No, I shall pay for the tea! My time spent in London cost me nothing since George pays for all my needs while I am his guest,' Charlotte said. 'Where is the porter? Ah! He has my trunk still. Surely that isn't all your luggage?'

She looked in some surprise at the neat bandbox her friend was carrying.

'I travel light,' Ellen said, a mischievous look on her face. 'Now that crinolines are so wide I attach various garments to my stays. My hoops are replete with underwear. It saves having to carry heavy bags around or hail porters in vain!'

'In my next letter Mary Taylor will certainly be told!'

'It was Mary who suggested it,' Ellen said.

Rather to her relief, Mr Nicholls chose to absent himself from the scene during Ellen's short visit and Papa, evidently having some thought for her own feelings, refrained from making any comments.

But when Ellen had gone the atmosphere darkened again. It was impossible to avoid Mr Nicholls altogether when he emerged from the Brown house to take services in church or to stride off over the moors. She was aware of his eyes following her as she took her seat in church and more than once she glimpsed his tall unyielding frame standing stolidly in the lane and staring fixedly towards her window.

'Would you mind if I paid a brief visit to Mrs Gaskell and then spent a few days with Ellen at Brookroyd?' Charlotte asked her father.

'I think the visit would do you good,' Papa said. 'You will then have the summer in which to begin your new novel. Mr Nicholls will have left by then and we shall neither of us be troubled by his nonsense again. I have engaged a Mr De Renzy to assist me and so the slight inconvenience of his leaving will be minimal.'

Going to stay with Mrs Gaskell felt like escaping from prison. Charlotte loved the large, bright, airy rooms, the walled garden with its sweet-smelling plants, the flattering eagerness with which her hostess listened to the story of her tribulations and to the recent tragi-comic saga of Mr Nicholls's wooing.

'Is he so very unsuitable as a husband?' Mrs Gaskell wondered.

'For another woman he might be very suitable indeed,' Charlotte admitted. 'He is not ill-looking and he has given every satisfaction in his parochial duties – though the villagers don't like him much. He has a severe air and no humour at all! His mind is narrow and his tastes are not intellectual. Martha, our servant girl, told me that she hates him.'

'Why should a maid servant hate him? Has he offended her?'

'She thinks he is unworthy of me I suppose. He dogs my foot-steps when I walk home from church or the village in a positively weird way!'

'But Mr Nicholls has a new curacy elsewhere? So he won't trouble you again.'

'At Kirk Smeaton I believe. He goes after Whitsun and then I can concentrate on my new novel.'

'Have you made progress?'

'Not really,' Charlotte confessed. 'I make beginnings and then the mood flees; inspiration turns her back. I cannot write until I have reproduced the situation, the feelings, the dialogue in my own being. I lie in bed at night and try to place myself into that particular situation mentally before I sleep and often in the mornings I wake with the next part clear in my head! That hasn't happened recently.'

'You have had other concerns.'

'Mr Nicholls, yes! And I have ended my friendship with Miss Martineau. I am sorry to do it but the critique she wrote about *Villette* in which she castigated the amount of loving in the tale – how can I go on communicating with a woman who, admirable as she is in many ways, is so utterly at variance with my deepest convictions? My conscience will not allow it. Mr Sidney Dobell has written to me though. His account of my dear sister's novel has moved me very deeply. Emily would have been so glad to read such praise of her novel by one who understood the true beauty in it! The praise comes too late for her but I was grateful for her sake.'

'And you go to London again soon?'

'When I have written more of my next novel. I have its title,

Emma, but who she is and what part she plays in the unfolding story I have yet to fathom!'

'All London will wait anxiously for the book,' Mrs Gaskell said.

'Another reason for my staying single. I could not cope with wedlock and fame as gracefully as you do, Mrs Gaskell.'

'It can be trying,' Mrs Gaskell murmured.

'And with young girls to rear too! I admire your energy.'

'Your own is limited I fear,' Mrs Gaskell said with concern.

'I am very far from being an invalid.' Charlotte frowned slightly. 'Cowan Bridge stunted my growth but my health is generally good. I still walk Flossy regularly on the moors though I no longer have human company.'

'Your poor sisters – what sad lives they led!'

'Yes,' said Charlotte.

Dear Mrs Gaskell was determined to cast her in a tragic role! But life, even childhood, had held much joy in mutual interests, tramps across the heather, mutual teasing, and private jests. The problem was that the last weeks and days of her siblings overshadowed brighter memories. Branny turning somersaults in the graveyard and inventing fantastic tales about those cradled in the stone, Emily joking with Tabby and breaking away as they walked the dogs to whirl and dance, her long dark hair whipping about her, Anne with her dry little comments dropped into the conversation like plump raisins into a rice pudding.

'Yes,' she said again. 'Yes, our lives have been sad.'

When she reached home again there was the Whitsun service to endure.

'Mr Nicholls will take it,' Papa said. 'I have no intention of attending. My chest has been rather tight and painful recently. The congregation presented him with a leaving gift of a gold watch if you please! They are so pleased to see him leave I believe they would've bribed him with a gold clock if he had threatened to remain!'

At the service itself, kneeling at the Communion rail, Charlotte was aware of the black-and-white cassock looming before her, of the long pause before the words of the blessing were uttered almost inaudibly. She felt in the midst of her shrinking embarrassment a sense of power. She too was now in a position to rise and walk away, with no *Madame* to make certain that Mr Nicholls reached Kirk Smeaton without saying a private farewell.

Yet the unfinished aspects of the affair left her feeling as she did when a novel she had begun refused to progress and had to be laid aside.

He came that evening to say goodbye to Papa. Charlotte, lurking on the landing above, heard the parlour door close quietly and the front door open and close with the same final click.

She hurried softly down the stairs and through the kitchen, reaching the lane by the back route unseen from the parlour windows.

'Mr Nicholls! I merely wish to bid you goodbye and to hope that you are content in your new curacy,' she said impulsively.

Mr Nicholls, leaning against the gate, raised his head and gave her a long steady look.

'May I write to you?' he asked.

Her own question once to Heger, and for a while he had replied to her letters, but she had made the mistake of leaping the limits, of writing with vigour and passion.

'Yes, of course, Mr Nicholls. If you address your letters to Currer Bell they will escape notice in certain quarters,' she said. 'You understand that there can only be friendship?'

He bowed slightly, turned abruptly and walked away.

'We shall see now,' she thought, 'how you enjoy waiting for a reply. We shall see how passionate your missives become.'

Then she too turned and went back into the house, pausing in the kitchen to give the glowing coals a triumphant poke.

Yet the new book she was working on refused to advance. She set it aside and took out another fragment, poring over the tale of the old house presided over by a familiar spirit, owned by a cruel older brother who mistreated his younger brother, tried to marry it to the adult Willie Elfin visiting a fashionable girls' school where a pupil called Matilda was revealed as a fraud – found herself thinking instead about her next visit to London. Letters from Cornhill continued to arrive. George was frantically busy but still kept the tip of his little finger entirely for her, a boon she had jestingly requested in one of her own letters.

Sometimes his own letters ended abruptly or tailed off into long meaningless sentences that served only to fill up the page. They troubled her because she had noticed signs of overwork in him during her last visit, moments when she had sensed he was about to speak but then had retained his silence.

'Mr Nicholls is writing to you!' Ellen on a brief visit stared at her in consternation.

'Hush or Papa might hear! His hearing is still acute. Yes, he writes regularly, still pressing his suit.'

'But why? Surely you made it clear that you had no intention of marrying anybody?' Ellen said.

'I was never cut out for marriage,' Charlotte said. 'But, it is rather flattering to be courted at my age!'

'You are thirty-seven,' Ellen said flatly. 'That's not so old!'

'Exactly! It is not the first flush of youth either,' Charlotte retorted. 'Letters are really very safe!'

'You have answered them?'

'I replied after the sixth one,' Charlotte said. 'He wrote to say that my reply had consoled him very much and he requested that I write again!'

'Charlotte, you're playing with fire!' Ellen exclaimed. 'Mr Nicholls is a good decent man and you are holding out false hopes to him! They are false hopes, aren't they? You have not abandoned our dream of one day having a home together? I have relied on that dream for a very long time. It helps me to cope with my mother who grows frailer and with Mercy who cannot be trusted to do anything properly!'

'I write to many people,' Charlotte said.

'Yes, but —'

'Ellen, you and I made a pact that we would care for our parents, your mother, my father, until fated to be together. Writing letters does not alter that pledge! As Currer Bell I must leave home in order to visit people who have the same interests as myself – the mind requires stimulation. Mr Nicholls will recover from his present infatuation – were I not to write to him it would become an unhealthy obsession – and George Smith I also write to in the way of business. You write to Amelia and Joe and half a dozen other people.'

'That is different,' Ellen said.

'Only in that my letters touch more on intellectual pursuits and less on family news and local gossip! Now I am going to ask Papa if we may take our tea with him. You are a great favourite of his you know! He has always considered you very charming!'

'I can also read and write,' Ellen muttered, so low that the words reached Charlotte's ears as no more than a faint buzzing.

TWENTY-FIVE

Mrs Gaskell's visit was over and done and had proved a most welcome diversion, with Papa taking a decided shine to her visitor and paying her compliments in his high flown manner. Charlotte too had enjoyed the visit and was pleased that since the structural alterations and the acquisition of curtains and new carpets the parsonage looked bright and welcoming. It was a pity that recent storms had blighted the heather on the moors but the weather had been fine enough for her to escort her guest out for a daily walk.

'My sisters loved the moors,' Charlotte said softly. 'They are truly magnificent at every season of the year but in summer they are an Eden!'

'They have an underlying savagery,' Mrs Gaskell commented.

'Oh, we're a savage lot in Yorkshire!' Charlotte told her. 'I could relate tales of the families hereabouts that would curdle your blood! There is a farm high on the moor where a widowed farmer kept his daughter prisoner, using her in an unprintable way until she escaped one day and drowned herself.'

'Surely not!' Mrs Gaskell had paled.

'It was some hundred years ago,' Charlotte admitted, 'but in our own time there was found the body of a newborn babe hidden under one of the large setts outside the apothecary's shop. Someone had prised up the stone and put it beneath. Someone had carved a cross on the stone. Enquiries were made but its parentage was never settled. Papa decreed the bones should be left where they were. I can show you the exact spot for the cross was carved very deeply.'

'My dear Charlotte!' Mrs Gaskell looked distressed.

'As I say this is a savage region. Flossy! Here!' She called to Anne's spaniel as it chased an imaginary rabbit.

'Your father still carries pistols,' Mrs Gaskell said.

'He always has ever since the days of the Luddite riots. You will have heard him firing his pistol out of the window first thing each morning? That too is a habit! He likes to discharge the shot. When his sight was very bad he still insisted on aiming and always hit the church tower. He taught my sister Emily to shoot too. She often walked alone on the heights and he wished her to have some protection.'

'Your sister Emily sounds . . . unfeminine.'

'She was a law unto herself,' Charlotte said.

As they turned for home, Mrs Gaskell, casting a glance at her shoes which were somewhat muddy, asked tentatively,

'You mentioned that a Mr Nicholls had offered for your hand but that Mr Brontë objected. He has left the district now I assume?'

'He has a curacy at Kirk Smeaton. Mrs Gaskell, I do receive letters from him,' Charlotte told her. 'I have answered them. Papa would be furious were he to find out. He thinks a mere curate far beneath me, and I myself have no yearning towards him but on the day he left here, my heart was wrung by his agonies! He stood at the gate sobbing like a woman and would not stir until I had promised to answer his letters. Of course nothing can ever come of it and by and by his own strong emotions will fade.'

'Is it wise then to continue writing?'

'That is my friend Miss Nussey's opinion,' Charlotte sighed. 'To be frank with you she and I have had a falling out about it. She no longer writes to me or issues invitations. I am very fond of her but like many single women she is somewhat possessive about her female friends. Her own life has been dominated by family concerns and the chances of marriage grow fewer as the years pass.'

'I shall hope for a happy outcome,' Mrs Gaskell said.

Or perhaps a surprising one, Charlotte thought, as they walked up the lane. Even Mrs Gaskell with her flair for drama would never guess where the letters from Cornhill were leading!

'Good day, Miss Charlotty!' Mr Greenwood, the stationer, limped past them and halted as Charlotte said:

'Mrs Gaskell, may I introduce our local bookseller and stationer, Mr Greenwood? He supplies me with all my writing materials and was one of the first people in the village to divine the identity of Currer Bell.'

'Aye and I've read thy books too, Mrs Gaskell, ma'am,' he told her. 'Not being a fit man I spend much time reading. I used to wonder why the young ladies from the parsonage bought so much paper! Often I've walked into Bradford and back to be sure of getting some! Aye, Miss Emily and Miss Annie were so pleased when I had paper for them.'

'Ah! you knew them!' Mrs Gaskell said, interested.

'Aye, since they were little lassies. Miss Annie was a nice little thing – very shy, and Miss Emily – eh, she were a beauty! Her eyes were like blue stars —'

'Mr Greenwood, excuse us but Papa will be wanting his tea,' Charlotte interposed.

'That I will, Miss Charlotty! Good day to thee, ma'am.' He tipped his hat with awkward courtesy and limped on.

'Mr Greenwood has some education,' Charlotte remarked as they entered the gate. 'Emily always took the trouble to stop and say good-day to him. She wouldn't give a look or a word to most people, but if they were crippled in any way she would stop and talk.'

She opened the gate and ushered her guest within.

The last of the summer was gone and the leaves that lay on the path were crisp and brown. The wind had sharpened and had in it an edge of ice. Mrs Gaskell had gone back to her husband and her four daughters, Papa was grumbling about Mr De Renzy who as a replacement for the efficient Arthur Bell Nicholls was sadly inadequate.

Letters from Cornhill had dwindled into hasty scribbled notes. Charlotte, seated alone in the dining-room after Papa had retired for the night read them over with a worried little frown creasing her brows.

George was clearly troubled and she had a very shrewd notion of what the trouble was. He hesitated to declare himself because she had always drawn back from a too intense involvement with him. Indeed she felt no intense involvement but she did feel affection and the stirrings of what she admitted to herself was surely physical desire.

She took paper and pen and wrote to the Wheelwrights asking them to reserve lodgings for her in a quiet corner of London as she had private business to transact in the city. Once she was there she would send round a note to George and a private meeting would provide him with the opportunity to say what she knew in her heart he wanted to say.

Meanwhile she wrote to Mrs Smith, begging to be remembered to the family, and enquiring after her son's wellbeing.

The answer from Mrs Smith arrived a few days later. Charlotte, hesitating between her pink-lined bonnet and another edged with grey squirrel, opened it eagerly.

Ten minutes later she sat, numb and pale, by the dining-room fire. Mrs Smith had written kindly but with an undercurrent of unease to tell her that George was engaged. He had met a Miss Elizabeth Blakelock during an evening at the theatre and fallen in love with her at first sight. Both families being agreed, they would marry in February.

Past scenes rose in her mind. Herself teasing George after he had escorted her to the House of Commons, the pair of them going together to a phrenologist and styling themselves Mr and Miss Frazer in order to have their characters analysed, George going with her to the studio of Mr Laurence to inspect the drawing of her the artist had made, George gripping her hand as they climbed up to Arthur's Seat in Edinburgh – such happy hopeful scenes.

The truth was that he had been kind to her because she was small and plain and awkward in brilliant society and because he wanted her to write further bestselling novels that would increase the profits of his publishing house.

Had she loved him she would have wept, but she was filled with a cold bleak anger that turned the blood in her veins to ice. When she had ceased trembling she rose, carried her writing-desk to the table and sat down to write – first to the Mrs Shaen in whose house she had reserved lodgings to cancel her stay, then to George, her nib digging into the paper as she wrote,

Dear Sir,
    In happiness as in sorrow few words suffice.
Accept my meed of congratulations,
                    Yours faithfully,
                        C. Brontë.

The books that Mr Williams regularly sent her to read were piled on a shelf. She made a neat parcel of them and included a brusque note.

Dear Sir,
   Pray don't trouble to send any more books.
These courtesies must cease some time.
                              Yours faithfully,
                              C. Brontë.

Not until letters and parcel had been posted did she tap on the parlour door.

'Papa, I have been receiving letters from Mr Nicholls,' she said abruptly.

'He has dared —?'

'And I have answered them, Papa.'

She watched the veins in his head swell, wondered if it heralded a seizure.

'In his last letter he told me that in the New Year he intends to come and stay with his friend Mr Grant at Oxenhope. I would like to invite him here, Papa.'

'He will not set foot in this house! He will not set foot in this village!!'

He had risen, still formidable, his long fingers sawing the air. If he had a seizure now she could walk out, take Flossy for a run on the moors, come back later to mourn him. Let it be a seizure and let silly, fussy Mrs Nussey who was even older than Papa fall down the stairs or be struck by lightning! Then she could stop writing encouraging letters to Mr Nicholls and find a cottage somewhere for Ellen and herself.

Papa had controlled himself with a Herculean effort, seating himself again, the hectic colour fading from his face.

'Papa, I am nearly thirty-eight years old. I am a published author. I have the right to meet Mr Nicholls and make up my own mind as to his character —'

'It's a bad one!'

'His character and my own feelings. He was for many years an excellent curate for you, Papa. You cannot deny that. He worked very hard to improve conditions in the village, has joined with you to lobby for a fresh water supply, teaches in the Sunday-school—'

'He did his duty!'

'And more than his duty, Papa! For ninety pounds a year!'

'He wants your money. There can be no other reason for his presumption! He's a jumped-up Irish peasant!'

'I don't think the Pruntys were reared in marble halls!' Charlotte shouted. 'You were born in a cabin with two rooms and your brothers labour on the roads and in the fields. Good God, Papa, my Uncle William even keeps a shibeen! You have advanced in the world but that ought not to ruin my chance!'

'Your money's the attraction,' he repeated stubbornly.

'Papa, I have earned fifteen hundred pounds through my own work and I have the legacy from Aunt. At the most it will yield me a hundred and fifty pounds a year. When you die I shall have no home. Mr Nicholls would be willing, I'm sure, to live here as your curate for the rest of your life.'

'Which your disobedience is shortening!'

'Papa, the children are gone now! Maria, Ellie, Branny, Emily, and Anne all gone! And I am a woman, an independent woman! You are being completely unreasonable!'

'He will not set foot in this house while I am master of it!'

If she stayed longer she would strike him, break every tenet of daughterly obedience.

She turned and flung open the door, blindly stumbling out.

'What's all the noise about?'

Old Tabby had limped into the hall and stood like the good witch in the fairy tale leaning on her stick.

'Papa refuses to allow me to see Mr Nicholls!' Charlotte cried.

'Thought it might be that!' The old servant chuckled. 'Master likes t'be master in his own home, Miss Charlotty!'

'And I have the right to meet whom I please!'

'Happen Mr Nicholls's too short of brass t'please thy father. I'll have a few words.'

'He won't listen to you!'

'Happen he might,' Tabby said with a grin. 'He'll have cold suppers for a month else! It'll take time, child, but he knows I speak plain and without fear!'

She patted Charlotte on the shoulder and went into the parlour, closing the door behind her.

Charlotte snatched down her shawl and went out into the lane. The wind caught the ends of the fringe and blew them outward. On the graves the brown leaves rustled and chattered together.

I don't love Mr Nicholls, Charlotte thought, walking the well-worn path between the granite headstones. I don't love George Smith though his marriage hurts my pride. I never loved *Monsieur* in the way that is regarded as loving – he fed my mind with manna, saw me as an individual – what his wife feared would never have happened.

She wanted to turn time round and bring them all back, to laugh and squabble and tease in the secret world. There was no secret world now, no eager plans for the future, no Ellen even, for it was months since she'd heard from Ellen.

They had all left her and gone away, even Mary Taylor who still wrote occasionally from New Zealand. Mary had wanted her to emigrate as well, but she had lacked the courage.

She sat down on the edge of a tomb, pulling her shawl closer about her, feeling herself decay into old-maid ugliness. The wind was a small gale now, tearing at her. She crouched, listening to the screaming as it tore across the moors and funnelled down the steep main street, but the voices she waited to hear were silent.

TWENTY-SIX

Today was not an actual day but a dream. Charlotte sat on the edge of her bed and watched the first faint radiance of dawn. It had been a long hard struggle, not only to bring Papa round to accepting the fact that she was going to marry Arthur Bell Nicholls but an equal battle within herself to come to terms with the fact.

'Papa, it means that Mr Nicholls will remain as your curate for the rest of your life. You know you dislike Mr De Renzy.'

'That's true enough! You will lose your home should the worst happen to me – but I still don't like the fellow! How much money have you invested?'

'Nearly two thousand pounds, Papa.'

'I cannot give my consent until your money has been secured out of his grasp. Mr Joseph Taylor comes next week. He can act as executor or whatever the legal term is and draw up a document giving you full control over your own money during your lifetime and afterwards – to be divided among any children you may leave —'

'Papa, I am thirty-eight years old. It is not certain —'

'And after your death should I be too infirm to continue my ministry – I will be destitute, Charlotte.'

'Should I die without children the money will revert to you, Papa! Mr Nicholls will agree to that and Joe Taylor may draw up the document.'

'It will be a safeguard for us both, my dear.'

And a snub for Mr Nicholls, she thought, making it clear that he would gain no financial advantage from his marriage.

To her surprise he had accepted the arrangement with no

more than a faint stiffening of his bulky frame and a reproachful glance.

Next there had been Ellen to placate. Charlotte winced as she recalled the hysterical letter Ellen had sent to her, accusing her of bad faith, of selfishness, reminding her of the plans they had made and of how, at Charlotte's behest, she had refused several suitors. After that there had been months of silence, enlivened by a welcome letter from Mary Taylor in faraway New Zealand, congratulating her heartily.

> 'Marriage is not and never was a road I would travel myself, but we must all make up our own minds on the subject. Ellen has no right to hold you to a promise made in girl-hood. I shall toast your future happiness with a mug of red wine!'

It was Miss Wooler, to whom Charlotte had written for advice, who had brought about a letter from Ellen begging pardon for her foolish attitude and Charlotte had replied at once, asking her to choose and buy the wedding garments and act as brides-maid:

> It will be a very quiet affair, my dear Ellen. You know that I take little interest in ceremony and your taste is far superior to mine. Charge everything to me of course. Try to under-stand that I enter into this arrangement solely to ensure Papa's comfort in his old age.'

Fortunate Mary, who had never regarded men as anything more than good friends! Signing and sealing the letter Charlotte envied her single-mindedness, her independence, when she herself veered unhappily between two kinds of loving.

She had refused to visit Ellen before the wedding, fearing that her resolve to wed would not stand against the reunion with her dearest friend and companion, and had paid a short visit to Mrs Gaskell instead.

There, with Mrs Gaskell's friend Katie Winkworth giving her own opinion on marriage she had loosed her fears.

'Mr Nicholls is not an intellectual. He cannot follow me into the realms of imagination. He is educated but narrow-minded, not a man who flourishes in company, and he must understand that I intend to continue my career and will need my own private space still.'

'But you will be glad to help him with his parish work?' Mrs Gaskell said.

'Yes, of course I will! I hope I shall always be pleased to do that!'

'And if he is terribly dull,' Katie Winkworth said naughtily, 'you can close your eyes and pretend he is somebody else.'

'Katie, as if a married woman would ever do such a thing!' Mrs Gaskell tried to look shocked, caught Charlotte's eye and broke into laughter.

There had been a letter from Cornhill informing her that George Smith was married. She sent frosty congratulations and the request that in future any moneys due should be invested in the name of Charlotte Bell Nicholls. She had written also to James Taylor in Bombay to tell him of her engagement. To Brussels she wrote nothing at all.

Ellen arrived with Miss Wooler, the only other female guest whom she had invited.

'Papa will not be coming to the ceremony,' Charlotte told them. 'He feels the emotional stress will be too much for him.'

What Papa had actually said was:

'I'm aware this marriage brings certain advantages but I still don't trust the fellow! I cannot give you away, Charlotte. You must find someone else to perform the task!'

'The Prayer Book does not specify gender,' Charlotte said to Miss Wooler. 'I would be greatly honoured if . . . ?'

'I will be happy to give you away, my dear. You know you and Ellen and dear Mary and Martha Taylor were among the brightest and nicest of my pupils,' Miss Wooler replied affectionately.

The dresses Ellen had chosen were laid out for her inspection. Charlotte looked at the high-collared gown of white silk with a border of green leaves embroidered round the hem of the wide crinoline skirt, at the neat white bonnet with its border of green silk leaves and the blonde veil. In this dress a woman she didn't yet know would be married.

'For going away,' Ellen said, indicating a second dress, 'I chose silvery grey shadow-striped in lavender with a matching cape and a straw bonnet with lavender ribbon.'

'And you are going to wear pale pink,' Charlotte said with a smile.

'With a straw bonnet and a cream cape. Miss Wooler has chosen cream with brown trimming. I hope you approve?'

'Your taste is impeccable as usual, dearest.'

What would happen if at the beginning of the ceremony she put up her hand and said:

'Excuse me but I actually don't want to get married. Could Mr Nicholls kindly choose one of my attendants who are both single and already very suitably clad?'

When she went downstairs the parlour door was closed. Tabby and Martha in their Sunday best, gifts from Charlotte, were setting off for the church and a small knot of people waited nearby.

'Shall we go?' Ellen asked.

'A moment!' Charlotte whipped off her spectacles, put them on the hall table and took up the bouquet of lilies of the valley that Martha had fashioned. 'Ready!' she said brightly.

The rest was dreamlike, colours blurred, sounds muted.

She heard whispers of admiration as she passed the villagers at the church door and felt her heart lift because someone had said she was as pretty as a snowdrop. It was, after all, a pleasant thing to be pretty on one's wedding day.

When she signed her name in the register she hesitated after the B of Bell, resisted the urge to write Brontë and wrote Bell Nicholls instead. This was a person she would need to get to know.

Then they were processing slowly towards the main door, her posy of lilies laid on the spot beneath which her family, save Anne high on the Scarborough headland and Papa, fuming in his parlour, lay.

When she went up the steps into the hall Papa, wonder of wonders, was waiting to greet them, embracing her warmly, shaking hands cordially even with Mr Nicholls.

The dining-room had been decorated with vases of wild flowers and a plentiful spread was arranged on the table crowned by a large cake sprinkled with sugar with fresh green leaves wreathing its base. There was white wine and a decanter of whisky and grenadine for those who preferred a non-alcoholic drink.

And then the gig was at the gate and there was a flurry of

farewells and a shower of flower petals as they drove away.

They were travelling first to North Wales to spend a few days there and then to Ireland to stay with Mr Nicholls's family. He had told her very little of his childhood save that an uncle had adopted him and his brother when both were small boys and that he had only heard later when his parents died.

'And as my life fell in pleasant places their deaths seemed something that belonged to someone else's life,' he had finished. 'My aunt is a kindly, hospitable woman who will welcome you heartily.'

Slapdash Irish! Charlotte thought and gazed steadily out of the train window as she recalled the brief conversation.

By the time they reached the inn in Bangor she was bone-tired. It was still light and the view from the window of the straits glinting with all the colours of the sunset roused her a little.

'I have ordered a supper for us in the private snug at the back,' Mr Nicholls said.

'First I must write to Ellen to let her know we have arrived safely,' Charlotte told him.

'Surely your father —?'

'Of course! to Papa also and to Miss Wooler.'

'Of course.' He glanced at her, observing not without humour, 'Writing letters is the ideal way in which to spend one's wedding night. I may drop a line to the bishop.'

'I'm sorry . . .' She turned helplessly from the window.

'My dear Charlotte, would it not be better if we made of these few days a pleasant sightseeing holiday?' he said mildly. 'It would be of help to you to – delay a little?'

'Thank you, Mr Nicholls!' She shot him a look of gratitude. By the time they embarked for Ireland at Holyhead the awkward and unfulfilling consummation had taken place, herself desperately shy and ready to close her eyes and imagine almost anyone else there, Mr Nicholls surprisingly deft, kind and quick. Men, she thought as she drifted off to sleep, must know some things by instinct.

Ireland was as green and beautiful as she had imagined, Dublin a handsome, elegant city where they stayed for a few days before making the final leg of the journey to Banagher where a crowd of relatives greeted them, headed by an elderly lady in a large mob-cap that reminded her suddenly of Aunt Branwell.

'This wife of yours has a bad chill, my dear Arthur!' she said, her arm about Charlotte's narrow shoulders. 'You shall have a good rest here, my dear, before you continue your honeymoon trip!'

Her voice held little trace of accent and the house into which they trooped was a large handsome one, scantily furnished but with turf fires burning in the wide hearths and an air of repose that was soothing.

'It seems quite like an English household,' Charlotte found courage to remark as a steaming tisane was brought to her.

'I was reared in England,' the other said. 'In London. As a small girl I was presented to King George the Third, though I can recall little of it now. Let me get another cushion for your back – may I call you Charlotte? I am Aunt Bell.'

Aunt Bell, Aunt Branwell – it was pleasant to slip back into childhood again, to be cossetted and coaxed to eat, to have Mr Nicholls shooed away to amuse himself with his cousins while his aunt sat chatting to Charlotte.

'Though we had a fair-sized family of our own we could not refuse to take Alan and Arthur when their parents' farm failed. They were brought up here and never went home again. Most of this house is used as a school of course but it makes very little money. Do you ride?' Charlotte shook her head.

'My daughter Mary Anne used to be a keen horsewoman but a bad fall left her with a limp and she has lost some of her confidence.'

'Miss Mary Anne is the pretty young lady with the dark hair?'

'Yes, she is the flower of the flock. She will not soon marry for we are Protestants in the midst of Catholics and there are problems with mixed marriages. Happily she keeps herself occupied and her temper is a sunshine one. Now I must cease chattering and you must get some rest.'

She went out, closing the door gently. The large bedroom was on the ground floor, its narrow windows looking out on to a garden where tall trees shaded the lawn and cast long shadows into the room. Flames danced on the wide hearth beneath a loudly ticking clock on the mantelshelf. The central part of the chamber was occupied by a large coffin, raised on trestles and draped in scarlet.

Charlotte sat, bolt upright on the *chaise-longue* where she was reclining and stared at the coffin. What on earth? She fumbled for her spectacles and put them on.

In the centre of the room a high bed held a folded scarlet quilt. Her heart resumed its normal beat and she took off her spectacles, not looking in that direction lest the coffin appear again.

'Haunted?' Mr Nicholls raised his eyebrows at her as she asked the question.

'What makes you ask that, my dear?'

'Charlotte has seen the coffin,' Mary Anne said.

It was the last day of their stay and Charlotte felt perfectly strong again.

'Yes, but it was merely the bed seen in a certain light.'

'Mother saw it when she first came here after her marriage,' Mary Anne said. 'The room held no furniture at all, and I have glimpsed it once or twice.'

'What does it portend?' Charlotte shivered slightly.

'Nothing at all, my dear Charlotte! It is merely a trick of the light!' Mr Nicholls said heartily. 'Come! we must be off or we will miss the best of the day!'

Only one incident occurred to mar the remainder of their honey-moon. Mr Nicholls had hired mounts and a guide to take them through the Gap of Dunloe when they stayed in Clare. Somewhat nervously she allowed herself to be assisted to the saddle but though the terrain was rough the pony was placid and steady and she found her fear evaporating rapidly.

'We should get down here, sir!' the guide called back to them. 'Sure but it's steep for the lady!'

'We shall manage! Go on ahead and keep an eye open for fallen tree trunks and the like!' Mr Nicholls called back.

The guide signalled obedience and went on ahead.

'This is rather a tricky section.' Mr Nicholls had dismounted and came to her horse's head. 'I shall lead him for a little while.'

'I really can . . .' Charlotte's voice died in her throat as her pony suddenly reared up, snorting and whinnying.

She tried in vain to keep her seat in the saddle but an instant later she was on the ground, shielding her head with her arms as the animal kicked and bucked above her, hoofs flailing within inches of her face.

'Hold hard, sir!' The guide was galloping back.

As quickly as it had occurred the incident was done. The pony stood, foam-flecked and trembling, and Mr Nicholls was helping her to her feet.

'Are you hurt, my dear?'

She shook her head mutely.

Why hadn't he gone immediately to her aid when she had fallen? Why had he not loosed the pony to spring away and reduce the risk of her being kicked or trampled?

'I didn't realize you had fallen, my dear. Come, we'll walk the rest of the way.'

But she had cried out. She knew she had cried out! Her skirts had flown up as she slid down and the loose stirrups had – she closed her eyes, took a long quivering breath and said as firmly as she could,

'I believe it is a sign that we should go home, Mr Nicholls. I feel that Papa may be unwell. You will oblige me in this?'

'Of course, Charlotte. We shall return to Haworth as soon as you please.'

That evening she wrote to Papa, wrote to Ellen, wrote to Mary, wrote to Miss Wooler and to Amelia, Joe's wife – detailed over and over the near disaster, her handwriting sloping wildly. It was foolish of her for she had suffered no hurt but there was a creeping dread at her heart.

'Tha looks well!' Tabby said, eyeing her critically after they had greeted Papa. 'Wedlock suits thee then?'

'Yes, Tabby! I believe that it does!' she said cheerfully.

It had been an accident. Of course it had been an accident!

She went into the little store room where the geese had once been housed. She had converted it into a study for her husband – having the walls papered with a design of green leaves and making green curtains for the window.

'My dear, I have drawn up a list of tasks which must be seen to as soon as possible.'

He looked up from his desk.

'Tasks?'

'For myself of course but you will not refuse to help me? We ought to give a tea for the Sunday-school scholars and it would be a nice idea to hold a tea for the parishioners in the school-house to thank them for their good wishes on our nuptials.'

'I shall be very glad to help, Mr Nicholls.'

'Arthur, my love?'

'Arthur, of course!'

As she went out she wondered if he had any thought of handing back the gold watch with which he had been presented when he left for Kirk Smeaton.

'Of course Ellen must come and stay for a few days, my love! I thought we might invite my good friend, the Reverend Sowden Sugden at the same time. He is looking for a wife.'

Ellen came, but the long private talk Charlotte had promised never materialized. When they walked out Mr Nicholls – Arthur she reminded herself – and his clerical friend went with them.

'How is your book going on?' Ellen enquired as they strolled across the grass.

'I have not had time to carry on with it yet, but I hope to do so very soon,' Charlotte told her.

'Mr Nicholls, you must give Charlotte leisure in which to write,' Ellen said, playfully scolding.

'I married Charlotte Brontë, not Currer Bell,' he answered, his tone bringing the colour to Ellen's cheeks.

'How could you be so – so dismissive?' Charlotte exploded when the guests had departed. 'My career means a great deal to me.'

'Let me hear what you have written so far.'

Eagerly she took out the pages she had laid aside and read them as he smoked his pipe.

'What do you think? I feel there is a story there unfolding.'

'The critics will accuse you of repeating yourself,' he said.

'Oh, I often make several beginnings! I have been thinking that I might use the back bedroom as a study when we have no guests.'

'We must think about it, my dear. Oh, Charlotte, could you check these addresses for me? I intend to shame them into whitewashing their outer walls if it's the last thing I do!'

She took the bundle of letters silently and went into the dining-room, the story of *Emma* sinking into the recesses of her mind.

Amelia came with Joe and their little girl and the visit went reasonably well though 'Timmy', as the three-year-old Emily had been nicknamed, took a sudden and embarrassing dislike to

Arthur, shrinking away from him and insisting instead on trotting round with her small hand held firmly in Papa's hand.

Writing to Ellen about it she jumped slightly as Arthur's shadow loomed across the page.

'Your letters to Ellen are very indiscreet,' he said irritably.

'Arthur, they are private —'

'Letters may fall into the wrong hands. You must order Miss Nussey to burn them as soon as she has read them. In fact I shall expect a written undertaking in her own hand to that effect, otherwise I shall have to censor your letters as a precaution, my dear.'

'You are not serious?'

'Entirely serious, my love. The obedience of a wife is the glory of any marriage. Now be done with it! I wish you to take a walk with me.'

'But —'

'I have given you an instruction, Charlotte. Finish the letter in the manner I have indicated and then go and put on your bonnet.'

He stood smiling at her in the doorway, tall in his black coat.

A young Carus Wilson, she thought suddenly and felt his shadow remain after he had left the room.

At least there was the visit to Brookroyd to anticipate but at the last moment word came that Mercy wasn't well, and the visit was postponed.

They went instead to stay for a long weekend with Sir James Kay Shuttleworth and his wife, which was a mixed blessing for the wife hardly left her room and Sir James and Arthur talked over her head as they walked in the grounds where a fine rain fell constantly.

Back in Haworth the snow began, shrouding the moors, dripping from the eaves. Charlotte sat down to write a long overdue letter to Mrs Gaskell but Arthur breezed in.

'It's a splendid afternoon! Come, we'll take a walk up to the waterfall and see it in its winter glory,' he said.

'I must just finish —'

'You are writing to Mrs Gaskell? My love, the Gaskells are Unitarians, are they not?'

'Yes, but —'

'We cannot associate with Unitarians, Charlotte! It would not be conducive to any future advancement! Come! I have a surprise for you!'

The surprise was a sledge. Dumbly she looked at him.

'I shall pull you up the slopes and you may set your own pace going down! I thought it would please you.'

'Yes,' she said with an effort. 'Thank you, Arthur. It will make fine sport!'

Chilled and frozen she huddled on the wooden seat as he dragged it up the hill and let it go sending her sliding at a dizzying speed to the bottom. By the time they reached the waterfall she was drenched through.

'We had best make for home! Can't have you catching cold!'

They walked back, she sinking up to her knees in the thick snow while icy flakes scorched and stung her face.

The next day the vomiting began.

BEGINNING

Day by day she was shrinking; day by day she was growing smaller. There was no child coming. She felt no swelling in her stomach, no fluttering in her womb. The doctor seldom came now. He had told her it would be a difficult pregnancy and she had obediently swallowed the various remedies that he had left, had tried to control the retching that shook her frail form. She had longed for Ellen to come but Arthur told her that Miss Nussey would upset her by fussing too much. She had penned a note to Amelia asking her to send anything that might do some good. Joe was sick of a serious liver-complaint and so was little Tim who had taken such a fancy to Papa.

She hadn't signed her will properly it seemed. Propped up in bed she had scrawled her name, hearing the slow tolling of the bell from the church tower. Poor old Tabby had died of a stomach complaint, almost certainly a typhus attack, Arthur told her. She had died at her sister's house down in the village since Martha, who wasn't well herself, could not be expected to deal with two invalids.

Arthur was very attentive, very kind. It wasn't his fault that she wished he would never enter the room where she lay, week after week, able only to write in faint characters the brief notes he dictated.

She had been wrong to marry, wrong to allow any man to violate her private space. He spoke gently but she could see the waiting in his eyes as he studied her face thoughtfully. In three weeks' time she would be thirty-nine years old, almost the age at which Mama had died. Only Papa had made old bones and came now to stand at the door, his voice breaking as he enquired,

'Are you a little better today, child?'

Perhaps he had loved her, loved them all, all the time in his own eccentric way. Perhaps she had always been special and not known it.

The angel hovered over the old cradle in the corner, face serene, the tips of its wings vibrating. Beyond she could see them faintly, Maria, Elizabeth, Branwell, Emily, Anne – not dead at all but still children playing in their secret world.

'Come and join us, Tallii!'

Branny was calling her. She could hear Emily laughing as she whipped her top and Anne humming a tune with her thumb in her mouth and her frock slipping off one shoulder.

The angel beckoned and drew aside the curtain of years. Charlotte raised her head and, stepping through into the tender shining, joined the others at their play.

AUTHOR'S NOTE

Charlotte Brontë died leaving all her possessions to her husband. The legacy amounted to about £60,000 in today's values.

Ellen Nussey arrived the next day and was greeted by Mr Nicholls who reminded her to burn any of his wife's letters she held. Since she did not we owe her an inestimable debt for our knowledge of the Brontë family.

The cause of Charlotte's death remains a matter of heated debate. Mr Nicholls remained for a further six years in the parsonage until Mr Brontë died and was entombed with his family. Then he returned to Ireland, having been refused the ministry at Haworth, left the church and took up farming having married his cousin, Mary Anne. The marriage was childless and he died in 1901. The servant Martha accompanied him to Ireland for a long visit and paid subsequent visits there until her death at the age of forty-six.

Neither Ellen Nussey nor Mary Taylor ever married. Among the former's papers after her death in her eighties a love poem written by her suitor, Mr Vincent, was discovered, perfectly preserved.

Sarah Garrs died at ninety-three in the state of Iowa. Among the mourners at Charlotte's funeral was Nancy Garrs who had walked from Bradford to be there. She died in the Bradford workhouse with one shilling and ninepence in her pocket.

After reading through over three hundred books about the Brontë family it would be invidious to single any out since all gave me something to ponder. Similarly I thank all the people who discussed my own theories with me and offered their own, and my renewed thanks to the staff at the Brontë Parsonage Museum whose friendliness and help make Haworth such a rewarding place to visit.